To understand the present, you mus past.

As Wewelsburg Castle burns, Eli carries Isaiah to safety. So much is lost. Malachi is gone, the Demon from Eli's terrible past is reborn into the world already at war, and to make matters worse, Gideon is back. Yet before Eli can even reach the sanctuary of his home, he learns a painful truth about Gideon, the truth about why he left him, and Eli can barely hold onto his own sanity. Eli quickly understands that not everything in life or death is black and white, and sometimes to protect the ones we love, we have to make the greatest sacrifice of all.

Something is coming. Eli can feel it, there, in the darkness, taunting him. The truth of his own mysterious identity. But the road to the truth is paved with the pain of a story that he has to hear, a story that will change his perception of history forever, a story of great love, and a story of two lovers who died to change the world. He does not want to hear it, he does not want to believe it, but if he is to understand who he was, if he is to understand why he was made Vampire, he has no choice but to listen as history unfolds before him.

With Morbius close at his heals, the truth is finally out. Eli can either allow himself to be crushed beneath the bu den of his own identity or allow the world to be consumed by the evil knocking at his door.

Death is just the beginning--Love is the end.

This book is a work of fiction. Names, characters, places, and incidents either are products of the author's imagination or are used fictitiously. Any resemblance to actual events or locales or persons, living or dead, is entirely coincidental.

Dead Camp Three
Copyright © 2016 Sean Kerr

ISBN: 978-1-5207-0097-7
Cover art by Latrisha Waters

Published by eXtasy Books Inc or
Devine Destinies, an imprint of eXtasy Books Inc
Look for us online at:
www.eXtasybooks.com or www.devinedestinies.com

Dead Camp Three

By

Sean Kerr

Dedication

To my husband Derek for his understanding of my literary love affair. To Craig, Krys, and Jayne, for their wonderful support. To my mum and dad who bought the books, even though I made them promise not to read them!

To my Laura, always and forever in my heart.

Books are nothing but words on paper without people to read them. So I need to take a moment to thank some incredible people who have helped to get Dead Camp out there, and whose kindness, help, and support has helped my books to be noticed by so many new people. So to these amazing friends, I say a huge thank you, and I dedicate this book to you. To Margie Lane, to Ronnica Bourgeois, Patricia Strehle, to Sta'Cee Wilson, to Leah Negron, Lori Ferry, to Brandyjo Newton, and to Janice Birnie, to Drew Lily, to Tounorris Walker thank you with all my heart for your amazing help and support, and for your kindness. And finally, to Nicholas Bella for bringing me into your world.

Prologue: The Agony Of Departure

My time is almost through. I tried to help them—I tried to love them, but nevertheless, I will die for them.

I see my agony running down my broken body, dripping onto the hot sand, droplets of grief melting into the granules of my never-ending despair. I suffer for them so that they may suffer not, but will they have eyes to see? Will they have ears to listen? Do they have the desire to understand? Do I die in vain?

My body feels so very heavy, weighed down by the cruelty of man. It pulls on me, and it wants me to fall, it wants to rip me away from the spite of mankind that so painfully pins me in place. The pain is beyond my comprehension.

No more, no more fight left in my body, no more life, no more suffering. For that was my life, one long moment of struggle and pain leading up to this one moment of exquisite agony.

I did it all for them.

I did it all for him.

Pain, more terrible than the physical torture endured by my body, rips at me heart and tears at my black withered soul because I know that he is dead. I know that my eyes may never look again upon the beauty of his face, that my body may never know the comfort of his arms or the comfort of his smile, because he is dead.

He died because of me. He died because of the crushing weight of guilt I placed upon his undeserving shoulders. The

1

certainty of my own destruction became the certainty of his own death.

It was my idea, to die for them, to make myself their hope and inspiration—that in death, mankind could be reborn. I asked him to do it, I begged him, pleaded with him to betray me. It was the only way. Therefore, I killed him, as surely as if I tied that rope around his neck myself. I killed him, and my heart died with him.

I saw the pain in his eyes that afternoon, as we played our final act out before a voracious audience. His lips trembled as he kissed me. He begged me to change my mind, to turn away from the path laid so inevitably before me, a path of humiliation, of cruelty, and death. How to explain to his yearning face that he and I went beyond the joining of two hearts, the longing of two souls? We belonged to the people, we all belonged to the people, and as such, our fragile, transient lives meant nothing. For my plan to work, for mankind to survive, I had to die. The light died in his eyes as my words sank in, and his heart withered and died inside his chest as his lips pressed against mine for the very last time.

We were thirteen, twelve wonderful men and one incredible woman, but one amongst them loved me more than all the rest, and I loved him above all others, trusted him above all others. Only he knew the truth, only he shared the burden of my imminent sacrifice. How could I tell my friends whom I loved so very much of my impending fate without destroying the faith that made them so strong? So we kept it between ourselves, our secret, our own personal pain.

As my death approached, every day a little more of him died, the knowledge of my end killing him little by little, eating away at the man who once stood by my side so strong, so defiant, so magnificent. I saw the darkness crush his light until nothing but anger and bitterness remained, and he channelled it towards me. So I took his loathing and his scorn, because he needed that much of me. He deserved that much of me.

I could not save him. I could not save the man I loved. The darkness took seed in his heart and blossomed with a kiss to extinguish his life for all eternity. I have failed, for if I could not save him, he whom I loved above all others, what hope is there of saving man? Faith, for that is all that I have left, dictates my path and leads me by the hand towards the light. Faith is the only comfort left to me as I die for mankind, so I let it guide me to my end.

Why so much pain? Why do I have to suffer so? I am alone, dying alone, suffering alone. Why have they abandoned me? Where is my Father who asks this of me? I am sorry, I do not mean to doubt, I understand the need to suffer for their beliefs, but do I have to suffer this torment alone? Why do I have to be so afraid?

My eyes are so dry that I cannot close them. Blood and sweat encrust my flesh, rivulets of dried salt tightening my skin that blisters beneath the onslaught of the sun. I feel my shame running down my legs—my body weeps for me. I long to feel the relief of water against my parched lips, just a drop of succour to reprieve the desiccation of my mouth, but all I can taste is the bitter aftertaste of vinegar. Even my own tears torture me—I feel their sting against my cheeks.

Life is slipping away. Death is creeping around the corners of my vision. It taunts me with faces, the faces of my thirteen—except they are not thirteen because he is not there, he is dead. So why can I see him? Why are they there watching me die, enjoying my dying? The deceiver stands between them, holding their hands, long fingers entwined with those whom I love, and he is smiling at me. He too watches me die.

I am frightened, so very frightened. Father, why have you forsaken me? I thirst. Father, forgive them, for they do not know what they do. It is finished.

Father, into your hands I commit my spirit.

Chapter One: The Ghost Of A Chance

Hear my soul speak. The very instance that I saw you, did my heart run to your service. Shakespeare

As Related By Malachi

Oh, and it so did, the very moment that his hunky countenance filled my vision. I, the King upon the stage, and he, the dazzling beauty whose gaze sought me out from that audience of adulation. Was I not a star? Was I not a God upon the stage of Heaven? Yes! I, the star in ascendance, more dazzling than any other meagre thing that London had to offer. And yet, there in the dark, I saw him, his eyes, so bright, so moved by the brilliance of my performance, eyes that sought me out, and love lay lost at my feet. My heart belonged to him from that very moment. There, upon that stage, I fell in love with a dream. I fell in love with a beauty that blinded all else, and every word, every emotion that I invoked, all of it I directed towards him, my muse in the dark.

That was before he killed me, of course.

It took every ounce of strength left in me to leave him. Poor Eli. He looked so hopeful standing there on that hill overlooking Wewelsburg Castle, naked. Where to focus my eyes? I had to scrape my gaze away from his hard, muscular body and that thing hanging between his legs and remind myself that there stood the man who killed me. Eli ripped open my throat, and he drank my love away, every drop, and he cast me away, an empty thing, a savaged testament to his own insurmountable grief. As we stood upon that hill of decisions, I searched his eyes, and I saw his guilt glistening inside there, the pain that sparkled with such sharp definition, cutting away his insufferable confidence as he faced me. I heard my Bard inside my head, his words never truer to my ears. *The smallest worm will turn, being trodden on.*

"I am not coming with you, Eli." I had said the words, I meant the words, yet even so, the suffering they caused upon that beautiful face pained me so. A darkness washed over him that had nothing to do with the weak sky or the sun that fought to rise above the mountains, it had to do with me. I never thought I had it in me, the strength to leave him, the one thing that kept me bound to the Earth, the one thing on Earth that I truly loved, even more than Shakespeare.

So I turned my back on him, and I walked away. Without flesh to contain my emotions, it felt worse somehow, as though my own despair could not stand to stay inside me. I could almost see my own heart aching inside my chest, a pathetic, broken thing, shattered like myself, beyond recognition. My tears streamed down my cheeks in a torrent of misplaced love, as wasted as the years I spent at his side, yearning for his affection. And like my tears, I too felt wasted. I wanted nothing more than my time upon the Earth to come to an end, to release me from my pain.

"Daniyyel! Ask me, Daniyyel! Please ask me, I am ready." How pathetic my voice sounded as I bellowed into the sky, so weak, so ineffectual, so inconsequential. That just about summed me up.

I waited, sitting in the long grass outside the concentration camp, staring up at the sky, waiting for the gentle flutter of wings to herald my salvation, but the Angel did not answer my call. He had promised me he would ask me the question one more time when he thought me ready. Was I not ready? Was my business upon the Earth not concluded? The truth, no matter how foul, no matter how unpalatable to me, now lay revealed — I had nothing left to bind me to the world of the living. I wanted to go, it was time for me to go, to leave behind my pain, to leave a world in which I no longer belonged.

I lay down in the long grass, my vision filled with sky, and I wanted to feel the grass against my skin, to feel its coolness brush against my flesh, but I could not feel it.

Did I feel different? Oh, where to begin with that! Malachi the ghost, Malachi the actor, Malachi the murdered, Malachi the betrayed. Malachi the lonely. Love did not want me, love had no place for me in life or in death. And yet, just a very short time ago, I felt love, a different kind of love, a love that burned, a love that wanted all of me.

Possession leads to damnation. Well, in fairness, they did warn me. I just did not listen to them, I did not want to listen to them. I would risk my eternal soul for Eli, and risk it I did. The Demon took possession of my soul in a fury of unconditional love. It felt so liberating! To do and to say whatever I pleased, to feel the Demon's insidious fingers fill every crevice of me, to look upon the world with eyes that did not care and did not feel. Not a fleck of unrequited love to blacken my heart, because as a Demon, I had no heart, just desire, just love. To be free of such crippling emotion, from the constraints of civilised behaviour, the Demon unshackled a part of me that I never knew existed. Well, apart from the fruitiness. I always was a bit on the fruity side, as many a Russian sailor could testify. The Demon filled me with a confidence that made me feel so attractive, so sexual, and I loved it.

"Did it hurt, dear heart?"

His voice startled me, and a little yelp squeaked between my lips. Melek lay next to me, lying on his side, his handsome head resting in his hand, the yellow of his eyes burrowing into me.

"Please, how very dare you! You gave me quite the turn."

"I would love to give you a turn."

I turned onto my side, my own head resting in my hand, mirroring his sublime position, looking at him, drinking him in. Wow. His beauty really defied description, and as I gazed at his pouty, full lips, I found that I wanted to kiss them. Kissing meant trouble. My lips never failed to land me in it, every time they touched someone. Yet, they were there, just in front of me, crying out for me to kiss them.

"Tell me, Malachi, I want to hear it. Did it hurt?"

"What? When Daniyyel ripped my Demon from my body and made me a floating fart again? Of course if hurt."

Melek reached out his hand towards my face, and I felt him, his touch, his warmth against my skin, and my body shivered at his caress. Better the Devil you know.

"Then tell me about it, share it with me, my beloved, I want to hear it from your lips."

Lips. Even just the mention of lips made me quiver.

"You saw me, I was magnificent, was I not? I wanted to release all the Feral. But when Eli ran off to save the prisoners from them, Daniyyel appeared before me. Are you all so beautiful?"

"No, I am more so. Do go on."

"He did not say a word. I was about to rip the cross off another box, and it was raining. Everything looked so grey, so gloomy, except for me, because I glowed with fire, my body burned with love, a blazing light in the darkness of mankind's darkest moment. I felt his hand upon my shoulder, and I spun around, and there he stood, all silver wings and silver armour."

8

"Wow, he had his armour out? He usually reserves that for special occasions. You were honoured indeed!"

"Do you want to hear this, or do you just want to make sarcastic comments?"

Melek laughed, and as he laughed, his eyes sparkled, they burned with life, they burned with something I could only describe as pleasure. It was all I could do to stop myself from touching him. His hand, however, well his hand continued to touch me, moving down my neck, stroking my collar bone, and I could feel every exquisite sensation. *They do not love that do not show their love. The course of true love never did run smooth. Love is familiar. Love is a Devil. There is no Angel but love.*

"As I said, he did not say a word, but he reached inside of me, his hand through my chest, and I could feel it in there, gripping my heart, pulling my burning Demon out of me, and the pain... oh, the pain... I screamed. My Demon screamed. It felt as though he pulled all the love out of my soul. It felt as though he pulled my very existence out of me. My poor Demon tried to stay inside, he tried to hold onto my soul, but the Angel thrust his other hand inside my chest, and the world exploded in a blaze of agony, and I could barely see through my agony, I could barely believe the pain. The light left me, I felt it leave my feet, leave my legs, I felt my arms dim, the fury that burned so hot inside me extinguished in the hands of the Angel. When he pulled his hands out of me, I think that I died again. I think that he killed me, and he stood there with nothing but a handful of ashes in his hands, and left me empty. My Demon, he took my Demon, and he left a ghost."

My pain bled from my eyes. I could feel the tears pouring down my face, my voice a trembling quiver upon my lips. "I am more a ghost now than I ever was, and I feel so empty."

Melek leaned over, and his lips touched mine. It took me by surprise, not the fact that *he* reached over to kiss me, but the tenderness by which he did it. So much sensitivity presented itself through that kiss, so gentle, so careful, so heartfelt. I almost fell forward onto my face as he pulled away. I did not want it to stop.

"And what will you do now, my dear Malachi?"

I knew what I wanted to do, but I dared not give my desires voice. "A lot of people died today. There will be a lot of others in that camp like me, and they will need help, and that is something that I can do, I can help them."

"Come with me."

Melek leapt to his feet and held out his hand towards me.

I took it, feeling his strength in the palm of my hand. I knew not why I could feel him, he above all others, but I felt deeply grateful for the connection we shared, for the feel of him, for his ability to touch me. I had nothing else.

We walked in silence, hand in hand through the grass, the Devil and the ghost. If they could see me now, those little friends of mine. Did we look like two lovers? It felt so, two people enjoying each other's company, and such a simple gesture as holding one's hand lifted my spirits so that they soared into the stratosphere in a whirl of giddy pleasure. The sun deemed fit to shine on us, a fleeting beam of warmth that broke through the grey misery, and for the first time since I died, I felt completely at peace.

We stopped on a small hill overlooking the remains of the camp. The sight below froze my happy moment in my heart.

"Tell me, Malachi, what do you see?"

"I see dead people."

So many of them, aimless things, memories drifting on the pain of their own departure. Grey spirits, some more defined in their shape than others, ghosts milling about aimlessly amidst the fire and the bodies. It broke my heart to see such a thing, to know that I too was once like them, a thing broken, a thing unwanted. I knew, in that very instant, that I had to help them.

"There are so many of them."

"Yes, dear heart. And do you think that you may help them all? Is that your wish?"

I stole a glance into his face, and I saw within it such deep sorrow, a grief that I did not expect. A tear, a single black tear fell down his cheek. "Melek, what is wrong?"

I could see that he wanted to tell me something, something that hurt him most deeply, and I felt him so completely in that one shared moment of grief that my heart stuttered.

"Just a memory, dearest, a memory of dark souls left in the cold. But this does not matter, what matters is you."

"I will help them—I have to help them, do you understand?"

"I understand more than you could possibly know, dear heart. And afterwards, what happens afterwards? Will you go back to Eli?"

"*My grief lies all within, And these external manners of lament Are merely shadows to the unseen grief That swells with silence in the tortured soul.*"

"Is that a yes or a no? Shakespeare always was so confoundedly enigmatic!"

Would I ever go back to Eli? That was the question.

"He hurt me, Melek, he lied to me, he murdered me."

"Answer the question, dear heart. I need to know if I stand a ghost of a chance."

Those eyes. They gazed at me with such intensity, such longing, I could barely speak.

"A chance of what?"

"A chance of you loving me."

Oh, wow. If I needed breath, it would have frozen within my chest. "I have no love to give, for he took it all. No, I will not go back to him. I cannot go back."

"Then I will ask you the question."

"What?" I did not expect him to say that. I did not know what I expected at all, not from him, the Devil standing before me, but I did not expect that.

"I am asking you to come with me. I am asking you to be mine, I am offering you a home, at my side. I want you, Malachi, so I am asking you the question. Leave this world that does not want you, and come with someone who does. Me."

Chapter Two: The Roman Question

As Related By Gideon

Running, again. All my life, running. Paderborn forest flashed by in a blur of verdant violence that hurt my retinas it looked so lush, so majestic, all so fucking beautiful. It made my skin crawl. Everything around me looked so bloody... green. That was Eli's thing, not mine. I preferred the immutable hardness of concrete, the undeniable strength of steel. Give me brick and marble as opposed to never-ending trees and grey mountains, anytime.

While Eli cowered from the world surrounded by the thick stone walls of Alte, I hide amidst the pumping hearts of the living, yet we both remained fugitives against our own history. The truth, that thing that I feared for so very long, finally there for all to see, fucking us in the ass. History now hammered at our door, and nothing could keep it at bay.

How much did my blood reveal? How much of the truth did he drink? The look on his face as my blood hit the back of his throat, it burned my flesh away to reveal the liar he always suspected me to be. I saw it in his eyes, it blossomed there like a bad joke, the dawning realisation of all that I had kept from him, the sudden knowledge that I made him.

Still, not all the truth filled his mouth. That shit storm would come soon enough, more crap than I could shake a stick at. Everything that happened in Judea, everything that transpired in London, all of it, all of it there for him to see at last. A stranger once told me that the truth would eventually bleed out, no matter how far from Eli I ran, and there I stood, bleeding.

"Don't let me go back to Eli," I asked of him.

"You love him that much?"

"Yes." I did love him that much, enough to spend twenty-six years entombed in a block of ice.

It was my choice, my decision. To remain free meant returning to Eli, for I could not resist his pull any longer, and *they* would have followed me, as *they* always followed me, straight into the arms of my beloved Eli. I could not allow that to happen. I had to protect Eli at all costs.

Centuries of love, and still not enough time. A man must know his worth. A man must know his own name. A man must learn the truth of his own heart. I remained but a teacher, and Eli my pupil, and now I would have to set him free.

My God, had it come to that? The end, finally here? The weight of history pounding at the door. I could hear it, I could feel it tearing at my skin, trying to get in, telling me that it was over, that Eli no longer needed me. Time. Fucking time. Endless bloody time. Now, there was none. I was free, running through the forest towards him, towards one of the most important figures that history had ever known. So yes, the time had come, my freedom proved that, but it was the pain in my heart that told me so.

I stopped, my world spinning around me in a dizzying frenzy of utter panic. Bile filled my mouth. The final end. History, about to convulse in agony, and we would be at the centre of it.

They would be coming for me. They would be coming for Eli. They would be coming for the Spear.

I felt the cold fingers of fear grip my chest and squeeze my heart with cruel intent. The pain, so sharp, so terrifying, ripped through my body until I lay on my knees gasping, trembling, blinded by agony and helpless. My hands dug into the nearest tree, fingers digging into the bark, digging into the wood until the sap ran freely over my knuckles, the tree indelibly wounded, as I, myself, lay ineradicably wounded. The thing, the splinter, moving inside me, burning its way through me, seeking out my Vampire heart, ate away at my resolve, and offered me visions of a past mortality.

Blood drawn to blood. History drawn to history. Death drawn to death.

I heaved myself to my feet, determined to move, determined to go on. There was still time, time for me to tell my story, time for me to lay it bare before the one I loved. Time for him to forgive me.

For so long I denied Eli my blood, but in that one moment of pity, as he lay on that hill above the ruins of the camp, tired, desperate, I allowed him to feed. My blood is strong, the strongest of us all, and it filled his mind with so much information, all of it so fleeting and momentary, a cacophony of images that would burn anyone less than he. Thank fuck he did not have time to see it all, not there, on that mountainside under the shadow of so much death. It would not seem fitting somehow.

It would not befit the man that he used to be.

I feared what it would do to him, the knowledge of his own identity. If he had looked into my blood long enough, he would have seen the burden of his own dark history staring back at him. And I feared that it would destroy him now as surely as it destroyed him then, all those years ago in a world that did not know any better. It remained a burden that killed a part of me with every passing day. I lost Eli on the day I turned him, and from the moment that he first looked upon me with his Vampire eyes, I knew that he could never truly be mine. Another owned his heart, and the truth of it tortured me for hundreds of years. Eli was but on loan, until the day that another should claim him as their own.

That stranger in Rome, he knew, he knew this day would come—he knew everything, that funny little man who became my friend.

Rome, 1920, was a city undergoing a profound change, a city on the verge of embracing Mussolini's fascist wet dream. But I loved it. So much stone, so much hardness, a thriving city of untold beauty filled to the rim with sharp-jawed, olive-skinned men of utter perfection.

I sucked my way through Italy, in more ways than one.

I could lose myself in Rome. It became my go-to destination when I needed to cower from the world, when I needed to re-connect with myself, my true self. Strange that a Vampire should find such solace in a land bursting with Christianity, but it was exactly for that reason I returned again and again. To remember.

As I walked the cobbled streets of the Borgo Vecchio towards St Peter's Square, with St Peter's Basilica glimpsed tantalizingly between stone and brick, anticipation would rise within me in a steady build of barely concealed excitement, until, with an ejaculation of euphoric adulation, I stood upon the square itself.

Bernini's masterpiece, two sweeping Tuscan colonnades, four columns deep, curved around me. I remembered when Bernini designed them, sketching them on a coarse piece of canvas as I lay naked next to him, his vision of the maternal arms of Mother Church reaching around the square to embrace each visitor, a stroke of genius. He was a genius, and I told him, repeatedly. The scale of it rivalled the Rome of old, and it thrilled me just as much.

I placed my hand against the Egyptian obelisk at the centre of the Piazza, the setting sun illuminating the red granite with an internal flame that glowed and pulsed with a deep knowledge of the past. I closed my eyes, feeling its power ripple through my Menarche body, hearing the cries of distant shadows beckoning to me through time. Caligula himself had the obelisk moved to Rome. It stood the only thing in that Piazza older than I.

They had been following me for some time. I saw them out of the corner of my eye, stalking me behind the stone colonnades, as tigers trapped behind bars, their hunger just as palpable.

How fucking dare they. Did they not know who I was?

As far as the rest of the world was concerned, the Corsican Guard no longer existed. Tensions with the French saw to that in 1662. However, Pope Alexander Chigi was a friend of mine, and a little word of caution in his ear saw to it that a small contingent of Corsicans remained in the service of the Pope, as his own personal guard, of course. The French loathed Chigi, desperate to sabotage his efforts to create an anti-Ottoman alliance, and I would not put it past their cunt of an Ambassador to make an attempt on Chigi's life. The frog was an imbecile, albeit a very attractive one.

Future Popes enjoyed the clandestine services of the Corsican Guard, known only to a select few nearest the incumbent Pope, but they owed their continued existence to *me*, so how dare they treat me in such a manner.

Something had changed. Whenever I visited Rome, I would present myself to the Corsican Guards, and they, in turn, would arrange my audience with the Pope, in the utmost secrecy of course. This time was different. From the moment I arrived in Rome, I became aware of their presence, lurking in the shadows, following my every move for weeks. Curiosity demanded that I see their little game play out. So I allowed it to continue, feigning ignorance, but as I stood in the middle of the Piazza, I felt somehow cheated, violated.

I felt unwelcome in a city that I had helped to create, and I did not like it.

As I moved away from the obelisk, towards the steps of St Peters Basilica, the twelve acted as one, a carefully choreographed dance that saw them move between the pillars either side of me, all pretence at subterfuge abandoned. I stopped at the base of the steps, unable to conceal the smirk that crept across my face. They thought they hunted me, when all the time I hunted them, for I had the scent of their blood in my nostrils, each individual as distinct to me as a rose against shit, and I would be able to find them wherever they might be. So I beckoned to them. I stretched out each of my long, muscular arms, and I beckoned to them.

As one synchronised body, they emerged between the pillars, six on either side to surround me, and I could not help but laugh.

"You know, I could rip your fucking throats out before you had the chance to piss your immaculately pressed pants."

One man stepped forward, a rather ugly creature with a nose that pointed south. No amount of black slicked-back hair could ever hope to mask his unfortunate face. His hand moved to the lapel of his jacket, and I tensed, ready to spill their blood upon the steps of St Peters without a moment's hesitation.

I was brash like that.

He pulled the lapel to the side to reveal his inner pocket, and the crucifix nestled within. I felt its power immediately, the overwhelming wave of nauseating faith, but I held fast, unwavering. As one, the others did the same, each flashing a cross of silver until my eyes burned with their reflected light.

"Really, what do you take me for? Do you know whose blood runs through my veins?" I felt my fury flash through my face as my teeth extended, just enough to wipe the smirks from their Corsican faces.

"You dare to threaten me, on whose authority?"

Broken nose closed his jacket, and the others followed suit amidst nervous glances. I trained the original Corsican Guard, I taught them how to deal with Vampires, but they surely had forgotten their training over the years, or else they would not have attempted such a futile gesture.

"We seek only your compliance sir," he grunted, like the Neanderthal he resembled, "by the authority of his Holiness Pope Benedict XV."

"Am I no longer welcome into the arms of Rome? Is that the meaning of this insult?"

"His Holiness would wish to welcome you personally sir, but as for the rest of Rome, I could not say. You will follow me, please."

Follow me meant being surrounded by twelve burly men as they escorted me into the Basilica. Under any other circumstance, I might have been flattered, turned on even, but instead, I felt angry, insulted, unwanted.

It hurt. The rejection, the lack of respect, the total disregard for my importance, it hurt me. I had come to Rome to escape such pain, to be embraced by the one institution I knew to revere and love me. The one institution to know me for whom I really was, not to be pushed aside like some unwanted child, the shit to be wiped from the bottom of one's shoe.

It would not do.

We moved through the narthex, then through one of the ornate bronze doors into a cruciform space so vast as to dwarf one's mind. St Peter's is bigger on the inside than it is without, dominated by the largest domed ceiling ever constructed. Lavish decoration covers every surface for as far as the eye can see, punctuated by enormous marble sculptures, so vast as to seem as giants, a testament to the

Church's penchant for stealing marble from the very beginnings of Rome itself. The Pantheon, even the Colosseum, all fell foul to the pillaging of the Roman Catholic Church during the construction of the Vatican.

Such was the singular genius of those few responsible for its architecture that at certain times of the day, the chancel glowed with crepuscular rays, or God rays, bright fingers of light that illuminated the nave in a show of breath-taking beauty. And so it was that I stopped beneath those fingers of light, and I felt *him* fill me. Rome, the Catholic Church, it belonged to me as much as it did them, if not more so.

To my guides horror, I dipped my fingers into the font to the side of the chancel, causing the water to bubble and boil at my touch. Steam hissed from my unharmed flesh as I knelt before God, fingers to my temple as I made my sacramental. I heard them gasp around me, but I paid them no heed, taking my moment with God despite the agony that ripped through my body.

Christianity, faith, it burned me from every angle—I felt it pressing against my skin, trying to evict the monster that dwelt within my soul. Those less than I would crumble to dust beneath such messianic might, but I was Menarche, more than Menarche, older than Christianity, and the holiest being to ever step through the doors of that Basilica.

I would not burn. It hurt like a fucker, though.

My little show of reverence over, I saw the outrage on the faces that surrounded me. It made me smile, my teeth flashing over my lower lip as the last of the holy water evaporated from my flesh. They would have killed me then, if they knew how, such was the disgust and the indignation my actions inspired. Fuck them.

"Do not presume to know me! I have as much right as you to show my respects before God, if not more so. So close your fucking mouths and take me to your pissant Pope!"

He stood in the northeastern niche beneath a towering marble sculpture, one whose history I knew all too well.

"Saint Longinus by Gian Lorenzo Bernini, completed in 1638, for which he was paid the handsome sum of 3,300 Roman scudi."

Pope Benedict turned around to face me for the first time, his heavy white cassock brushing against the cold marble floor, the fabric as crisp and brittle as the creases that lined his face. He was an old man when he took office, as was every Pope before him, but the greyness of his pallor and the black rings beneath his eyes betrayed a man weighed down by some heavy shit. My heart fucking bled for him.

"I see now how well Bernini caught your likeness."

"As well he should, he was fucking me at the time."

Benedict flinched, cold beads of perspiration blossoming across his scull capped brow. Strange, the man was nervous as hell, but he remained unafraid of me. I could smell fear, and he stank of nothing but day old perspiration.

"The records are not wrong in recording your bluntness. I'm so happy to see that your legendary humility persists." He glided forward and extended a glittering hand in my direction. "You may kiss my ring."

I took his hand and pulled it closer, until the tiny image of the Fisherman filled my sight. My lips brushed its golden surface with a subtle crackle, sending up faint tendrils of steam.

"There, formalities over. Now we may talk as friends." He meant his words to sound warm, but somehow they felt hollow, empty things that tumbled from his lips without care.

"Friends do not send guards to summon them, or spy on them."

"You must forgive the subterfuge, Gaius, we live in dark times, and those once thought friends of Rome have all too often proved otherwise."

"The Germans?"

"No, the Italians."

"Ah, the same old argument, then."

"Indeed, they fail to recognise my sovereignty over Vatican City while we refuse to acknowledge Italian sovereignty over Rome. The Roman Question, the only question worth answering if we are to see peace in our time, but it is a question that will be answered soon I think. Yes, very soon. You, however, are another question altogether. I can hardly believe that you are standing here before me."

I leant into him, smelling his frailty, his mortality, but still he stood there without fear. Brave man, I had to give him that much.

"I watched as this Rome of yours arose from the ashes of Christ's death. There is more of your *God* pumping through my veins than you will ever dream of—believe it."

"Is that why you always return here?" He began to pace before my statue, his hand brushing its glass-smooth surface. He was rubbing me up, and it irked me.

"Do you feel closer to him when you come back here, is that why you come, again and again? Like an errant child returning home when the going gets too tough? You have been here for four weeks already, and yet, it is only with my assistance that you present yourself. Why is that?"

"I come when I am ready. I had no idea that it should be otherwise." He was pissing me off.

"My predecessors may have been more—lax about such things, but by all means, consider this an affirmation of our new terms. How long do you intend to stay in Rome?"

"As long as I bloody well like."

"You have not visited the Colosseum as yet. Do you intend to?"

"You seem remarkably well informed."

"It is my job to be informed. The records are quite clear concerning your fascination with that dreadful place. You spend time there whenever you visit Rome, do you not? I find myself wondering. Why?"

"It's the thought of all those sweaty muscular men going at it, it makes me hard."

Benedict threw up his arms in exasperation and let out a loud, disgruntled groan. "You make this so hard for me, why? Could it be that you are trying to hide something? What is it that fascinates you so much about the Colosseum, could it be that there is something there of particular interest to you? Could it be that you have hidden something there?"

The hairs on the back of my neck bristled, and it was all I could do to keep my teeth sheathed. The man pushed me too far, but I couldn't very well drain him on the spot—he was the Pope, after all.

"Spit it out, enough with the bull shit."

"Indeed, as you wish. The Spear, where is the Spear, Gaius? Have you hidden it here, in Rome, perhaps in the Colosseum?"

I stepped towards him, my voice a thunderous, guttural growl as I allowed my anger to fuel my words.

"No Pope, in the history of this institution, has ever asked about the location of the Spear. Tread carefully, holy man, you are walking on thin ice."

It was the first time I saw it, the briefest flicker of fear flash between his eyes, but then it was gone before I barely had time to taste it.

"Curiosity, only curiosity I assure you. I am but a man, after all, one friend to another."

"Words, just words, empty sounds that mean nothing. That is all I hear."

"But I do so want to be your friend, Gaius, let me be your friend. Let me be the friend that shelters you from those who pursue you so vigorously."

"Who said that I was running?" That wiped the disingenuous smile of his insincere face. I had caught him out. Something did not feel right—the whole situation stank of shit. Something else lay behind those words of that arrogant, misinformed Pope.

"We are all running from something, are we not? Moreover, you forget, I know you, your story and your history. I know that when the burden of your existence becomes too much for you to bare, you come home to the loving arms of Mother Rome for solace and comfort."

"I come to Rome because I helped build it!" My anger growled through my lips, and I felt the Corsican Guard squirm nervously around me, but the Pope held up his hand, and they backed off. "I know every stone, every brick, every fucking painting! I know every piece of marble that you ripped from the breast of *Mother* Rome, the real Rome, *my* Rome."

I tried to calm myself, to give reason to my voice, but the red veil that clouded my eyes required satiating. I moved towards the statue of Gaius, the Gaius from so long ago, my hands caressing the cold marble of his still form, almost wishing that I could be him once again, in those times so distant and innocent. Innocent compared to the world that I now inhabited. I felt the Pope beside me, his eyes questioning, demanding answers, demanding my supplication. He would have a long fucking wait.

"Do you know why the cross does not frighten me?" I asked gently, reaching out to touch the simple crucifix around his neck. He did not flinch. The gold stung my flesh, but it was nothing more than a mere irritation.

"The cross does not frighten me because I have faith. I know the power it holds over man because I feel it too, I feel *him* too. Did it not occur to you that I, more than anyone of you, have more reason to believe? I was there! I saw him! I saw him die!" For a moment, the emotion of the memory caught in my throat, and I had to turn away from him, not wanting him to see the pain that flashed through my eyes or the agony of remembrance that tormented my face.

"Tell me how your faith could possibly be stronger than mine. Tell me how you could possibly believe more than I." I swung around on him then, bitterness flying from my lips. "What did you see? What did you feel? Fuck all, that's what. Don't tell me of your desire for a Christian state, because it means nothing to me, I who was there and saw it all with my own fucking eyes!"

His arrogance fell away, replaced instead by shock and confusion as his eyes searched out the truth of me. Even his voice sounded contrite.

"I had no idea, I had no idea that you had faith, that you could even feel such a thing, you... you who are..."

"Monster?"

"No, I don't think that you are a monster. I was going to say, you who are older than faith itself. The records do not speak of your passions. My predecessors made no mention that you are a creature of faith. Please, forgive me, I did not expect to hear such words from you."

"They were words spoken in confidence, words spoken to friends. They earned my trust, and I theirs."

"It seems that even in my twilight years, this old man may still learn a few tricks. You have shamed me, my friend, and I fear that we have started our friendship on the wrong foot. Would you forgive an old man?"

His words spoke of contrition, but his eyes glittered with ill-concealed duplicity. The man was hiding something, and it was eating him up.

"Then perhaps the next time we meet, Rome will greet me with a little more consideration."

The Pope opened his arms wide and then grasped me firmly by the shoulders.

"When we next meet my friend, it will be with the entire might of Rome!"

Something about that phrase unnerved me, and I pulled away from him sharply. I looked at him then, hard, trying to see beyond the façade of smock and cross, the man hiding behind his faith, trying to see the truth of him, but he remained blank to me.

With a slight smile that spoke more of regret than warmth, he nodded at me and swished around, moving away from me in a tornado of ermine and Corsicans.

"One more thing, Gaius." He spun around, his shadow entourage almost tripping over him. It was all I could do not to laugh. "The Colosseum is currently undergoing some major preservation work, and as such it is closed to the public. I would suggest that if you intend to make your traditional pilgrimage there, that you should do so by night."

"I will take your suggestion under advisement."

"Yes, well, you just do that my friend." He spun away more irritated than ever. "You just do that."

I watched him scurry away, a bitter aftertaste fouling my mouth, something that tasted remarkably like betrayal. If the Church no longer wanted me, then what was the point? In a world that changed so rapidly around me, was I that alone? Did any of it matter anymore? If that was the case, if the Church had truly abandoned me, surely I could go back to Eli. I wanted to go back to Eli and tell him everything. I needed to confess.

How I missed him. I missed his arrogance, his dark humour, his cock. To feel his bulging arms around me once more would bring much-needed comfort. To feel his unwavering love fill me would sooth my aching soul. If I could tell him the truth, if I could lay it bare for him to see, would he understand? Maybe. If I could tell him the truth, then we would stand a chance. I could let all my barriers fall, love him, truly love him, perhaps for the very first time.

I looked up at my statue, but my statue stood silent, lost for words.

"Do not be so hard on Pope Benedict, Gideon—he is a good man at heart."

My muscles tensed, and my hands clenched into fists at the sound of that voice, that insufferably smooth, cherubic voice.

"Daniyyel."

I could not turn around—I could not bring myself to look upon his beautiful face, with those huge gold-flecked eyes, eyes so full of compassion, eyes so full of unremitting love. I could not stand to gaze upon that perfect body, so hard and slender beneath his tightly fitted clothes, clothes that clung to each curve, and each bulge, with blasphemous intent. To look upon the Angel was to gaze upon temptation, and I was nothing if not a man of many needs.

How I loved Daniyyel, who above all others knew my pain. He witnessed it first-hand. He above all others understood me. He above all others knew the sacrifice I made of my love. And as I stood underneath my own shadow, I felt my love trickle down my cheeks, cold rivers of despair to quench my loneliness.

"What is the matter, old friend, can you not turn around and look upon one who loves you? God will not mind, of that, I can assure."

I fell into his arms, me, the big man, the hard man, wrapped in the arms of an Angel before the accusing fingers of God.

"Oh my friend, my poor Gideon. I felt your pain, I heard your heart crying out, and I had to come. How could I not?"

"I cannot do this anymore, Daniyyel, let me go back to him, please, let me go back. At least *he* loves me." Desperation heaved each word from my trembling lips, and I knew in that instant that I was lost. There was nothing left for me without Eli.

"Oh my friend, you are loved, believe me, by those who matter."

I pulled away from him, leaving the comfort of his arms to stand alone in the cold once again.

"Then let me go back to him. I need him, Daniyyel, I need to be with him, I need to tell him the truth, please, let me tell him."

"Do you remember what Melek told you so very long ago?"

I remembered. I never forgot his words. I remembered them every time I looked into Eli's face. Those words eventually drove us apart.

"How could I fucking forget? He told me that Eli was not for me, that he did not belong to me, that another would come to claim his heart. Melek told me not to fall in love with him." My words caught in my throat. To hear them spoken aloud after so many centuries of hearing them inside my head burned me more than any cross.

"Believe me when I say it gives me no pleasure to remind you of those words my friend, or the pain that accompanies them."

I felt my despair clawing at the back of my eyes, tearing its way to freedom.

"But what about me? What is there for me? Don't I deserve a happy ending?"

Daniyyel reached out an immaculate hand and wiped the tears away from my cheek with a finger.

"I know you love him, but you cannot go back to Eli, Gideon, he belongs to another."

I punched his hand away, barely able to conceal the anger tightening my muscles.

"Gaius! My name is Gaius Cassius Longinus! Use it."

"I know who you are. I knew the man that came before, and I know the man that came after. You have changed so much, you were so angry back then, so rough. But look at you, now. Look at the man you have evolved into. I am so proud of you, and I consider it my honour to count you amongst my friends."

"Words, Daniyyel, they are just words. Stop using so many fucking words."

Daniyyel laughed, a sound that almost broke through my despair, but not quite.

"It is good to see that some of that roughness remains beneath that polished exterior. So let me ask you this, Gaius, what would it do to him? If you told Eli the truth, what do you think it would do to him?"

Fucking Angel. I knew he was right—he was always bloody right. I knew when I came to Rome that my time with Eli was over, as I always knew it would be. We had walked the path of history together, he and I, but his path lay elsewhere. The truth, about me, about his true identity, would destroy him as surely as it had so many centuries before, and I could not see that happen to him again.

"So what am I to do?"

"Do you see that man over there, the one trying so very hard not to look at you?"

I saw him then, standing by the nave, his eyes dancing over every detail, but seeing nothing. He glanced my way, and the both of us looked away from each other quickly.

"What about him?" I found that I was talking to myself. At the time of my greatest weakness, he had appeared to me to strengthen my resolve, vanishing as quickly as he had appeared. Daniyyel remained nothing if not enigmatic.

I looked again at the stranger, and our gazes locked across the floor, the human and the Vampire. To my astonishment, something quite extraordinary happened—he smiled at me.

He looked a handsome man, and I estimated him to be in his late twenties or early thirties, slight of build, wearing a crisp tweed suit, obviously new to him. He looked uncomfortable in it as he fiddled with the plaid necktie around his sweating neck. There sat a man outside of his natural habitat, as unused to the constraints of modern fashion as I to the changing world. One glance at his brown oxfords told me that he had laced them up incorrectly. He stood a man out of his time, much like myself.

The stranger gestured to a pew, and the smile he offered felt genuine, warm. I could see no reason to refuse his invitation—I had nothing better to do, after all. Either he knew who I was, or he was on the pull. Either way, my curiosity remained aroused.

I slid along the pew and settled next to the stranger, both of us staring straight ahead in silence, hands clasped nervously in our respective laps. It felt like a first date. I could not help but taste his nerves. Anxiety leeched out of his every pore, but there was no fear. He was not afraid of me.

"I have wanted to meet you for so very long that now I find myself unable to speak."

Suddenly, I realised that it was not so much nerves that I tasted, but his excitement. I looked at him, at his eyes that glittered with so much life, that shone with such awed fascination. Such an open face, so full of kindness and sincerity, but what struck me the most was the intelligence that illuminated his wonderful features. It positively radiated from him.

However, I saw darkness there too, something clinging to the corners of his vision, something seen, something felt, something terrifying. Something that lived with him every day of his life, mirrored in the way he held himself, echoed in the slight sadness that creased the corners of his mouth. It felt as though I looked upon myself.

"And who is it that you think you are meeting sir?"

I could have destroyed him on the spot. I could have sent him screaming from that place, never to close his eyes again for fear of the nightmares to come. But I had the feeling that his nightmares were already considerable, so I thought better of it and gave him a chance.

"Gaius Cassius Longinus."

Did everybody know my fucking name? Was I walking around with a big fucking sign on my back with my name splashed across it? Centuries of anonymity lost in one mind fuck of an afternoon. It was making me edgy. I didn't know whether to kiss him or kill him.

"Then you are the first mortal to hold me at such a disadvantage for a very long time. Who the fuck are you?" I heard the old abrasiveness tarnish my voice. One may polish marble until it shines, smooth and perfect, but break it open, and it is as rough as any other lump of stone.

"Direct, to the point, yes, I understand. Isaiah, my name is Isaiah Nathan Silberman, and I have to say, it is an honour to sit here before you."

He offered me his hand, the stranger actually offered me his hand, and what's more, I took it. It was a confident move, and a very assured handshake, a strong handshake with a firm manly grip, further evidence of his indifference to my supernatural condition. I must admit that Isaiah had me perplexed.

"So I know your name, but what is in a name? Names are just a convenient string of letters tied together in order to form a label by which we may be recognised. I know that you are human, but what manner of human I have yet to understand. What manner of human are you, Isaiah Nathan Silberman? And how the fuck do you know who I am?"

The shadow fell upon Isaiah in an instant, a dark cloud of inescapable doom that clung to every crease on his youthful face. Such pain blazed from the depths of his eyes, and I found myself wondering what tremendous evil they had witnessed to burn them in such a way, for seldom had I witnessed such a look of despair from a human. In that one moment, I knew that he had seen the darkness too. Isaiah Nathan Silberman was the human version of me.

"I am just a man, just a simple man trying to protect the wife that I love so very dearly." He looked at me, his eyes so empty, hollow wells of torment that saw no end. "What would you do to protect the one you love? What would you do to protect Eli?"

My eyes flashed black, and my teeth unsheathed, drawing blood from my bottom lip. I would have killed him, there, before God, anything to protect Eli, and then his words registered in my enraged head, and I realised what he was saying to me.

"Anything. I would do anything."

Isaiah tried to smile, but it did not stop the single tear that fell down his cheek.

"I know, I know you would, I know you have, as have I. My wife, my Eva, unlike your Eli, she knows everything— you see, she was there when it all began."

I listened to his story, a tale so dark as to rival my own. It was a story of a friendship turned sour, and the discovery that monsters walked the Earth. It did not surprise me that the Mother and Father, my old enemies, and the leader of the Thule, should be involved. And it did not surprise me to learn of the ongoing hold they had over Isaiah, to undertake certain tasks when called upon, or Eva would suffer the consequences. The horror that took place in that crypt would have destroyed any other man, but Isaiah stood strong, and he stood brave, so very brave. But it was the revelation of the atrocity committed upon the figure of this Hitler that really surprised me. They called him the Black Messiah.

I slumped back into the pew. All around me, the world carried on as normal. All around me, humans continued to worship, to express their faith, to live. They didn't know what was coming. Echoes of London, ringing mercilessly through my ears. The Black Messiah cometh, and Heaven would fall.

Time, so fleeting, so transitory, running through my fingers. The world was running out of time.

"I have never told that story to anyone before."

I saw so much sincerity in his face, and I found that I wanted to kiss him, to kiss his humanity, to embrace his innate goodness, to take some of that faith into myself.

"Today is a day for such revelations my friend. Today, all of history has decided to visit upon me, and I find myself wondering why. Why Isaiah, why tell me all this, why are you here before me?"

He looked darkly serious, if that was at all possible, considering how terribly serious he had been up until that moment. He scooted forward on the pew until we touched, his voice lowered to a conspiratorial whisper.

"They are coming for you, Gaius, which is why I am here, in Rome, now, because they know you are here. They are working with the Pope."

My fingers dug into the seat beneath me, splintering the polished wood beneath my angry nails.

"I fucking knew it! I knew that old git was up to something! I will rip that sanctimonious head off his pissing shoulders and mount it on that obelisk outside for the birds to feed on."

Isaiah laid a reassuring hand on my arm, and he flinched slightly as he felt its hardness.

"No, Gaius, it's not like that, he doesn't know. He doesn't know who they are or what they are. The Thule came to Rome with an offer. They want information on the Spear, and in return, they will help the Catholic Church to resolve the Roman Question. Pope Benedict thinks they are nothing more than a powerful, influential business consortium collecting important historical relics. All he can see, all he wants to see, is a solution to the splintering of Rome."

"In exchange for me?"

"They have filled his head with tales of your duplicity, how the blood that runs through your veins gives you the divine right to all that the Church has and all that the Church believes. The Thule have convinced Pope Benedict that you are going to take the Church away from him, away from all Catholics. That you will pervert it to the ways of Vampirism, and he will do anything, anything to protect it, to his dying breath if necessary. You have been made a monster in the eyes of the Church, and in particular to this Pope, so they will do anything to remove you."

"Why are you telling me all this?"

Isaiah looked stunned for a moment, as though I had said the most ludicrous joke in the world.

"So you can run. I'm trying to give you the chance to leave this place, before they have the Spear, before they have you."

"They will never have the Spear. No one will, not while I live."

"But they will have you, and what then? Will they go for Eli?"

"No!" The word exploded from my mouth and echoed around the massive interior, drawing unwanted eyes in our direction, and I withered beneath their accusing glares. Did any of them know? How many of those eyes knew who I was? Did they all want me?

The inevitability of the situation hit me, and suddenly I felt tired. Not even a Menarche could fight futility.

"If they have me, then they will not look for Eli, he will be safe."

"I don't understand."

"My greatest fear is that I will return to Eli, and if I do that, I will tell him everything. I cannot lie to him—I just can't do it. There is so much that you don't know, Isaiah, and I am running out of time."

"They are planning to freeze you. Do you understand me, Gaius? They are going to imprison you in a block of ice until their plans reach fruition."

Such was the audacity of their scheme that I could almost admire them. A bold plot indeed.

"To be like a fly trapped in Amber, unable to affect the world around me or the people around me. I'll do it."

Isaiah could not have looked more shocked if I had gone on my knees and pulled out his cock.

"You cannot possibly understand what I am telling you..."

"Yes, I do," I snapped, my situation swimming nauseatingly around me. "I will be locked away, away from the Church, away from the Mother and Father, but more importantly, I will be locked away from Eli. I have visited enough pain on him already. I love him, Isaiah, more than this existence, more than the blood that pumps through my veins. I love him, and if I go back to him, I will destroy him. No, lock me away in your prison of ice, save the world the indignity of my existence. Save Eli from me."

"You love him that much?"

"I love him that much and more."

He shrank away from me, something like shame weighing him down. I felt for him. There sat a man filled with good intention, but the words that came out of his mouth filled me with dread.

"You will be conscious at all times. The machinery that will encase you will keep you frozen, and your body will be nourished through tubes, but you will be awake. You will be more dead than even you are now, yet through it all, you will be awake."

His words filled me with horror, a raw gut wrenching horror that nibbled at my bowels and squeezed my balls with iron fingers.

Yet Eli would be safe, safe from me.

"Then so be it. Take me away from all this life."

When Isaiah looked at me, it was with tears in his gentle eyes, and I loved him for it.

"I will get you out, somehow, someday I promise you. I will find a way."

"I have long since learned that promises made in haste are the hardest ones to keep."

He started to protest, but I placed my finger against his lips, gently, smiling at him all the while. "Tell me how and tell me when."

"The trap will be set tomorrow night, at the Colosseum, using liquid nitrogen injectors before installing your frozen body into the machinery hidden beneath the amphitheatre."

"Clever."

"The German responsible for creating this ticking monstrosity is nothing short of genius. Mad as a box of frogs, mind you, but genius all the same. I shudder to think what else he concocts for them."

We sat in silence, both of us looking at our feet. There was nothing else to say. Rome was finally about to defeat me, or so it thought, but I knew that the victory remained my own to savour, despite the terrible cost.

"What is it like?" There was so much emotion in his gentle voice that he almost broke. "To have his blood in your veins? What was *he* like?"

"Ah, my friend, that is a discussion deserving of a good meal and a bottle, or two, of the finest port. Tell me, Isaiah Nathan Silberman, if this is to be my last night on Earth, will you not join me for dinner? My last supper, you might say."

"You can eat?"

"Oh yes, I enjoy it immensely. Just don't hang around afterwards, it's not pretty."

We left St Peters, not as two strangers, but as two friends, the mortal man and the Vampire. As the sun cast its dying light across the Colosseum, streaming through its innumerable arches with fingers of violent red and orange, we sat outside a small intimate Bistro, and I told Isaiah my story. I told him everything. The words poured from my lips in a never-ending torrent of revelation, and as each carefully chosen sentence reached his attentive ears, I felt the weight of them lift from me until I felt light-headed.

Never before had I told it. As the sun died, I vomited my secrets and lies to a man whom I had only just met, on the eve of my frozen, indefinite imprisonment. It felt fucking good. When I told him who Eli was, his true identity, Isaiah finally understood the full implication of my dilemma, and his emotions streamed unchecked down his flushed cheeks in rivers of sympathy. I, however, had no more tears left to shed.

When it was over, two bottles of Italy's finest port lay empty on our table, and I silently thanked my Menarche condition for my lack of inebriation. Isaiah, however, was not so fortunate. He stood on uncertain legs and fumbled for my hand, shaking it with so much enthusiasm as to remove it from its socket. I stared at him long and hard, waiting for it, searching for it, but it did not come.

"What?" He slurred, breath pungent with alcohol.

"The Spear, not once have you asked about the Spear. Why?"

He staggered slightly to the side and then straightened himself, tugging the bottom of his jacket to straighten it. "I want to know. I'm not going to stand here..."

"Stand?" I could not help but smirk.

"... Stand here before you and tell you otherwise. It was that thing that got me into this in the first place."

"So why haven't you asked me where it is?"

"Is it safe?"

"Yes."

"Then that's all I need to know. Maybe one day I will see it with my own eyes. One day, but not this day."

I leaned over, and I kissed him on the cheek. Isaiah was as straight as they came, his heterosexuality oozed from his every pore, but I could not help it all the same. He moved me, and it was more a gesture of deeply felt friendship than ill placed hope.

"I will see you tomorrow, Isaiah Nathan Silberman, my friend. Good night."

I left him holding his hand against his cheek, and I walked into the arms of my other friend, the night.

What to do with my last night on Earth? There was only one thing for it. I needed a fuck, and I knew just where to find it.

A twinkling, pierced sky shrouded the oval magnificence of the Colosseum in a blanket of darkness, the perfect cruising spot for those in the know. Around its immense crumbling base, lonely men roamed in search of cock, hunting for eager holes to fill. It was my last night on Earth, and I fully intended to join their ranks.

Fire and earthquake had ravaged the Colosseum, with the entire outer walls of the south side long destroyed by the unforgiving fingers of Mother Nature and the neglecting hand of man. Huge parts of her lay naked, her skeleton revealed to the world, but the original layers of pilasters and arches in the remaining north side made for convenient hiding places in which to receive, or give. It was beneath such a secluded arch that I stood, with my back against the time-worn stone, awaiting a hungry mouth to feed.

A shadow of a man appeared, tall and slender, elegant as only the Italians seem to manage, and I felt my excitement press against the lining of my trousers. He saw me in the shadows, he stopped, waiting for some sign from me to confirm my intentions. I noticed with some satisfaction his hand stroking a rather impressive bulge forming between his legs. I sank back further into the shadows, and he followed.

Blue eyes, pale clear blue eyes set amidst a perfect olive complexion, so very attractive, so very pretty, so utterly delicious. I liked my men pretty. He had lips to die for, plump and moist, cock sucking lips that I intended to put to good use. He reached out a hand and traced the outline of my throbbing bulge, and I gasped at the sensation, at the intimate touch of another being, denied to me for so long. I was fit to burst.

I saw the shock register across his chiselled face as he felt the size of my cock and the sheer hardness of it beneath the thin fabric. His fingers gripped it, rubbing and pulling in long hard strokes that made my legs tremble with anticipation. Without taking his gaze from my face, he knelt down, and suddenly I gasped as his teeth bit into my girth. I closed my eyes, the sensation of his warm wet mouth through the cloth of my pants making me groan. His lips traced the twitching outline of my dick, his mouth clamping around my bulbous head, and I could not believe the ripples of pleasure that pumped through my groin, threatening to end my pleasure early in a wet sticky mess of ecstasy.

"Well, dear heart, nice to see that old habits die hard."

My eyes snapped open in shock, and the young man at my feet sprinted away into the darkness in a fit of panic.

"Oh dear, have I spoilt your fun?" Melek, immaculate as always in a beautifully tailored black suit, leant against the arch with his arms folded across his chest, smirking at me with his insufferably handsome face.

"Fuck off!" The very sight of him inflamed my blood and made me feel sick.

He laughed gently as he moved forward, the sound of his voice sending a cold shiver down my spine, a confusing blend of fear and exhilaration. Melek reached out an immaculately manicured hand and grabbed the bulge in my pants. My cock jumped in recognition of his touch.

"Your words say no, but your cock says yes. It always did get so impossibly hard. You need to take that in hand."

Anger burned me, tearing through my muscles, ripping through my eyes in an explosion of fury, and I grabbed him by the shoulders roughly, slamming his back against the arch in a shower of stone dust.

"You don't get to speak to me!"

Melek pushed away from the wall, and his hands slammed into my chest, sending me careening into the darkness, where I crumpled to the ground in an indignant heap. Before I could blink the dust from my eyes, he sat upon me, his weight on my chest, his yellow eyes filling my vision, his wet, lascivious mouth mere inches from my lips.

"Who said anything about talking?" Melek's tongue slid into my mouth, urgent, passionate. For a moment I lost myself in his desire, pressing back with my own eager tongue as my bulging arms wrapped themselves around his neck, pulling him closer.

Was I that desperate? Was I that horny? Fuck, yes.

My hands slid under him until they lay flat against his hard, well defined, smooth body. I placed my hands flat against his chest, and I pushed. With all of my considerable might, with every ounce of my Menarche strength, I sent Melek flying into the darkness, his howl of rage cut short by the impact of his hard body first against a wall, and then against the floor.

I sat up with a start, my dead heart pounding inside my chest as my dead lungs sucked in great whoops of air, not because they needed it, but because I was excited beyond the capacity of my body to cope. Melek stirred in the darkness, the yellow of his eyes shining like beacons of contempt. I felt their glare rest upon me, and I withered beneath their might.

"You do not get to kiss me!" I didn't want him to stop, more like it.

Melek's voice drifted out of the darkness in melodious waves of desire, each word laden with so much sensuality that I nearly drowned in it, he made my head spin so.

"Who said anything about kissing?"

He moved so fast that even I could not see him. All I felt was my body leaving the floor and the stone of the Colosseum smashing into the cheeks of my face as he slammed me against the wall. Melek pinned me into place, thrusting his groin against my ass, rubbing his massiveness against me. To my dismay I realised that I wanted him to put it inside me — I hated him, but he also knew how to turn me on.

"Do you like the feel of that cock against you?"

"Yes." I felt the whisper of his lips against my neck, the foulness of his breath against my skin, and I felt lost, barely able to spit the word out from between my clenched teeth.

"Do you want me to fuck you?"

"Yes."

"Do you want me to fuck you hard?"

"Yes!"

Expert hands untied my belt, slowly and deliberately, prolonging the agony of my anticipation, easing my garments down to expose my buttocks to the night. I felt wetness against me as his spit hit my ass, and then his fingers probing, moistening, stretching my hole until I whistled. He pushed in, his massiveness splitting me apart in exquisite agony until he drove it home, all of him inside of me, pressing against me. I pushed away from the wall, but he shouted, "No!" and he gripped my hands in his, slamming them against the stone above my head, pinning me into place with each thrust of his cock.

Melek took his time, his penetration slow. I felt the length of his shaft sink inside me, each push deeper than the last, but I could not move, only feel, my dick pressed against the stone, hard and aching. Teeth dug into the base of my neck, and I moaned as my flesh parted, his tongue lapping the blood that welled to the surface and filled his mouth. I knew he had changed, I knew the Devil beast that devoured my flesh and pierced my body, but I was beyond caring.

Suddenly my hands were free, his claws gripping me by my sides as his pounding became urgent, faster, fierce. My own hands reached down to my cock, taking it in both my hands to stroke its entire length, my head against the stone my only support. Harder and harder Melek thrust with agonizing precision, my body swallowing his entire length, again and again, harder, faster, my hands manipulating myself as I felt my orgasm rise. My entire body tensed to the ejaculate flooding my organ.

Melek's teeth ripped away from my neck with a rough tearing of flesh as he screamed, and I felt his warmth fill me, flooding inside my cold body in thick heavy streams. I closed my eyes, my balls tightening, my hands moving so fast as to rip the skin from the head of my cock, until with my own cry of satisfaction my body released my ecstasy across the stone wall in thick pumping rivulets of pleasure.

All my anger, all my energy left with that ejaculation, leaving me spent and weak. As I turned to look upon my defiler, I had no will left to argue, no desire left inside me to fight—just contempt for the Devil before me.

"Ah, my shoes—look what you have done to my shoes!" His shiny black patents clung to his enormous feet, scuffed and torn. "Well, no harm dear heart, I fancied a new pair anyway. I've seen a darling pair of spa..."

"I told you to stay the fuck away from me." A little of the old anger started to creep back into my voice, and I felt emboldened. "Do you know what you did to me? Have you any idea how much you have ruined my life?"

"Oh, I wouldn't say ruined exactly. Was it my fault you fell in love with Eli? I did tell you not to."

Before I knew what I was doing, my hand flashed out and collided with his cheek. Melek brought his own hand up to the glowing flesh, and a smirk curled around his fingers.

"I suppose I deserved that, but really sweetie, what you are about to do goes beyond stupidity. Does it not occur to you that by placing yourself into the hands of the Thule, that you bring the spear closer to them, and by association, closer to me?"

"Fucking spear! That's all you ever cared about isn't it? I was never part of the equation, not me, you just wanted the spear."

"You may very well think that... but you were a rather pleasant distraction, all the same."

Suddenly I lie against the wall again, his hands flat against the stone either side of my head, his yellow eyes burning into me.

"Give me the spear? Oh, go on, you know you want to. Give... me... the spear." His tongue snaked out and licked my lips, sliding across my cheek.

"Fuck off."

"Would it help if I said please? Just think of it, all this could be over, you could be free."

"Tough shit, Melek, the spear is safe."

"But Eli isn't."

"Don't even try it, you worthless piece of shit. Eli is safe, the Covenant ensures that, and you fucking know it. You can't touch him, you can't tell him, you can't so much as piss in his direction without Heaven knowing about it. And you wouldn't want to piss your Father off now, would you?"

I enjoyed the look of fury that flashed behind his fanatical eyes, but it remained a small victory, because I was the one contemplating eternity in an ice cube.

Melek turned away from me chuckling to himself. It was the most infuriating sound I had ever heard, and I wanted to silence him with my fist.

43

"I know now, Gaius, my friend, I understand. You think that you are buying him time, Eli, until his one true love turns up. How much of a fucking martyr does that make you? Fool! Take him back, go to him and take him back!"

"No."

"But you love him—you have always loved him. Go to him, Gaius, go to him and tell him!"

"No!" My fist hit him square in the jaw, pain shooting up my arm with nerve-shredding ferocity, but I didn't care, because the sight of him lying in the dust rubbing his jaw was too delicious to miss.

"And that is the last time you will ever fucking touch me, you arrogant cunt! Kill me... if you dare... otherwise, just fuck off!"

For a moment, I thought that he would, that the creature glaring at me with such hatred would reduce me to ash with a flick of his manicured fingers, but he simply picked himself up and brushed the dust of his Italian suit.

"Really? Now I will have to go shopping. What a drag!" He stretched out a hand towards me, and I flinched, but his finger slid down my cheek and caressed my lips gently. "You are beautiful, you know, I always thought so. Play for time if you will, lock yourself away from the man you love, see if I care. You will be out soon enough, I assure you, and I will be there waiting for you."

Melek turned his back on me and sauntered away, the blackness of the night curling around his slender form until he looked indistinguishable from the night. Nothing remained of Melek except the throbbing in my asshole.

Pain, sharp and unrelenting, flashed through my stomach, and I gripped my stomach with one hand and used the other to steady myself against the wall. I closed my eyes, forcing myself to calm, willing the pain to leave, to give me time. I needed time. Fear consumed me from the inside, and soon there would be nothing of me left.

The pain faded, melting away into my abdomen, and I could only think of the following night when I would remove myself from the world. I was happy about it, because it was better than knowing that Eli would love another.

Alte reared out of the ground before me, draped in a light dusting of snow. I looked at her stone towers, at her windows burning with life, and I felt sick. Eli was inside. Isaiah was inside. My entire existence stretched out before me in one never-ending lie, all of it leading to that one moment of truth, when I would break the heart of the man I loved. Nothing would ever be the same again, Eli would never be the same again, and in that one moment of agonizing clarity, I knew that I would lose Eli forever.

Chapter Three: Reunions

As Related By Eli

The sky fell away from me in a dizzying whirl of *what the fuck?* Through icy clouds, my body spiralled away towards a ground that rushed ever closer, and Isaiah was slipping through my fingers. Alte lay below, a glistening beacon of sanctuary, if I could just last long enough to reach it. I felt exhausted, running on empty, the flight from Wewelsburg Castle sucking me dry, and the sky fell away from me.

"Hold on old man, I'm going down, and this isn't going to be pretty."

Isaiah clung to my neck for dear life, and I held onto him with every ounce of strength I had left. Isaiah would not die, not in my arms, not because of my weakness, not before I returned him to Ethan.

Stone, sharp and unforgiving, moved towards my immaculate beauty with alarming speed. Even in the face of excruciating pain, I could not stand the thought of my devastating good looks smashing against the rocks.

My beautiful naked body, my lithe, hard muscles, my rock hard rippled abs, my bulging arms, dashed against the ground like a fly against a window pane. How very fucking rude.

Time and place Eli. Time and place.

"I'm falling!" Isaiah slid down my body, and I clutched the collar of his jacket, pulling him up as another fifty feet of sky disappeared beneath me. He climbed me like a mountain, feet digging into places that made me wince, but suddenly I was spinning head over ass as I plummeted towards the ground, a comet of flesh streaking towards an Earth eager to consume my Menarche bones.

I pulled Isaiah into my chest, my arms and legs wrapped around him, and I remembered that time, not so long ago, when I did something similar with a Feral in my arms. That hurt like a fucking bitch, too.

Did that really happen? It all felt like a dream, another life, another existence, but then, that was a different man, from a different time, and he didn't exist anymore.

Twenty feet. Fifteen feet. I had to try, with everything I had left in me, I had to try.

Ten feet. With a scream that shattered the weeping sky, I pulled up, hovering, a momentary instant of reserves, and then I dropped Isaiah safely to the floor. Pain surged through my veins, agony that collapsed my arteries, and shrivelled my heart, and I plummeted to the floor like a stone.

My eyes throbbed, veins lacing across my vision in pulsating filaments of hunger. My body, shattered and broken, started to shut down, my organs collapsing without the lifeblood to sustain them. I would wither away into a broken husk in the shape of a man, alive, conscious, a living lump of dried shit smeared upon the landscape. What a fitting end to such an ignominious life.

A shadow fell across me, and I saw eyes, worried old eyes. "Feed on me."

"No."

"For the love of God Eli, feed on me, I beg of you."

The smell of his flesh so close to my mouth brought my Vampire to the fore, and I felt my teeth slide down across my hungry lips. I didn't want to drink him, to taste his life renewing my own. I didn't want to press my teeth against his wrist until their tips pierced his skin, so I pushed him away, covering my monster with my arm, hiding my shame. "No Isaiah no, you cannot know what you say."

"Yes I do, of course, I do. And I know what you will see, I want you to see, I want you to understand."

The smell of blood filled my nostrils, crimson life exploding across my nasal membranes in pinpricks of invitation. I was hungry, so very hungry.

"What will I see?"

"Gideon, you will see Gideon, you will see why he left you."

My teeth hovered over his flesh, over skin so brittle that as I pressed down, it popped without resistance, and his blood, his rich, warm blood, filled my mouth. It filled my mind, an infinity of red corpuscles exploding across my tongue in a symphony of revelation.

Through the darkness that engulfed me, I heard his voice, Melek's voice, as he chided Isaiah in the Black Vatican.

"Feeling a bit guilty are we dear heart, because trapping him in ice was your idea?"

Gideon, trapped in ice, trapped by Isaiah, and it was his idea.

Suddenly I was there, I was Isaiah, seeing Gideon through his eyes.

I ran full pelt around the third level of the Colosseum, where so many thousands sat in years gone by. The Thule ran ahead of me, silver canisters glinting on their black-suited backs, like an infestation of Death Beatles scuttling through the night.

"Force him down into the hypogeum, use the ice packs!" I tried to sound as confident and as commanding as I could, for I needed to sound convincing.

One by one, they unhooked the trigger units from around their belts, the clockwork mechanisms whirring into ticking life as they pointed the units towards the pierced night. With a shriek, each unit gushed a fierce jet of liquid nitrogen into the sky, and for a fleeting moment, I was running through a blizzard as fine ice particles drifted to the hungry ground.

Something leapt ahead of us, a dark shadow standing on a crumbling pillar. I froze, my Thule entourage surrounding me, sensing the danger, the Quellor Demons on their backs aroused by the presence of another supernatural being, but in the blink of an eye, the shadow melted into the surrounding darkness.

"Don't be fooled, he's fast. You must be faster."

My heart banged inside my chest. Could they detect my duplicity? Did the Thule know about my pact with Gideon?

They would kill me if they knew. They would kill my Eva. Without hesitation.

With a flash of gut-churning speed, Gideon exploded from the darkness above in all his bestial fury. He crouched close to the ground, snarling, his face a twisted parody of all that was human. Pointed ears and bulging cheekbones ripped away his once handsome face, and teeth, long and cruel, dripped from his salivating mouth between pale, languid lips. Yet, it was the eyes that frightened me the most, such black burning holes of pure hatred that regarded us with the utmost contempt, and they wanted blood.

Gideon saw me then, I felt his darkness brush against my skin, and I saw a look of such pain etched into those monstrous features that I felt my own eyes fill with emotion. We understood each other, and I think, in that place so steeped with death, we respected each other. We were two people fighting for the survival of those that we loved, the human and the Immortal, more alike than we could ever have imagined.

Gideon moved with a speed that terrified me, so fast that his twisted body became nothing more than a blur to me, and before my astonished gaze, a Thule fell to the floor, blood pumping from the stump of his neck. The sudden attack seemed to galvanize the others, and as one, their units belched forth crystalline destruction into the dying night.

The cold fingers of death swirled around my feet as everything turned white. I heard a scream, a sound as cold as the liquid ice that blinded me, and with a whoosh that pressed against my ears, I saw Gideon leap into the air above the gas, and then he was gone.

As the gas cleared, the Thule looked around in confusion, fear evident across their pitiful faces. I should have felt sorry for them, as one human to the next, but they were not strictly human, and I had no sympathy left inside of me that night.

"You bloody fools," I bellowed, trying my hardest to mask my own tremulous panic. "Cross the streams! I told you to cross the streams!"

They refused to listen to me. The superior race listened to nobody, let alone a Jew. But then I saw the object of their attention, one of their own, standing in a defensive pose with his arms raised to cover his face, unmoving.

"No, don't touch him," I warned, but it was too late. One of the Thule touched his elbow, just the lightest brush of his black-gloved finger, and the figure splintered, a million tiny fragments of crystalline humanity that fell to the ground like a column of collapsing sand.

"Leave him," boomed a voice, a deep sibilant voice that I had learned to loathe and fear so much. "My child will not be undone so easily."

The Father stepped out of the shadows, his impossibly long legs carrying him forward in great elongated strides that made me shiver. He stood before me, towering above me with his half-formed features, his eyes so piercing as to shatter my soul.

"But he is dead," I said nervously.

A smile crept across his inhuman face as he bent down to whisper in my ear.

"My poor little Jew, and still he does not understand. Look."

As I watched, I saw the impossible. Bit by bit, each shattered piece of Thule began to pull itself together, moving across the bloodied ground, joining with the next, merging. Something slithered amongst the carnage of human flesh, something shapeless and alien to the human form, tentacles flashing across the bloodied ruin, assembling the impossible jigsaw before my very eyes.

Something brushed against my foot, and I recoiled in horror at the sight of a disembodied head crawling across the ground, pulling itself across the stone on tenuous strands of red gore. The headless corpse twitched, fingers reaching out to accept the head. And then I saw it, the thing on his back, its great yellow eye blazing with hatred as its flaccid grey tentacles reached out and pulled the head onto the still bleeding stump of its neck.

"What is this?" My words choked on the vomit that threatened to pour from my mouth. That thing on his back, that monster assembling the shattered body of its fallen comrade — I had seen it before, back in Berlin, born from the womb of the Mother and placed onto Adi's back.

"My children, little Jew, and that is what this is all about."

"Your children? I thought this was about the Spear, I thought you wanted the Spear?"

"Oh, I do. You will see to that." The sneer that broke his inhuman face sickened me. "But first, we have a world to destroy."

I staggered to the edge of the railing and stared down into the darkness of the hypogeum, overcome with the urge to jump, to free myself from such fathomless evil, such madness. What had I done? Shame coursed through my veins and inflamed my heart, darkening my spirit with the knowledge of my own treachery, my betrayal of the human race. Just one more step into the awaiting darkness and it would be over — the horror of my life would end.

Eva's life would end.

"Why are you doing this? To what end must the world suffer so?"

The Father stepped forward to the edge, and together we watched the Thule hound Gideon through the Colosseum, jets of icy death forcing him ever downwards into the bowels of history, and it was all my fault.

"Do you love her?" The question shocked me, and I dared to look into his face, into those cold, heartless eyes. "That bitch from Berlin. Do you love her?"

"Yes, with all that I am, for what it is worth." The words caught on the edge of my lips, and I held my emotions there, trembling.

"And what would you do for love, Isaiah? Would you destroy the world for love?"

"Anything. I would do anything for love, but I won't do that. I would die for Eva, and she would die for me."

His smile crept across his pallid features as a fault-line creeps across the ground, deadly, and immeasurably dark.

"Yes, my friend, as you demonstrated so proficiently in Berlin with your tight virgin ass in the air, as you continue to demonstrate now. As I would do for my son, as I will do for my son. I will have Morbius returned to me, little Jew, and the blood of that cunt out there will allow me to do just that, amongst other things."

A ball of red light drifted upwards from the heart of the hypogeum, a slow impending omen of doom that exploded across the ruins in a shower of red sparks, and for a moment, the Colosseum lay bathed in blood once more.

"They have cornered him, that's the signal."

"Then finish your work, little Jew, descend into the bowels of time and capture a piece of history for me. Put the bastard on ice!"

I ran from the Father, eager to place as much distance as I could between his unearthly presence and my trembling bones. As I ran headlong into the pits of hell, I could not help but pray the darkness would consume my treacherous soul. Every step I took, every breath I inhaled felt stolen, as though I had cheated mankind with every beat of my heart. How I hated myself for living.

The hypogeum was a maze of intricate corridors and cells that once housed the various animals and gladiators beneath the arena floor of the Colosseum. Time had exposed the guts of the Amphitheatre to the machinations of nature, turning the inner workings into a maze of moss ridden brick and crumbling architecture, into which I plunged headlong.

Blackness wrapped its Machiavellian fingers around my traitorous body as it pulled me into the heart of darkness, the heart *of silence. The world vanished in shadow and brick, my ears ringing with the sound of utter emptiness, for not even my feet disturbed the air as they brushed against the ground. I could barely see, and my mind existed in such a state I could hardly feel. I stood in the middle of Rome, groping in the dark, surrounded by monsters.*

My fingers felt along dry dusty walls, my skin thrumming with the beat of my pounding heart. Something moved to my right, a stone bouncing against brick with a sharp ping, and I froze, my lips clenched tight against my own irrational fear. I felt sure something lurked within the shadows, just on the edge of a split between two walls, and I moved forward tentatively. I had to find Gideon, I had to know that his mind remained resolute.

The sky exploded as another crimson flare lit up the night, and Gideon stood before me. My mouth split in an instant of sudden shock, the scream perched on the edge of my lips, but Gideon swept forward and clamped a cold hand across my mouth.

"Have I done enough Isaiah, are they convinced that their trap has worked?"

He removed his hand from my face, and I stared into the countenance of one who looked desperate. His eyes burned with pain, with a helplessness that wounded my heart.

"You still want to go through with this then?"

"Put me in that fucking ice and never let me out! Do you know what I did last night Isaiah? I nearly went back to him, to Eli. I can't stand it anymore, I can't stand to be away from him, I can't stand not touching him, and I can't fucking stand lying to him! So yes, my friend, I still want to go through with it. Lock me away and never let me near him, for Eli's sake."

A tear, a sparkling diamond of despair trickled down his pale cheek, that hulking man, that gladiator from days gone past, breaking before my very eyes. I pulled him into my arms, and I held him close, feeling his loneliness seep into the fabric of my suit, and I felt closer to him then than I had any other being since Eva.

Gideon fumbled in his jacket and produced a book, a thick volume of papers that he shoved into my hands.

"What is this?"

"Answers my friend. A story. If I do not ask for it back, if I am unable to do so myself, you must give it to Eli, will you promise me this Isaiah? Would you do this for me?"

I pushed the book into my own pocket, feeling its bulging volume against my chest, safe next to my heart.

"It will not come to that my friend. When this is over, you will give it to him yourself, of this I promise."

"Time has been a cruel thing, Isaiah Nathan Silberman, but in the last seconds of my time upon this Earth, it has delivered me into your hands, and I thank it for you."

"In a moment I want you to hit me. Do you think you can do that Gideon? They will be upon us quickly, so you must make it convincing."

"I could never hurt you, Isaiah," he groaned as he pulled away from me, concern masking his pain.

"You must, Gideon, you must make it so."

The man, the Vampire, the being closest to God, pulled himself up and looked into my face with a steely resolve. It was time.

"Gaius, call me Gaius. I was born with that name, let me die with it too."

"You will not die this day, Gaius Cassius Longinus, now bloody well hit me. He's here! Over here!"

With a speed that surprised myself, I pulled the flare gun out of my pocket and fired into the air, just as Gideon's fist collided with the underside of my jaw. My vision exploded in a kaleidoscope of red stars, and I found myself weightless, floating amongst the glowing embers of my own consciousness.

My breath exploded from my lungs as my body crashed onto the top of one of the walls, and for a moment, I thought the blackness would win out as the world spun around me in a dizzying whirl of pain and nausea. Above me, the flare began its slow, graceful descent, a flickering ball of incandescent light that blackened the sky and diminished the stars. I struggled to sit up, pain throbbing through my jaw, and I turned around, perched *precariously upon the wall above the hypogeum as I was, clutching the brick for dear life.*

Red flickering light illuminated the scene below. Figures dressed in black with glittering canisters strapped to their backs advanced down the many branches of the maze, a dozen black beetles converging on Gideon at the centre, but he did not move. One by one, the Thule unhooked their triggers, and the night filled with the sound of ticking.

My eyes strained against the agony that wanted them to close, that wanted me to submit to the welcoming arms of oblivion, but I had to see, I had to watch. I had to make sure.

The flare flickered in and out of existence so that the action below appeared to strobe in slow motion. Like the killers they truly were, the Thule stalked their prey, sliding forward in unison until they surrounded Gideon, their guns firing icy blasts of gas until his body vanished in a cloud of white.

The world started to fade as the flare started to fade, its dying light offering mere fragments of the carnage below. As I fought against the darkness that so wanted to consume me, I saw him, Gaius Cassius Longinus, the soldier who stabbed the side of Christ two thousand years ago, the first Vampire to walk God's green Earth, frozen in time, unmoving in a prison of ice.

I withdrew my teeth from Isaiah's wrist, and I was blind. Grief, despair, pain, all crashed over me in a tidal wave of bitter realisation.

Gideon left me to keep me safe.

Gideon left me to protect me from the truth.

Gideon loved me.

The sky blurred through my cold tears, my lips curled at the brink of a frozen scream, and the remains of my blackened heart broke into a thousand pieces.

My Gideon. Gaius Cassius Longinus. The man who made me Vampire. The lying cunt who made me Menarche.

I felt my hands dig into the snow-encrusted ground, pain throbbing through my fingers as I dug deep, splitting flesh, splintering bones, and I wanted the pain, I needed the pain, to fill me as his lies filled me.

"Papa!" The voice came from behind me as I lay there staring into a Heaven that fucking hated me. For a moment, Ethan's face appeared above me, and even through my despair, I could not help but be struck by his fascinating beauty.

The sun broke through defiant clouds, and for a moment, just the briefest of moments, Ethan's head lay crowned by a blinding halo of light.

"Son!"

The sound of a muffled embrace tickled through my dizzy brain, but the world had no embrace for me, the world had no love left for me. I stayed but a Demon ground into the mud like so much shit pumped out from a horse's ass.

"Help me, my son, help me to move him into safety."

Hands, so gentle, so human, lifted me from my resting place and carried me towards Alte, my lonely Folly in the middle of nowhere, as remote from the world as I, and just as desolate.

My feet dragged across the earth, as unable to grasp the soil as my mind remained unable to grasp reality. Isaiah's chest wheezed with the exertion, but I was no more capable of helping them than I was capable of changing history.

Gaius Cassius Longinus, the man who speared Christ on the cross, the man who made me Vampire. He was fucking history.

They lowered me into a chair next to my dining table. I loved that dining table, it was so grand, so ostentatious, so fucking expensive, and I had to have it. My finger, weak and trembling, traced the fissure that marred its perfect surface, a fissure made in a fleeting moment of anger. My anger.

"I spared... no expense..." The words tumbled from my trembling lips and fell upon the painted surface in a whisper. Broken. All of us broken.

"Where's Malachi?" Ethan's question sliced through my flesh with icy precision, and my heart cracked open as easily as the table before me. I looked up into his beautiful face, his eyes so wide and clear, so full of concern, so fucking full of empathy.

"He left me... I killed him, and he left me. They all leave me." Shock flittered briefly across his face, but he was quick to conceal it, his face lying to me with sympathy and concern.

They all lied to me. Faces were nothing but animated lies, and words were nothing but lies given form.

"Ethan, bring him blankets, we must get some warmth into him, he's in shock."

A smile, small and cruel, curled at the corners of my lips.

"I'm a fucking walking corpse, a fucking Vampire, warmth means fuck all to me unless it's the heat of your blood filling me!"

Isaiah looked at me with such compassion that I wanted to knock his pissing lights out. He knelt before me and took my cold hands in his, his old, coarse skin rubbing the cold of my unyielding flesh.

"I know very well what you are, my friend, make no mistake about that. Ethan, do as I ask."

My gaze followed Ethan's tight ass as it bounced up my massive stairs, his cheeks, so firm, so fucking tight. For a moment, my desire dampened my anger, and I yearned for my tongue to slide between those cheeks and seek out the soft inner flesh, but then I turned my anger upon Isaiah, and he flinched beneath its fury.

"He thinks you are not his father. Is it true?"

Isaiah paled as his fingers clenched around my fists. It was cruel of me to say such a thing, to spill it so callously upon his lap, but I was so fucking angry, so fucking bitter, and why should I suffer it alone?

"He has read my diaries then?"

"Is it true? Is he yours?" I made no effort to conceal the spite in my voice, and he withered before me.

"That is a conversation for another time."

I swayed in my chair and slumped forward, my head resting on the old man's shoulder as my suffering poured into the tweed of his jacket. Pain heaved through my body and cleaved at my shrivelled soul as my life crashed upon Isaiah's shore.

"He lied to me, all those years lying to me." My voice, so pathetic, so weak, dissolved into his shoulder, and when I looked up, Isaiah was crying too, tears streaming through the old rivers of his face.

"Don't lie to him, Isaiah, don't ever lie to him."

The hall echoed with the sudden explosion of Alte's huge wooden doors as they flew inwards. With a speed that belied his age, Isaiah leapt to his feet and swung around, but I could already see the massive frame outlined in the doorway.

Gideon.

Isaiah walked forward, and to my astonishment, they embraced, as though two old friends, arms wrapped tightly around each other.

My muscles tightened, rage filling them to the point of bursting.

"Papa?" Ethan stood half way down the stairs, blankets clutched to his chest. Isaiah stepped away from my ex-boyfriend, and Gideon's jaw nearly hit the floor in shock as he saw Ethan for the first time.

"Jesus fucking Christ!"

The sound of his gruff voice acted like a catalyst. Every muscle, every sinew, every nerve in my body released me from my stupor, and I launched myself out of my chair, a seething, hissing mass of fury. Before Gideon could react, I wrapped my talons around his neck, lifting his hard, bulging body from the floor, the points of my teeth mere inches from tearing into the flesh of his neck.

I became the monster, and my fury burned.

"How dare you do that to me, you fucking cunt!" Gideon's massiveness flew through the air and crashed into the balustrade running around the upper level. The marble quivered at the impact of his bulk, and then Gideon slammed to the floor in a heap of flesh.

"Eli, don't," pleaded Isaiah as he placed a gentle hand upon my bulging arm, but I turned on him, snarling into his oh so concerned face, my anger unleashed in a fury of bitter words. "Fuck off old man, before I fuck you up too!"

Through the blur of darkness that cocooned me, I saw Ethan rush forward to pull his father away from me, but it was the squirming piece of shit on the floor that had my full attention.

"Get up and face me, you lying, worthless bastard."

Gideon picked himself up, slowly, carefully, his gaze never leaving my face. Not even a flicker of Vampire manifested itself across his handsome features, and he remained handsome, every bit of him as hard as those eyes that bore into me.

"I will not fight you, Eli."

"No, you never were one for giving out, were you?"

I lunged at him, my hands colliding with his magnificent chest, and for a second, just the briefest of moments, I remembered how he felt beneath my fingers, beneath my lips.

It infuriated me.

Enraged, I sent my feet into his rippling stomach with a force befitting my anger, and Gideon slammed into the plaster wall behind him, crumpling to the ground with a groan of pain.

"All those years," and I picked him off the floor, lifting him above my head, "lying to me. All those years of fucking lies!"

All his lies, all his betrayals, the horror of everything that he was pumped through my veins and inflated my muscles to send him flying through the air onto the upper level with a satisfying crash. My body lifted, rising above Isaiah and Ethan, and I landed on the edge of the bannister overlooking my twat of an ex.

The blue of his eyes blazed back at me from within a tangle of thick limbs. I used to love those eyes, and now I hated them.

"You made me, you fucking made me! All those years of looking, of wondering who I was, who I am, and you knew, you knew all along, and you never told me."

"I couldn't tell you, Eli, I couldn't."

I leapt down off my marble perch and hunkered down beside him, my lips skipping over the hardness of his neck, my nostrils inhaling the manliness of his scent. My tongue brushed his cheek, tasting him, remembering him, and to my horror I felt my cock stiffen, aroused by my memory of his magnificent body.

"Why couldn't you tell me?" I breathed the words into his ear, and his flesh erupted with goose pimples. "You are my creator, are you not? You made the choice to make me Menarche, so why couldn't you tell me?"

"Because I forbade him too."

The fucking Angel stood over us, Daniyyel in all his sanctimonious glory.

Something inside me snapped.

We were flying through the air, the Angel and the Vampire, and my hands squeezed the life out of his throat. Words, obscene, erupted from my mouth in a torrent of abuse, spittle, blood, bitterness, flecking his pretty face as we hovered above the hall, a spiralling commotion of wrath.

I was no match for the Angel, I knew that. He could tear me limb from limb without stopping for breath, but I didn't care. My fingers dug into his flesh, my teeth snapped at his face, and my legs wrapped themselves around his body in an effort to purge his body of its life.

I might just have well have fucked a bloody statue.

The floor hit my face so hard that the marble cracked beneath my cheek. Pain, dark and intense, surged through my skull and down my spine and exploded in my ass in a burst of throbbing agony. I tried to lift my head, but a hand, a strong hand, ground my face into the ruined floor.

"Stay down, Eli."

My hands fumbled behind me, trying to dislodge the Angel on my head, but it was like trying to move a mountain with a fart.

"I said stay down."

My fingers clawed at the flesh of his hands, but my anger dripped from my eyes, consumed by the dust beneath my flesh as despair filled my soul and broke my heart. I was nothing but a pathetic creature lying in the detritus of my own failures.

Somebody pulled me to my feet and wiped the tears and the dust from my face. For a moment, I did not know who he was, who any of them were in that room, looking at me with eyes filled with so much fucking pity.

I stumbled over steps, but firm hands kept me upright, guiding me in a blur of movement about which I had no comprehension. Images flashed by my vision, indistinct shapes and colours that meant nothing to me, a voice that whispered in my ear, words lost to me in a fog of utter desperation.

Something soft beneath me. It felt so comfortable, yet somehow alien, as though comfort belonged to some other world.

My legs moved, lifted from the floor and onto the mattress. My naked flesh sank into that wonderful surface.

Naked. I lay naked. Why was I naked?

The concentration camp at Wewelsburg Castle, the gas chamber, Joseph dying in my arms. The Black Vatican. Morbius, back from the dead. Gideon.

The scream that flew from between my lips shattered the silence. I sat up suddenly, my gaze darting around my blue room, my bedroom, straight into the face of Ethan.

"Ssshh, you're safe, Eli, you are safe now. Nothing is going to harm you."

He placed a surprisingly strong hand against my hard chest and pushed me down onto the mattress, leaning over me. His lips were so close, his beauty blinding me to the horror in my head.

"Trust in me Eli, trust in me." Those words, they flickered through my brain to ignite some distant memory, words from the past, words spoken by those lips, by that beautiful man, words he had said to me before.

"Who are you?" It was such a stupid question, spoken in barely a whisper, but he laughed at me all the same, a gentle sound that filled me with a profound feeling of hope. I wanted to cry.

"Your friend, Eli, I am your friend. I want you to lie still so I can wash you, can you do that for me?"

I lay back, suddenly calm, his voice so soothing in my head, and I closed my eyes. Through the darkness of my despair, I heard the swoosh of water, a sponge squeezed of excess water, and then the sensation of his hands upon me. The sponge moved across my chest, firm yet gentle movements that left a cold trail of moisture across my flesh. Droplets of water slid down my side, and then he refreshed the sponge.

I had to keep my eyes closed. I had to stay in the dark. If I opened my eyes, I would see him bending over me, touching me, and I could not stand it.

Fingers wiped the hair away from my face, and the sponge followed, swift circular movements to wipe away the horror of the last few days. But I could see them, there behind my eyelids, more horror than I could stomach, and I feared that I would throw up, but my stomach remained as empty as my cold dark heart.

Cloth, soft as snow against my skin, wiped away the water from my face before the sponge returned to cleanse me. If I opened my eyes now, would he be looking at me?

His hands worked with purpose, inch by inch down my rock hard body, around the massiveness of my arms, down the edges of my legs, around my calves, sliding wet and cold, their touch an epiphany of sensation. I dared to move my hand, sliding slowly across my chest, the hardness of my nipples rubbing against my palm, sending a tingle of excitement through my nerves, and I had to bite my lip to stop the gasp of air that awaited there.

My back arched slightly as the wetness reached my groin. Cold water ran freely between my legs, down my testicles, which tightened at the sensation. I knew my cock stood hard, I could feel it throbbing, moving against the flatness of my stomach as it twitched in sympathy with each stroke of Ethan's hands.

The sponge moved around my erection, the side of his hand brushing against my veined shaft, making it dance. I slid my arm up over my head to cover my eyes, to cover the shame that trickled down my cheek, wishing it to be over, to hide from the world that hated me so very much, but then his fingers entwined within my own, pulling my hand away from my face.

"Look at me Eli." I dared to open my eyes, and I looked into the face of a God. "Do not be ashamed, you have nothing to be ashamed of."

"I have everything to be ashamed of." Damn the emotion that strangled my voice.

Ethan's free hand slid onto my chest, fingers gliding down the musculature of my stomach until his palm lay flat next to my throbbing cock. His gaze never left me, the emerald green of his eyes penetrating me, fucking me, and I wanted to give in to him. I wanted him to touch me until I lay spent.

The silence felt so profound that it hurt. I could feel the heat of his hand next to my dick, and I could not stop the throbbing, as though my cock wanted to jump into the palm of his hand no matter how I tried to resist. Still, he looked at me, his gaze unnerving, the look on his face unfathomable to me, intense yet gentle, searching, questioning, wanting.

I had wanted him from the moment I saw him. From the moment I pulled him out of the mud, he belonged to me.

And I belonged to him.

My bedroom door flew open, and Gideon filled the doorway. He stopped, something akin to surprise registering across his hard manly face, and Ethan jumped to his feet. I pulled the sheet over my nakedness.

"I'm sorry..."

"No, no it's okay," stammered Ethan as he quickly walked towards the door, "I was just leaving."

As Ethan moved to the door, Gideon sidestepped away from him. It was an odd gesture, because Gideon seemed reluctant to touch Ethan, and all the time his gaze never left him, a look of utter disbelief upon his face. Even when Ethan closed the door behind him, Gideon looked at the door, through the door, eyes wide, bewildered.

"Get out of my fucking room."

"It used to be ours."

"Yeah, and then you abandoned me. Fuck off, you lying cunt, I've got nothing to say to you."

Gideon walked forward and stood over the bed, his eyes taking in the smoothness of my body, the contours of my muscles, the bulge still twitching beneath the thin sheet.

I thought he was going to touch me, it seemed to me that he wanted to. His hands twitched by his sides, his arms bulging with muscles, and I wondered if I would let him. My cock told me that I would, moving as it did against the sheets, but my head told me otherwise, and my heart insisted that I hated him.

"Get dressed." It was a demand, not a request, as gruff and as straightforward as only Gideon could be.

"The days of me doing what you want have long fucking gone, you pompous prick. Don't march back in here and tell me what to do!"

Gideon stomped over to a chest, ripped open the drawers and pulled out a handful of clothes.

"Get fucking dressed," he demanded, throwing the clothes at me. "You may not want to talk to me, but I fucking want to talk to you."

"I don't want to hear it!"

He leaned into me then, his rough, handsome face filling my vision.

"Listen to me Eli, and listen to me well. Right now, I would like nothing more than to rip that sheet of your fucking tight body and ride that stiff cock of yours until my asshole bleeds for more. Fuck me into next week for all I care, but we haven't got time, for your bruised feelings or any of this bullshit! I have a story to tell you, one that you all need to hear. Now, before it's too late."

Chapter Four: The Passions Of Men

As Related By Gideon

I woke up with Pontius Pilate's cock up my ass. As wake up calls went, that was not so bad.

Pilate was not my first, but he did ruin me. He was a syphilitic cunt, all too fond of sticking his dick into anything warm and wet. Every time his wife ran off to her rich father in Rome, Pilate partied, for days, orgies that became a legend in their own right. Pilate knew how to retain the loyalty of his men, knee deep in wine, cunt and semen as we were, for nothing bought a man's silence more than the sucking of his dick, and nothing happened in Judea, or the Empire, without Pilate knowing it. Such remained the hold that Pontius Pilate held over his men, one hand on their hearts with the other firmly gripping their bollocks. His influence stretched as far across the Senate as his dick stretched my hole.

As a Praetorian Guard, I remained one of a small contingent of protectors for the Prefect of Judea, Pilate, an important position within the vast Roman Empire, in an area besieged by political and religious unrest. Not that I understood a fucking word of it. I was there to protect him, and my comprehension of the political status was unimportant. What did the machinations of a corrupt Rome matter to us, those chosen few in his favour, licking his dick and enjoying the privileges of our position?

Everything that happened, everything that I became, all the horror and the agony, all because of that one moment, all because he chose me to be the receiver of his rotting dick. It sucked.

We were men, real fucking men, hard, rough, crude bastards with bulging arms, and more muscle than brains. That was me, that was my life. A walking lump of meat with a sword in my hand and a sword between my legs, and I was not afraid to use either of them. I should never have left Migdala Nunia, not that I had much choice considering what happened.

Nestled upon the shoreline of Galilee lay the small fishing village of Migdala, with an even smaller, very tight, community of people. As with all small communities, everyone knew each other's business, and in that lay the problem.

I grew up with Mary, as much one of the boys as any of my male friends. Shit, that girl knew no fear. Who was it that persuaded us to steal a fishing boat one night so we could catch fish for father's breakfast? We got ourselves stuck on an outcrop of rock, stranded until our parents came to our rescue the next morning. Mary laughed, she thought it funny, especially when our fathers tore a strip off us boys, leaving Mary unscathed and blameless. Those were good fucking times.

Mary and Gaius, two names forever joined together in the same sentence, two souls joined at the hip by the deep bonds of friendship, inseparable. Everyone assumed that we would marry, everyone assumed that we loved one another, and we did, just not like that. I tried a lady garden once, and I swear that thing had teeth, and I knew early on that women did nothing for me. Mary always knew, of course, as only women seem to know such things. While men always talked to her tits, I always talked to her eyes, so she knew — we just never really talked about it, we didn't need to. More often than not, our gaze would linger upon a particularly pert ass, or sweaty, rippled torso — such things abounded in a hardworking village full of robust men. And we found pretty quickly that we had very similar tastes in men. She didn't judge, she didn't laugh, she just understood. And while those observers, none the wiser, watched in eager anticipation as we wandered along the shore of Galilee, hand in hand, we did so as two friends, best friends. We understood each other with the same love, and the same heart as any brother and sister. Intelligent, astute, witty, all words that best described Mary Magdalene, but more than that, she was kind, and she was generous, and she was my friend.

Leonidus changed all that. He came to Migdala as part of a Roman battalion stationed on the outskirts of the village, a tower of blond hair and muscle that turned my eye every time I saw him parade through our little village. Every part of him glistened in the sun, his skin so bronzed with veins that bulged across his muscular arms and legs. He was fucking gorgeous. He always made a point of looking at me, at all of me, and I always felt my face flush beneath his hard, penetrating gaze. He liked that, it always made him smile.

Mary saw it too, she was no fool, and true to her love for me, she arranged our first meeting. As far as our families knew, Mary and I went out to enjoy another moonlit walk along the sands, but in reality, I was sucking Leonidus's cock dry in the net sheds.

We met every couple of days. I was seventeen, barely a man, but I knew what I wanted. He was twenty-two, and I wanted him.

One of the fishing boats arrived home late one night. I didn't know that both my father and Mary's were on that boat. Leonidus threw me over a barrel and stuck his cock of death inside me, and it felt so fucking good, and just as I reached the peak of my orgasm, our fathers walked in. That signalled the end of my life in Migdala.

I left that very same night, having found that my own front door remained firmly closed against me. As did every door in Migdala. The scandal travelled around the town like a fart on the breeze, even to the point that my neighbour threatened me with a knife. Small towns have small minds, closed minds, afraid of anything different. However, to see my mother and father standing on their doorstep shouting at me as I walked away from them, screaming at me to leave, declaring me an unfit human being—well that broke my heart. A parent should always love their child, no matter what they may be, but I lost them that night, I lost my parents forever, and I never saw them again. To this day I don't know when they died, or where their bodies lay, and I never went back to find out, it hurt too much. So I left.

Mary cried. Leaving her behind hurt like hell. I would never forget her face as I left her on the outskirts of Migdala, the grief that poured from her eyes as I hugged her for the last time. She wanted to come with me, she pleaded to come with me, but I wouldn't let her. Would things have been different if she had? Would I have lived my life as a human? Died as a human? Who knows? But I left Migdala and I joined the Roman Legion, and although I never found Leonidus again, I did find a whole new vocation.

Pilate picked me out of a lineup. All of us, slaves and guards alike, paraded before the devouring eyes of the Prefect of Judea for his titillation and entertainment. He moved along the line as though shopping for fruit at the markets, hands testing the firmness of his wares. Tit or cock, he did not care, not with his wife away.

When he stood before me, he stopped, his watery, beady little eyes regarding me as a scorpion regards its prey, and I could almost feel him taking in every contour of my hard, proud body. Pilate felt my bulging arms, his fingers tracing the veins that pushed through my bronzed skin, feeling the outline of my muscles that glistened with sweat in that interminable heat. My arms seemed to please him. His fingers moved down through the valley of my rippled stomach, his gaze never leaving my face, and I met that gaze, unwavering as his hand reached between my legs to grab my manliness at its root.

I did not flinch. I dared not flinch. I didn't want to flinch. Clammy fingers fondled my balls, caressing my sack until the skin tightened around my scrotum. Pilate smirked. His fingers gripped my swelling shaft, tugging on its thickness until it stood tall and proud.

Blood filled the cheeks of my face as surely as it filled my cock, and that made Pilate laugh.

"Bend over."

I bent over, my fingers touching my toes, and that made Pilate laugh all the harder.

"The other way you dimwitted fool. Turn around."

I turned slowly, suddenly nervous as I glimpsed Pilate wetting his index finger with his mouth. Even so, nervous as I felt, I bent over.

It didn't hurt as his slippery digit slid into my hole. The sensation felt really rather pleasant. Indeed, during masturbation, I had inserted my own exploratory finger into my ass on more than one occasion, enjoying the prolonged orgasm it extended me.

Pilate pushed his finger in deeper, and I felt it moving inside me, his fingertip probing the base of my prostate, making my stiffened cock twitch with sympathy. So I clenched my muscles around his finger, opening and closing my hole, much to Pilate's amusement. He pulled his finger out roughly, and he spun me around, a slight smirk creeping across his not unattractive face.

"Tight, just the way I like it. You'll do."

Something caught hold of me, a moment of madness, and I reached out a hand to grab Pilate's shaft beneath his gown, which I noted with satisfaction lay hard in the palm of my hand.

"Hard, just the way I like it."

For a moment, I thought I was fucked, that I had pushed it too far, but his look of shocked disbelief soon melted into laughter.

"You are a cheeky one, aren't you? I like that. I hope you are as bold in bed, for I intend to put that mouth of yours to good use."

From that moment on, I became Pilate's bitch. Whenever his wife travelled, a frequent occurrence as she preferred the civility and luxuries of Rome, her position in bed belonged to me. I remained his bodyguard and a body to use, and I can't say that bothered me one little bit. No longer did I suffer the stifling and overcrowded atmosphere of the barracks. Instead I lived in my own small room within the Villa, easy access for the Prefect of Judea, and whomever else he saw fit to visit upon me. Again, I did not mind, such visits often accompanied heavy purses of coin. I felt happy in the knowledge that my fortune had changed for the better, and that one day I might return to Migdala a wealthy man and buy back the affection of the family that once abandoned me. A foolish, naive thought, but one that sustained me all the same.

Most of my visitors consisted of senators, visitors from Rome after some cock while their wives remained conveniently absent, but one man, in particular, stood high above them all.

As Prefect of Judea, Pilate had relations with all the important players in the region, and no one stood more important than Joseph Caiaphas, Jewish high priest and head of the Sanhedrin, the highest judicial body in the land. Caiaphas had control over the entire Jewish population, second only to the Romans themselves.

Pilate presented me to Caiaphas as a gift, as reconciliation for a fierce argument between Pilate and Caiaphas over someone they called the Messiah, but like the cum bucket I had become, I just laid back ready to take whatever he wanted to give, cock, spunk, and money.

Never a more striking man than Caiaphas had I seen, handsome, painfully handsome, with long black hair that glistened over his shoulders, tumbling down his back. His cheekbones framed a face of utter beauty, high and angular, defined, and his lips looked moist, plump. Nothing, however, could compare to his eyes.

Most men's eyes looked dead as they fucked me, nothing living behind them, no emotion, no interest, no love, just the insatiable need to spread their seed in something tight, something that would not lead to unwanted offspring. Caiaphas, however, he didn't just fuck me, he made love to me. His eyes burned. Never had I seen such a look on a man's face as he entered me, and he wanted me on my back, he wanted me to see his face as he pushed his huge dick inside my ass. He kissed me, bending my body in half as he bore down upon me. His lips crashed against my own, his tongue seeking me out with such eagerness, such unbridled passion as he pushed in deeper and deeper, filling me with his cock, splitting my ass in half with his immense manhood, and I fucking loved it. There was something animalistic about it, bestial, and the ferocity, the hunger that blistered across his sublime features aroused me so profoundly that I found myself orgasming without aid, my semen shooting across his snarling face as he, too, shot his load inside of me. Yet his eyes burned, bright, alive, glowing with a desire that set my skin on fire, eyes that burned in the dark.

He did not speak as he adjusted his robe, tucking his manhood away, but his gaze never left me as I lay straddled and spent across the small bed. He seemed to look at me with a deep satisfaction, and something else, something that

I could only describe as approval. His hands, such big hands, with long immaculately manicured fingers, brushed my cheek, and for a moment my heart beat so fast within my chest as to burst through the ribcage. Such was the sensation of his touch against my skin that a tingle of unexpected affection surged through my flesh to arouse me yet again.

He paused in the low door, and he turned, his handsome face so commanding to me, bewitching, but then he smiled at me, a smile so big that I thought it a trick of the light, for no man could split his face so wide. Something flew through the air and landed next to my hand, and I picked it up, weighing the bag in my hand — a heavy bag, full of silver.

That was the first time I met Joseph Caiaphas. The second time I met him changed the course of history.

So began the day that would forever remain in the collective memory of mankind. Pilate emptied his balls into me with a grunt, slid off me without a word, and began to dress. I sat on the edge of the bed, a huge thing surrounded by billowing panels of translucent fabric, and I stared at the floor, my head spinning.

I could barely see the tiles beneath my bare feet.

The pain in my head, the blurring of my eyes, all of it worse with every passing day. Some days I could see just fine, sometimes the world existed behind a sheet of shimmering fog. However, that morning, sitting on the edge of the bed looking for my robes, it felt as though I looked through layers of moving gauze, a sickening, nauseating sensation that left me disorientated and dizzy. My eyes throbbed, my head hurt, and when I rubbed my eyes, I found them to be coated with a thick, sticky substance that glued my eyelids together. The blisters also returned, painful sores that lurked at the edges of my rectum, throbbing now due to the pounding inflicted upon me by Pilate.

My condition, the sores, the trouble with my sight, came and went in ever increasing intervals. Each time my sight grew dim that bit more, and it frightened me, for what good was I as a soldier? Indeed, what good was I as a man, if I could not see? Already the other men ostracized me, a soldier turned prostitute in the eyes of men, and they were right. I lived the life of a fucking prostitute, and I took the money gladly, a means to an end, I kept telling myself, my ticket out, my way back home, but I only fooled myself with such naïve beliefs. I allowed men to fuck me for money, and the disease that ravaged my body stood as my just reward.

I couldn't tell anyone about my shame, and I certainly couldn't show my weakness. The Guard did not tolerate such frailty within their ranks, and if I revealed my condition, all my worldly goods, my armour, my money, even my life, would be forfeit. I had seen it happen. A blind man left to fend for himself in the wilderness of Judea. Might as well be a dead man, and the Guard would just as likely pierce my heart at the point of a sword and call it mercy. So I kept my secret as the world around me diminished in a cloud of darkness.

Darkness. I had yet to understand the full meaning of the word, but darkness would make me comprehend its deepest despairs.

It took me longer than usual to climb into my white toga. As Pilate's personal guard, we did not have to wear the full segmentata. The overbearing heat made such things almost impossible to wear, and besides, if anyone made an attempt on the Prefect's life, we could move more freely without the restriction of leather and metal. However, that morning, Pilate had a meeting with the Sanhedrin, and such formalities required the complete regalia, segmentata, breastplate, helmet, and spear. While incredibly articulate, it weighed a fucking ton!

I stepped out of the Praetorium into a day filled with bright white light, the harsh glare of the sun making me blink rapidly, tears streaming down my face. For a moment, blindness won out, and I found myself lost to a world of murmuring shadows until my hand found the back of Pilate's Judgment seat. I steadied myself there, blinking away the panic from my vision until the world came into focus, revealed to me as a throng of human chaos.

So many people, over a hundred, crammed into the area outside the Praetorium. Known as the Pavement, the high walled garden outside the Praetorium, with its blazing braziers and arched colonnades, usually admitted small groups of dignitaries, senators, important visitors wishing to gain an audience with Pilate, but on that unforgettable day, the area seethed with people, people baying for blood.

Danger hung in the air, a palpable sense of impending jeopardy that immediately saw the Guard forming a protective stance around Pilates throne, and as my vision began to clear, so did the faces that surrounded us. Anger, fury, poised upon every lip, a seething cauldron of unrest that could bubble over at any moment, and in the centre of the throng stood Caiaphas and a man who's pained face would live with me for all of eternity.

Much has been written about that figure crouched on the floor, bound with rope, clothes in ripped shreds across his soiled body, hair long and matted about a face etched with such deep pain. I just saw a man, beaten, bruised, but unbroken, whose eyes blazed with a compassion that extended even to his accusers. Such a man would cast an intimidating shadow under kinder circumstances, for he was a man of great size and physicality, a man who had seen the toil of hard labour, and whose body had shaped itself accordingly.

So much beauty, visible even through his soiled anguish, radiating from him, both physical and spiritual. I could sense it. I could feel the fingers of his compassion wrapping themselves around my beating heart. His eyes, so green, so pure, filled with a light that danced, a light that seemed to shine from within, a dignity that shunned the shame of those who cried for his destruction.

"Crucify him! Crucify him!"

The cry united the crowd, a terrifying scream for blood that made my veins run cold.

Caiaphas held up his hands, and such was the command of that imposing man that the excited crowd fell silent.

"And so Herod sent him back! Not even that fat cunt would deem to soil his hands with this man's blood. Herod will not kill him!"

The crowd roared, their cries threatening to shatter the stone upon which the Pavement arose.

"Crucify him! Crucify him! Crucify him!"

Caiaphas paced the flagstone pavement before the throne in a fury of gesticulating arms and flowing white robes. Even his long raven-black hair seemed agitated.

Pilate squirmed in his throne, a man trapped by his own fears and inactions. "Be reasonable, Caiaphas. Herod may hate my guts, but he is afraid of you, of the Sanhedrin. The accused lies humiliated even now, a man broken, what possible threat is he to you now? Surely, is that not enough?"

The sky darkened, thick black clouds obscuring the heat of the morning sun in a show of nature's wrath, but it was nothing compared to the blistering fury that poured from Caiaphas. He stopped his wild pacing and swung around to face Pilate, his beautiful hands clenched into fists at his side, his beatific features contorted into a maelstrom of rage, but it was his eyes that made Pilate shrink back into his golden throne, for they burned with a ferocity that outshone the sun.

"You have no fucking idea, do you, little man? Will he be our puppet King? To do as we see fit? Ours to control? No! Instead, he whips up the little people into such a state of religious fervour as to bring them away from our control. That limp wristed sycophant spouting his sanctimonious bullshit! And they turn to him, in their thousands, do you understand that? In their thousands. Where will it end? When we are but nothing beneath his sandaled feet, trodden into the earth that he claims to love so fucking much. If he won't be controlled, if this self-proclaimed Messiah will not bend to my will, then I will see him dead at my feet!" In a blur of movement that sent a shiver down my spine, Caiaphas glided towards the throne and thrust his face towards Pilate. "Crucify him."

I moved forward, reluctant, suddenly afraid of that powerful, magnetic figure that threatened the Prefect. I placed myself between them, the Prefect and the High Priest, but to stand between them felt like hell itself.

Slowly, Caiaphas turned his head towards me, a serpentine movement that made my stomach churn.

"Hello sweetie, I wouldn't, if I were you, wouldn't want to damage those lovely muscles of yours now would we dear heart? What is wrong with your eyes?"

My skin turned cold as the blood drained into my feet. Caiaphas winked at me and then stepped away from the throne, but I found that I could not tear my gaze away from the man. He terrified me, but at the same time, he excited me, the danger that exuded from him, the strength of being that radiated from his fine frame, the magnitude of his huge personality, all combined to draw me in, and I liked it.

Caiaphas spat at Pilate. "So what is it to be, Ponty boy? Are we to remain friends? Or are we to argue over the fate of this Jewish King?"

"Don't push me, Caiaphas. This man has done nothing wrong, not in the eyes of the law."

"Roman law! If you hadn't noticed, old chap, this is fucking Judea! Here it is *my* law that matters. Test it, go on, see what happens, see what the people want, then tell me what matters."

"Crucify him! Crucify him!"

Three figures stood behind Caiaphas, on the periphery of the crowd. Two of them, a man and a woman, stood head and shoulders above the rest, dressed from head to foot in long flowing robes of glistening gold that shimmered in the heat. Even with my weakening eyes, I could see how wrong they looked, unnatural, and they just stood there watching, so cold and impassive with their enormous eyes, eyes so dark that they appeared black. However, it was the young man between them that really caught my attention, a creature of such exquisite beauty that it took my breath away, yet it was a cruel beauty, marred by the derisive sneer that broke his stunning face as he regarded the proud remnant of the man at Caiaphas' feet. Never had I seen a look of such pure hatred, of such pure malevolence, a look that could kill.

Pilate shot out of his throne and bellowed into the unyielding crowds.

"This man is innocent! He has committed no crime!"

Caiaphas grinned from ear to ear, and I got the impression that he had won something, that somehow Pilate had played right into his hands.

"Why, does he not proclaim himself King? Does this not break the law? Is this not blasphemy?" Caiaphas finished with a smile, and then he turned his head towards me and winked.

"Listen to me, all of you listen to me." I had never seen Pilate so desperate, so lost. "In our cells there lies a true criminal, Barabbas, you know who he is, you know what he has done, so I give you this choice. One man shall receive my pardon. One man shall go free out of the two that stand here accused this day. Tell me, which one is it to be, this man who lies before you, this man who has done nothing wrong, or Barabbas, a killer, a man of true evil. Who shall I set free?"

"Barabbas! Barabbas! Barabbas! Barabbas!" The cry deafened me, and Pilate fell back, almost falling into his throne, shock and despair etched across his startled face. The two tall strangers looked at each other, a look of triumph that sickened me.

"Then he shall be flogged! Here, now, before your eyes, he will be scourged to cleanse his soul, and prove his innocence! You, tie him up, do it now."

Pilate looked at me. Nothing could have prepared me for that moment, the sudden realisation that he intended for me to carry out his command. As a soldier, I had killed many men during battle, as a Praetorian Guard, I had killed many men while in his service. The taking of a life, an action justified by status, demanded as service, done without question or remorse. Now he demanded that I beat a man, an innocent man until his flesh parted from his body.

I walked forward, the world a misty blur around me. The cries of the angry mob became whispers in my ears, because I could only see him, that man on the floor, looking at me with those incredible eyes, such green eyes. I saw no fear there, no regret, just pity, and something else that made me want to turn and vomit—I saw forgiveness.

I lifted him gently, my hand wrapping around his considerable bicep, drawing him towards a stone pillar to the side of the judgment seat. I tried not to look at the faces of the crowd, the faces full of hunger and thirst, faces that wanted to see his blood pour from the wounds that would never heal. The hatred that poured towards that man felt like a hand pushing against me, and I had to force myself forward, will myself to do the unspeakable.

As I tied him to the post, I looked up, straight into the face of Mary Magdalene.

The horror that filled my head as her gaze fell upon me made my bowels clench. My friend, my soul mate, there at the moment of my greatest shame. She just looked at me, shock, sadness, grief, etched across her pretty face. I wanted to say something, I needed to say something, but she simply shook her head so slightly, so discreetly, and that broke my heart more than anything. Why was Mary there? Why, in the midst of such horror? My mind could not grasp her reasons for being there. Then I saw the wretched soul standing at her side, and I felt my heart convulse within my chest.

He clung to Mary, tears streaming down his face in a cascade of glittering grief, and even through his torment, I could see his beauty, and I felt him, inside of me, his agony, agony for the man that I bound. And in that single, crystal clear moment, I knew that he loved him. Mary held the weeping man back, desperate to keep him in her arms, but the pain tearing him apart was so extraordinary as to rip at my heart, and I felt my own eyes stinging with his every cry.

As I tied the would-be king to the pillar, he looked up into the face of the crying man. He shook his head, an imperceptible movement that only I saw. However, it affected the weeping man in such a profound way, because he fell to his knees, his sorrow trembling upon his tear swollen lips, his eyes filled with so much sadness that I found my hands trembling as I ripped the clothes off the prisoner's back. Something akin to resignation alighted his perfect features, a strange calm that shuddered through his muscles, a hopelessness that bled from his eyes. Mary stared at me, and I felt my own shame blossom across my face. She offered me a smile, a small weak thing that curled at the corners of her lips. For a moment I felt lost in our past, the two of us on the shore of Galilee, hand in hand, two friends against the world, and I knew that she understood, as she always understood, that I had no choice in the actions laid before me.

I felt something hard press into my hand, and I looked down at the cruel implement placed into my palm. The flagellum consisted of three leather thongs connected to a wooden handle. Each thong ended with a cruel knot, barbs of bone and metal woven into the monstrous straps. Within my hand lay an instrument of torture, of unendurable pain, an instrument designed to shred flesh from a man's bones, and I had to use it.

I stepped back, unable to tear my gaze away from the beautiful man kneeling in the sand, from Mary holding onto his shoulders as he stared at his king so intensely, so intimately, and my shame dripped down my legs in rivulets of self-loathing.

"One!"

Pilates voice called out each stroke. His voice became just another sound, a mumble that mingled with the squelch of corrupted flesh as the flagellum whistled through the air to embed itself within raw muscle.

I had to rip it out of his skin with each new stroke.

Have you ever wondered why moments of extreme pain, the suffering of one's soul, the torture of one's heart, cause time to slow down, each moment of torment accentuated by the slow ticking of every insufferable second? Yet joy moves past at such a speed that you forget the detail of the event that elicits such wondrous emotion.

I felt every blow. It rippled up my arm in tides of unbearable pain, a thing felt so intensely as to shred every muscle in my bulging arm, moving through the fibres of my existence to settle in my heart, a ball of darkness that would forever become a part of me. My body wept for him, rivers of salty sweat pouring from my skin unchecked, joining the rivers of sadness and despair that poured from my eyes until there remained just water and blood. So much blood.

"Ten!"

A little piece of me died each time my arm reached the zenith of its arc as I took a piece of his life with each blow. He was a man, just a man, and I had hurt so many men before, in very many cruel and inventive ways. He was just one more. As a member of the Praetorian Guard, we taught ourselves to become desensitized to such things, to kill and to maim, as true Roman soldiers should, without thought, without question, and without remorse. So why did I grieve as with each slap of the flagellum, a new line of ripped flesh appeared?

Blood, so much blood, pouring down his shredded back, bits of flesh and ripped muscle, turning his flesh into a mush of red.

And the sun beat down, hot, unyielding, burning.

And he didn't scream once.

"Nineteen!"

Twenty. I was a soldier.

Twenty-one. I was a prostitute.

Twenty-two. I was killing him.

Twenty-three. Why was I doing it?

Twenty-four. Why was I crying?

Twenty-five. Why was I screaming?

He didn't scream.

I blinked the tears away from my eyes, but it did not matter. The world died in me, and I could barely see, my own guilt, my own shame, shielding my vision from the horror I inflicted.

"Thirty!"

The blood is the life. It dripped to the floor to stain the stone, drying black in the intense heat, a pattern of suffering seared into immutable granite.

Thirty-five. I could not breathe.

Thirty-six. My heart was breaking.

Thirty-seven. Rip my eyes from my skull.

Thirty-eight. My soul lay broken.

Thirty-nine. I was dead.

I fell away, crashing into the throne, my legs trembling, and I thought I would collapse. What had I done? What the hell had I done?

Pilate walked over to the shattered figure slumped inside the remnants of a man, and even Pilate trembled at the sight of his own command.

"What do you say now? Do you still proclaim to be King?"

Slowly, painfully, the ruined man lifted his head, barely able to force the words between his bloodied, swollen lips.

"That's... what you ... say."

A look of pure horror washed over Pilate, horror and defeat, the look of a man doomed.

"Crucify him. Take this thing away and Crucify him."

Silence. It filled the Pavement, as did Caiaphas' grin of triumph.

"Leave me. All of you leave me! You ravens, you vultures! You will rue this day, I swear to you, this is not my doing, this is not my fault. You made me do it!"

Pilate's eyes bulged with rage, his fury erupting from his crazed mouth in fountains of spittle.

"See! I wash my hands of it. I wash my hands of it!" He rushed over to a pedestal next to the judgment seat, upon which stood a jug of water. Like a man possessed, he scooped up handfuls of water and poured it over his head, and then he started to scrub his hands until they looked red and raw.

"See, I wash myself clean, this is your doing, not mine, not mine!"

But most of the crowd had already filed out, leaving just a few stragglers and Caiaphas, who viewed the scene with growing amusement.

As the Praetorian Guard dragged the broken prisoner away, Pilate could not tear his gaze away from him, his eyes bloodshot, and I thought perhaps that his sanity lay broken as much as the man he destroyed.

"Pilate, dear heart, rest assured my friend that you will be remembered for this."

Pilate looked at Caiaphas then, realisation dawning across his face.

"Yes," he groaned, "that is what I am afraid of."

"No!"

Pilate looked on in horror as a man, the man who wept for the prisoner, rushed forward and fell to his knees before the Prefect, clinging to the bottom of Pilate's toga. Mary tried to stop him, but the hysterical man pushed her away. She glanced at me momentarily before she turned and ran from the horror of that day, tears streaming down her face.

Pilate glared down at the stricken man in disgust, as though he could not believe what he saw. When the man spoke, his voice filled with emotion, a heart-wrenching sound that ripped away the last of my humanity with every word that spilled from his broken lips.

"Stop this, please, let me take it back, it wasn't him, I lied, please, please."

Pilate grabbed the distraught figure by the shoulders and threw him to the ground in disgust.

"Stupid fool! I could not stop this now any more than you. It seems that we must both live with our betrayal."

"No, no, look, I'll give it back to you, see, take it, take it back, I don't want it." He pulled a pouch out from the folds of his robe and tossed it at Pilates feet, and the pouch burst open to spill a river of silver coins onto the stone. Pilate seemed to react in abject terror, jumping back from the coins for fear that one would touch him.

"I don't want your fucking blood money! Get out, get out now before you suffer the same fate as that Messianic fool!"

"Please, I'm begging you, don't do this."

Never had I heard such desperation, such pain, such despair, and it cut me to my soul. I couldn't bear to hear the breaking of his heart anymore. I couldn't stand the sound of the anguish that tumbled from his mouth or the agony that nestled in his eyes. I just wanted it to end. I needed it to end.

But it wouldn't end. It would *never* end.

Caiaphas approached the crouching figure, and the intense look upon his face sent a chill down my spine. So deadly, so sharp, and his eyes burned with malice. He cupped the man's chin in his big, slender hand, and lifted his head to look at him.

"Handsome man, I feel your pain, I do, but it means nothing. He will die on the cross, and I will be standing there to watch as his life slips away, and I will be happy."

The wretch pulled himself free and scrabbled to his feet. He looked so lost, looking from Caiaphas to Pilate in defeat.

"Then I do as I must, and it is on your heads, the blood of this day sits upon your hands." He turned, and he ran from the Pavement.

"Follow him," demanded Caiaphas fiercely, before grabbing my upper arm, squeezing it with a strength that surprised me. "I want to know what he is up to, and I want you to report back to me, do you understand?"

His gaze met mine, and something passed between us, something more than master and servant, a flicker of desire that danced across his wickedly beautiful face, and I could not resist him. I did not want to resist him. He frightened me, yes, his power, his magnetism, his sheer force of will, never had I experienced a man quite like him. But that fear mixed with an undercurrent of attraction as he looked at me, a look that wanted to fuck me on the spot, and it excited me. Even then, despite everything, the power of him made me hard.

I gave chase, weaving through the crowds, hot, sweaty and covered in blood. Many a face recoiled in fear at the site of my dishevelled bulk, but I continued all the same, afraid to lose my quarry, not because of the distance between us, but because my eyes started to fail again. All around me passed in a blur of colour and shadow, faces appearing with startling clarity up close, before melting away in a haze of disease. My world disappearing in a mist of venereal misadventure.

Akeldama lay in the valley of Hinnom, a land where the earth bled red because of the rich clay that infused the land, earning it the name of Potter's Field. Little grew there, and the few trees that managed to gain purchase in the sparse soil grew stunted, twisted parodies of their species. One such gnarled specimen grew out from the side of an outcrop of rough rock, red stains bleeding over its craggy surface. It was there that I found him, atop the rock, and staring into the thick serpentine branches of the half dead tree.

In other circumstances, kinder circumstances, he would have been beautiful. Indeed, he was beautiful, but the grief and the sorrow that so completely overshadowed his soul, marred that beauty, leaving behind a broken shadow of a man, and to look upon such a sad human being left me with nothing but pity in my heart.

I moved closer, drawn to his pain, attracted to his despair, feeling his agony leech out into the surrounding land, a tainted bitterness that seemed to turn the sky itself black. Then I saw him untie the rope from around his waist and wrap it around a thick branch. My flesh ran cold as I ran across the stony ground.

"No!" I screamed. I don't know why, I still do not understand it, even now, but the thought of him hanging there, dead, rotting, bloated, it repulsed me so much that I felt compelled to intercede.

He looked at me with his beautiful eyes, startlingly blue eyes that glistened with tears, eyes that burrowed into my soul and settled within my heart, eyes so filled with loss, eyes so filled with deep pools of hopelessness as to drown me in them. I looked at him, really looked at him, and nothing could disguise his true magnificence. It burned through his grief like a furnace, a fiery beauty that blazed so intense as to rival the sun in the sky. Such smooth bronzed skin, with high chiselled cheekbones that gave him an elegant, almost regal countenance, and his body bulged with tight, hard muscle that pushed his veins to the surface of his skin, and all of him glistening with sweat in the heat. He made me swoon, not the dirty fucker swoon that Caiaphas seemed to instil within me, but more of a Leonidus swoon, the type that grabbed hold of your heart and stopped it beating within your chest. So handsome. So perfect. So lost.

When he spoke, it was a man lost, a voice so flat and far away, a voice filled with so much pain as to blacken the world with the sound of it. He just looked so broken, he sounded so broken, and even with my failing eyes, I could see that his sanity, and his mind, lay shattered.

"Will he be there do you think? Will he be there, waiting for me?"

Oh my God, that voice. Such a gentle sound, tremulous between his lips, and I could feel my own heartbeat quicken at the sound.

"Don't do this, please. Nothing is worth your life."

"*He* is. It was his idea, you know? We argued over it. I begged him to change his mind, but he wouldn't listen... if mankind is to survive, to learn, to have faith... he said that he had no choice, that he must die. I am the tool of his destruction."

"Then why did you do it? Why did you betray him?"

"I didn't betray him!" His anger hit me in a shower of spittle that flecked my check and dripped from my chin. "That was his idea! No one else knew... no one else. It had to be me, for them to believe... it had to be me. Do you understand?"

"It was a lie?"

"Yes! Yes... he wanted to die, he needed to die, so that men would believe, do you understand? So he asked me to... I kissed him, it was the only way, and then they took him. And now he will die."

"But *you* don't have to."

The look he gave me then, as he looked down on me from his rocky perch, cut my soul away from my heart. His agony bled all over me.

"Without him, there is nothing. I know now that I will be remembered for what I have done, my name will forever be associated with betrayal, with murder, how then am I to live with that?"

"You can try. Give life a chance."

"I have murdered him! I have murdered him! And he, in turn, has murdered me."

He moved with startling speed, and before I could move to stop him, the rope tightened around his neck as he leapt from the rock.

For a moment his body floated, and the look upon his face was not one of fear, but relief, sweet, blessed relief, and then his neck snapped.

My world darkened. The ground rushed up to meet my face as my legs collapsed beneath me, and all the time I could hear the terrible creaking of that rope. Bile filled my throat, shot out of my nose, and the light faded from my eyes as I vomited into the red.

Chapter Five: The Man With The Golden Tongue

As Related By Gideon

I needed to clean my body. I felt the grime of death in every pore of my skin, and it made me feel corrupted, it made me feel less than human. My muscles glistened with sweat and blood, and my skin itched from the sand and dirt that encrusted it, and I craved to scrub the filth away, together with the bastard memories of a fucking shit day.

When I walked into the communal bathroom, I felt relieved to find it empty. The thought of dealing with the taunting banter of my bastard comrades filled me with dread. They loved nothing more than to ride me, to push me to my limits until I snapped, until I lashed out. They knew exactly how to hurt me without bruising my body, such was the affection they held for me. They would kill me one day, of that I felt sure. Such was the life of a Praetorian Guard, especially one who sucked the royal dick.

I sat on the stone bench, the heat rising through the stone floor, spreading beneath the soles of my feet, seeping into my weary bones to offer me warm solace. I threw water onto the coals and allowed the moisture to envelop me, breathing in the hot vapours, filling my lungs, and it felt good. Rivulets of sweat poured down my hard, naked body that glistened as marble.

I held the bone carved strigil in my left hand and dragged its sharpened edge down the muscular contour of my right arm, scraping away the pain of the day in a stream of grime, repeating again and again until my muscles glowed red and burnished. Once I had finished my arms, I moved down to my chest, enjoying the slightly painful sensation of the strigil slicing over my excited nipples, down the valley of my rippled stomach to the forest of my groin.

Suddenly, I heard the door bang shut, followed by the clang of the bolt sliding home, and I froze in the blindness of white steam, wondering what new torment awaited me through the mist, but the voice that drifted through the haze belonged to someone far more dangerous than any of my comrades.

"No man should have to resort to scrubbing his own flesh. Or is this a soldier thing?"

The figure of Caiaphas drifted out of the steam with nothing but a towel draped across his shoulders. His lithe, naked body appeared through clinging droplets of moisture, rivulets of water already forming in the deep clefts of his hard muscles. What a striking thing he presented, with every movement, every footstep so placed, so calculated, so beautifully elegant that he seemed to glide towards me as a wisp of smoke carried on a gentle breeze. His skin glistened with oil, each muscle and sinew of his tight, slender body accentuated, and I found him beautiful.

Caiaphas lifted a finger to stroke the corner of my eye. "You will be blind soon. Do they know?"

I pushed his hand away without care, angry that he should say such a thing to me.

"Don't be angry dear heart, it will be our little secret. What will you do? When you can no longer see the ground beneath your feet, or your hand to wipe your ass?"

I held my temper, but I could feel my anger rising inside me like the heat rising through my legs from the floor. Yet still, he goaded me, moving forward, pushing forward, into my face.

"When the world goes dark, will it matter then who's cock is in your ass?"

Something akin to madness gripped my arm, and to my horror it lashed out, the strigil gripped in my trembling hand slicing through the air towards his captivating face.

He grabbed my hand in mid-air, effortlessly, as though catching a fly. His strength far exceeded my own, and it surprised me, and then he removed the would-be weapon from my hand with just a simple flick of his long, long fingers.

"Turn around, Barbarian, turn your back on one whom you would strike."

I could do nothing. The command in his voice left me dizzy, weak, and I had to obey that calm, calculating voice, it left me with no choice, no free will, and I liked it. I turned around.

I could feel my heart beating within my chest, my blood surging through my veins, pounding at my temples, throbbing behind my eyes. I almost gasped as the strigil touched the flesh between my shoulder blades, as its sharp edge dragged down my skin towards my exposed buttocks. Caiaphas showed no mercy, I felt my flesh strain beneath the pressure of the blade, skin crumpling against the bone, and fuck did it hurt. I feared that my flesh would lie in tatters at my feet, ribbons of myself falling onto the heated floor, and it made me tremble.

"Oh I'm sorry, am I being too rough? I'm sure you can handle it. Tell me, what happened? You followed him as I asked, that much I know."

"He's dead."

"By your hand?"

"No, by yours."

Caiaphas chuckled. "Give the man a bone, and see how bold he becomes. Bravo sweetie, bravo. So tell me, my brave

Barbarian, how do you feel about what has happened here today?"

"I have no opinion."

"Well, I know that to be a lie. I saw it on your face as you whipped him, as you tore strips of flesh from his back. You were in pain, were you not?"

I kept my mouth shut, afraid of my answer, unsure of my answer. The strigil dug deep, deep enough to tear skin, and I gasped.

"It is your eyes that fail, not your mouth, speak Barbarian."

"I don't understand why he has to die."

"He thinks he is a God, and that is my job."

"But he has done nothing wrong."

"He dared to think that he could beat me. No one beats me."

"But why make him suffer so much? Why not just send him away?"

"Because there are those who would follow him no matter where he went, and I cannot have that. When a man sets himself up higher than all the rest, he must expect to fall from a very great height."

"But not even Pilate wanted him dead, or Herod."

"Weak sycophantic fools. I don't think either of them have ever had an original thought between them. Who do you think it is that rules this land, Barbarian? Is it the Kings? Is it the Senate of Rome? No! I do. Turn around."

I did as he demanded, unable to deny him. My eyes throbbed, pain darting behind them, but I could have sworn his eyes blazed yellow.

"You are but a soldier, a slave really, so I do not expect you to understand the complexities of all that you have witnessed here. But I am a God, Barbarian, and no other shall raise himself above me. One day I will be the only God, and I will tread the old one beneath my feet, where he belongs, in the shit and filth of his own creation. That fool, that Messiah, I could not allow him to continue his cause. I had to crush it, as I had to crush him. That is all you need to understand."

He believed every word that he said, and somehow, I believed him too. Caiaphas—he looked like a man, but he did not act like one, he did not sound like one, and yet, he certainly looked like a God. So I believed him.

"Who are you?"

He grinned, a wide, chilling smile that split his face in two. "I am many."

His lips smashed into my mouth with such unexpected force that my back slammed into the stone wall behind me. His tongue, huge and wet, pushed into my mouth with a ferocity, and an urgency that stole my breath and made my skin tingle. I brought my hands up to pull him to me, but he pushed my hands away.

"You are not allowed to touch me. If you do, I will leave."

I felt my cock stiffen, pressing against his leg.

"Does that count?"

Caiaphas laughed. "Keep your hands to yourself and shut the fuck up."

His tongue silenced me, probing the back of my throat, licking the roof of my mouth, entwining around my own probing organ. Teeth bit into my lower lip, piercing flesh, drawing blood, his tongue smearing it around my mouth before forcing its way back down my throat. The urge to grab him, to pull him into me became unbearable, and I had to clamp my hands behind my back, crushing them against the stone for fear of touching him. Caiaphas pressed against me, grinding against my hard, throbbing cock with his own stiff member, and I desperately wanted to touch it, to hold that thick piece of meat between my hands and guide it into my mouth. Harder and harder he pushed, my hands crushed behind me, exquisite pain and ecstasy conjoined as his mouth swallowed my face and tasted my flesh.

"You are not allowed to look at me. Close your eyes, Barbarian. I will know if you look."

He lowered himself to his knees, his mouth level with my twitching cock, and then that tongue flickered out from between his plump lips and touched the head of my dick, sticky strands of pre-cum connecting tongue to penis. But then his eyes moved, turning inside his head, impossibly moving up and up until they looked at me.

"Close your fucking eyes. And do not make a sound."

I felt his teeth grate against the head of my cock, sliding down my shaft, his warm, wet lips encasing my dick until its entire length sat in his throat. The warmth that flooded my body made me want to cry out, but I caught the sound on the brink of my lips, swallowing it down as surely as he swallowed me. His tongue wrapped around me, all the way around my cock, and still his lips surrounded it, sliding along the length of my throbbing manhood right to the tip of my head.

The orgasm started at the base of my balls, I could feel it building inexorably, an explosion waiting to fill his mouth with each pumping movement. Suddenly his fingers pushed inside me, fingers exploring, forcing their way into my hole while his other hand pulled at my balls, squeezing my balls until the pain almost made me cry. I held back the scream as my orgasm held itself at bay, and then his mouth swallowed me, all of me, his tongue somehow licking around my balls as the back of his throat hit the head of my pounding cock.

Fingers pressed and stroked eagerly at that spot between my ball sack and my anus, and my legs shivered in anticipation, my strength sapped into the orgasm that once again began its journey down my length. It flowed from the head of my penis with a force unknown to me, pumping hard and fast, draining the life from my worthless body as it hit the back of his throat. Caiaphas did not gag, and he did not move, but savoured every drop, his lips caressing my shaft, his tongue squeezing every drop from me until I lay drained.

With a grin, he stood up, his lips once again against my mouth, and I opened my mouth to accept him. Semen, warm and thick, flooded into my mouth, my semen, and then his tongue pushed in, tasting of me as I tasted myself.

No one had ever done that to me before. All of me, all of my existence, all of my life, fired from my cock in one massive load, and I tasted it, I swallowed myself, and it left me wanting more.

"There, now tell me, am I not a God?"

Chapter Six: The Death Of Me

As Related By Gideon.

Love, an emotion so anathema to me. What need had I for love? I, the soldier, a servant, a killer, a piece of meat handed around like a plate of appetizers at a party, a receptacle for old men's flaccid dicks and erotic fantasies. What need did I have for love? Love certainly had no need of me.

My body represented my passport to money and privilege. My bulging muscles earned me bulging purses of coin, and all I had to do was to lie there and let them do as they pleased. Fuck my face, fuck my ass, fill me up. Yet, my body, once so fit, so strong, so reliable, now failed me. How long could I rely on my physic, would my beauty persist through blindness and disease? Would you fuck a blind man? Please sir, fuck a cripple?

He touched me. He put his hands near mine and then he touched me. I felt a sudden tingle when he touched me, a sparkle, a glow. My body burned, my flesh bristled as his lips tasted me, my body ached to feel him inside of me, and for once, I felt as though someone was making love to *me*, enjoying *me*, giving *me* pleasure. In that one moment of exquisite orgasm, Caiaphas wanted nothing from me, he expected nothing from me, he just wanted to give, and for the first time in my life, I knew how it felt, passion, desire, pleasure.

The memory of his lips stayed with me, I could still feel them, taste them, and it left me wanting more. Even the thought of him saw my cock stiffen between my legs. Was that love? The obsession, the desire, the wanting, the unending whispers in my head? Both heads. Every time I closed my eyes, I saw him. Every time I closed my eyes, I heard him.

Soon my eyes would close forever. Would he still want me then?

Yet he frightened me also, and on the fields of Golgotha, I saw just how calculating a man he could be.

Just outside the gates of Jerusalem sat a small skull cap of a hill, dry and barren, a rocky outcrop of suffering where the condemned lay pinned to great wooden crosses, left to die in the blistering sun as a deterrent to those who would seek to subvert the law. The place, known as Golgotha, felt as though it belonged within its own bubble of existence, for the atmosphere of death and suffering that clung to the area gave it an otherworldly aura that crept under your skin and infected your soul. The sky, a never-ending sea of sapphire blue, met a ground of golden sand and rock, that glowed like the finest jewels beneath the ever present heat of the sun. Yet I felt a shiver of intense cold ripple down my back as I stood there behind Pilate, a witness to the travesty of mankind.

It seemed that all of Judea had gathered to bear witness to his death. To the side of Pilate's chair stood the Sanhedrin, Caiaphas in all his glory at their head, a vision in long black robes that shimmered like oil in the sun. He caught my eye and he winked, and I found myself smirking, my cheeks flushing at his glance. However, my childish infatuation died when I saw another group standing away from the Sanhedrin, and my heart sank as I saw Mary. She seemed so stoic. I recognised the hard, grave face that she wore as a mask, the face she used to cover her own pain as she comforted an older woman weeping in her arms. I so wanted to be by her side, to comfort my friend, to reassure her that she did not have to endure her pain alone. The older woman wailed, her single harrowing cry echoing around Golgotha with nerve-shredding agony, and the sound bled through my bones to chill my heart. Then there were the revellers, the ghouls, the curious, the thrill seekers, jeering and jostling for a better view of a man as they nailed him to a wooden cross.

They dragged that poor, ruined man across the sand, to cries of approval from the gathered crowds, and they threw him down callously onto the ground next to a huge wooden crucifix. Broken, bleeding, and not far from death, he lay in a crumpled heap wearing nothing but a soiled loincloth. Never had my own humanity filled me with so such shame, and I wanted to tear my gaze away from the degradation inflicted upon such an innocent. But something compelled me to watch, some inner voice demanding that I witness every gruelling moment of his departure from Earth.

A roar of pleasure shattered the stillness as a guard, one of my fellow Praetorians, produced a woven ring of thorns and rammed it upon the condemned man's head, vicious barbs cutting into his tender flesh to send fresh rivulets of blood cascading down his bearded face.

He didn't flinch. Not a sound escaped from his cracked lips.

I will never forget the sound of hammer colliding with metal. It echoed around Golgotha in a discordance of horror. Bang, bang, bang, each blow a nail in the coffin of humanity, each blow a resounding affirmation of mankind's cruelty as the sound bounced around Golgotha with sickening clarity. Huge, nine-inch nails drove through muscle and bone without discrimination, and I wanted to weep for that man, for the unbearable pain that ripped across his face as death ripped through his flesh. One guard held his legs to the cross, while the other held a nail poised over the ankles.

I turned away. My eyes could no longer suffer the images fed into them. If I was to lose my sight, if my world was to plunge into darkness, I did not want that to be the last thing I saw.

Bang.

"Does this offend you, dear heart?"

Bang.

"It is no more than he deserves, no one sets themselves above me."

Bang.

"This will be the end of his pathetic cult. Who will remember him in days, weeks, months to come?"

Bang.

"Nobody."

Tears, hot against my face, trickled down my cheeks. The sudden emotion surprised me. Caiaphas laughed.

"Don't waste your tears on him, dear heart, he is not worth it."

"How could you be so callous? How could you be so cruel?"

His eyes glinted with amusement, and despite their fascinating colour, I saw coldness behind them.

"Is it cruel to put down a sick animal? Is it cruel to correct the deluded? Do you see her? The younger woman, cradling the mother in her arms?"

I did see her, my best friend, my Mary, her grief and her suffering pouring down her face. It broke my heart that no one wrapped their arms around her, that no one comforted her, that there remained no solace for Mary.

"Mary Magdalene. She was my friend, in another life."

Caiaphas looked taken aback. "Well, you are full of surprises, aren't you? Yes, Mary Magdalene. A farmer's daughter, another innocent. She dares to think that she can continue their crusade in his name, she dares to preach the word of God, a woman, above me. I think not! Watch dear heart, see how, with just a few words, I may ruin her."

"No, please, don't."

The look that he gave me froze my blood in my veins, and I withered beneath his penetrating gaze.

"Don't dare to tell me what to do, Barbarian. Ever. Now, watch."

Caiaphas leaned over and whispered into the ear of a woman just a foot or so from us.

"Look at her, the whore weeping. See how she grieves for the cock she has lost. But you know what they say, she has eleven more to choose from."

The woman looked at Caiaphas in surprise, her eyes opening wide as he fed her his obscene gossip. He shook his head in affirmation. The woman immediately repeated the gossip into the ear of the next woman, and soon the rumour buzzed around the crowd like hungry flies.

I felt anger, rage that burned, yet I stood there impotent, afraid, belittled beneath his towering might. I no longer knew who I was, what kind of person I had become, and I realised then that I did not like myself very much. No wonder I no longer had any friends.

Caiaphas looked at me, a self-satisfied smirk creasing his beautiful lips. My heart pounded within my chest, I wanted to hate him, I wanted to plant my fist in his mouth, ram my spear up his tight asshole, but I couldn't do it, because despite everything, I just wanted to kiss him.

"And that, sweetie, is the end of her. She will forever be known as the cocksucker *I* say she is."

"Why do you do this?"

"Because I can."

Slowly, inexorably, the cross with its tortured burden lifted off the ground, pulled into position by ropes until it stood erect, a silhouette of horror against an embarrassed sky. Silence, all-encompassing, muffled the onlookers as the crucifix shuddered, and all eyes fell upon the false God.

I saw such beauty there, beneath the blood. Beneath the scars and the beard and the blood, a beauty that went beyond the flesh, a beauty of purity and sanctity that radiated from him, even as death wrapped its cruel fingers so inevitably about his broken body.

Mary and the mother fell to their knees, lost, defeated, two women bound by the unbearable tragedy that saw their hearts and their souls shattered.

The crucified Messiah spoke, the man on the cross—he lifted his head to the Heavens, and he spoke.

"Father! Why have you forsaken me? I thirst... Father... forgive them... for they do not know what they do. Father... into your hands... I commit my spirit."

A sound, a low rumble, started to vibrate through my feet, through my bones and into my ears, and judging by the shocked faces of those around me, they all experienced the same nerve-trembling sensation. Something happened to the sun, a blackness that crept across its burning surface, as though the fist of God himself wished to block out the horror unfolding before our eyes.

The rumble turned into thunder, and the world plunged into a terrible darkness, screams of terror piercing the night as blackness consumed us all. The ground beneath us heaved, great roiling leaps of anger that sent bodies crashing against each other as panic and terror infused the mad exodus of mankind from that place of unbearable death.

I held onto the nearest person, Caiaphas, and he did not flinch. Instead, he laughed, an animalistic sound that terrified me as much as the chaos around me.

"Why are you laughing?" I could not believe his reaction. All around me, people trampled over each other in their haste to escape the oncoming Armageddon, but Caiaphas just looked towards the darkened sky and laughed.

"Well, it's so fucking funny, dear heart! Something has pissed him off don't you think? Come on then, you cunt! Come down here and face me! You so know you want to!"

The ground split and the Heavens above exploded in streaks of light that flashed across the horizon. The Praetorian Guard formed a wall around Pilate, and I joined their ranks as we shuffled him towards the gates, moving the Prefect through the screaming hordes towards safety. Light flashed through the darkness. A strobing maelstrom of lightning that seared frozen images of terror into my eyes, images of fear and confusion, so I closed my eyes to block them out, to hide myself from the terror of that moment, but still I could see them, burned into the backs of my brain.

Flickers of light danced across my closed eyes, the veins inside my lids highlighted against the dark. I could hear my own breathing, shallow and tight, blocking out the furore around me, until that too was all I could hear, my own desperate heartbeat pounding in my ears. I tried to push forward, unable to see, refusing to see, one foot in front of the other, but the world slipped away from me as my own terror threatened to squeeze the life out of my heart.

I opened my eyes. Shadows, nothing but shadows. Panic thrust its ugly head up through my bowels and forced its way past my lungs, freezing the breath in my throat. I lifted my arms, reaching out for help, desperate to feel the guiding hands of my fellow man, but my cries for help went unheeded as the world disappeared from my view.

Blackness. Nothing but blackness. I felt stone cut into my knees as I sank to the ground, and then dust filled my mouth before my mind broke, and the world left me.

I awoke in my room, peeling my eyes open, breaking the crust that held my lids together. I saw light, and I nearly cried, because I could see the light. Blindness had yet to claim me.

I rubbed the crust from my eyes, but everything remained a blur, indistinct shapes that swam alarmingly before me.

A hand brushed through my long hair, and I started.

"Don't be alarmed, Barbarian, you are safe."

I felt relieved at the familiarity of his voice, but it also surprised me that he should be in my room.

"What happened? How did I get back here?"

"You passed out. I carried you here. Don't worry, no one saw. They were all too busy running for their lives. What do you remember?"

"The sun! The sun went out. But it's light again now, did the sun come back?"

Caiaphas laughed, a strangely kind laugh, the kind of laugh an adult would offer an inquisitive child.

"It was an eclipse, nothing more. Such things last for just the briefest of moments, and this was no exception."

"But the ground shook, everything was moving."

"And now it is still again."

"How long have I been out?"

"Just a couple of hours, dear heart. Now tell me, how are your eyes? How well can you see?"

Something else sat beneath his question, something squirming, and I felt distinctly nervous.

"I can see well enough."

"Good. I have a job for you. Tomorrow is the Sabbath, and I can't have that body out there offending our eyes and fouling our noses, so do be a good chap and remove him?"

"You want *me* to remove him?"

"No, I want you to examine his body, and if by some miracle he is still alive, I want you to break his legs to finish the cunt off, *then* I want you to remove him."

"Why me?" The thought of such a thing horrified me.

"Because you are the only one I trust to do the job properly, Barbarian, and anyway, you started the whole thing, so I would like you to finish it. Don't worry about Pilate, I've already informed him of my intentions, and he is in agreement. The quicker that thing is cut down and stuffed away somewhere out of sight, the better."

"Now?"

Caiaphas reached forward and grabbed my cock. "Unless you have other, more pressing plans?"

I brushed his hand away, despite my stiffening cock, and got off the small cot too quickly, because my room spun around my head, making me stumble. To my surprise, and gratification, Caiaphas leapt to my aid and steadied me.

"You can't ask me to do such a thing, it's not..." I pulled myself out of his hands, even though I wanted those hands to touch me, all of me.

"Human? And if he still lives? If he hangs on the cross, suffering, in pain, do you not think it better to extinguish that suffering? Are you not doing him a favour?"

"You're a calculating bastard, aren't you?"

"What? Me? You might very well think that... but I couldn't possibly comment. Now go, Barbarian, and who knows, maybe I will be waiting for you when you come back."

Something about that man made me want to shove my tongue down his throat, he made me so bloody horny. The man oozed sexuality from his every pore, even his voice fucked me on the spot. Yet the oncoming blindness meant that I couldn't see him, not properly. Like the room he stood in, everything melted into an indistinct blur, a smear of colour, the details of his striking face stolen from my eyes by the disease that ravaged my body, and I could not help but wonder how much longer I had.

My spear stood propped against the rotten door frame, so I grabbed it. If that man lived still, he would exit the world at the end of its swift, merciful tip.

The walk through the streets towards the gate felt like a living torment. My feet knew those dusty paths as I knew my own body, so I moved through those twisting lanes with automatic accuracy, each step placed by memory as I stumbled through a world of dark phantoms. Things so familiar became grotesque, buildings and people a mass of moving, indistinguishable forms that seemed to tower over me, hemming me in. Every sound grew louder than the last, a discordant clatter that pressed against my skin and fractured my ears, and for a moment I thought I couldn't do it, that I couldn't go on, that I would have to cower there on the ground, bathed in dirt and despair.

My father always said that as a baby I never cried, that I was born into the world with a smile. As a child, I wanted to be just like my father, funny, generous and kind. As a teenager, I wanted nothing more than to toil the land and sea, to provide for my family as they provided for me. As an adult, I needed to escape that closed community and live the life I had cowered from for so long.

Now, as a man, I just wanted to see.

As I reached those fields of despair, even the onset of blindness could not obscure the sight of that huge wooden cross silhouetted against the sun as it sank behind the rim of Golgotha. It rose from the land like a splinter from a wound, a poisonous effigy of cruelty that made my stomach churn with dread and pain.

There is something about a body devoid of life that screams at you, a construct of meat and bone that is so devoid of humanity, of soul, that it seems to be unreal somehow, almost fake. Those tiny movements of breath, of skin, of muscle, are so obviously absent that it becomes nothing but a cold, white mass of flesh where once a human lived.

As a soldier, I was used to such things. As a man, I despaired of it.

I felt overwhelmed, standing in the shadow of that wood and flesh monolith. Unexplained emotions welled up from my guts to spill down my face, and I did not know why. I did not know him. I did not understand why he had to die. He meant nothing to me. Yet, somehow, as my failing eyes gazed upon his broken body, I felt that he knew me and that I mattered to him, that his death mattered.

The tip of my spear entered his flesh just below his armpit, entering the carcass without resistance.

Something hit my face, it squirted into my eyes, into my mouth, and ran down my cheeks and neck, something warm.

I brought my trembling hand up to touch it, wiping the glutinous substance from my skin, thick rivulets of it coating my fingers, thick rivulets of blood. I could taste it, feel it running down the back of my throat, coating my tongue. I swallowed it.

Somebody screamed behind me. I spun around, the sudden sound making me jump, my own terror engulfing me as I shrieked. A woman stood behind me, his mother, looking at me with such horror on her face, and I held my hands out towards her, hands soaked in his blood.

"Look! He still bleeds! He is the son of God!"

I ran from that place, stumbling through the crowd gathering around me, ploughing through their confused faces. Still, I could taste the blood in my mouth, his blood, so coppery, sliding against my teeth, against my gums. It was in my eyes, in my nose, it was all over me, and I ran in terror.

What had I done? The horror of it kept pounding through my temples. The man on the cross, a dead man, stone cold dead, and yet his blood flowed from his body as though his heart still pumped in his chest. It shot from the wound in his side, it hit me in the face with a force befitting the living, and yet he lay dead, just an empty decomposing vessel of flesh.

Faces all around me. I saw them through my panic, looking at me, scowling at me, this figure stumbling through the streets covered in blood.

His blood.

Home. At all cost, I had to get home to my little room, to wash that filth from my flesh, to make myself clean of the death that lay wet upon my skin. Yet so many people crowded around me, so many hands reached out to touch me, this crazed, frantic man running through the streets covered in blood. Then I fell to the ground, covered in dust, and screamed my terror into the street.

Hands on my shoulders, hands on my arms, my legs, my back. I wanted to throw them all off, to run through them at full pelt, to escape those questioning voices. I picked my spear off the ground, and I thrust it out before me, my voice screaming above the din.

"Leave me alone!"

Like a ripple spreading out across the water, they moved away from me, a wide circle of silent figures that just looked at me, their expressions glazed, seeing, yet somehow blind.

I got to my feet, spinning around on the spot, looking at their faces, their blank expressions, so still, so emotionless as I ran forward, barging through their number without any resistance. I held the spear before me, pointing it ahead in some frantic gesture of warning, and they let me pass, so silent, so obedient, a sea of people parting before me to grant me free passage, and I ran blindly through the streets unhindered.

Blindly through the streets. Not blindly. I could see.

I crashed through my door, slamming it shut behind me, the rough wood against my back as I held my hands up before my face, my bloodied hands that shook so violently before me, hands that I could see, hands that stood out before me in the minutest of detail. Every cut, every scratch, every smear of red. I saw them through my eyes with the utmost clarity.

My room. My tiny wooden bed. The bowl of water resting on a wooden dresser. The tiled floor. The mud plastered walls with their myriad of tiny cracks creeping across its pitted surface like a spider web. The half burned candles resting in their iron sconces. I saw it all, clearly, without the insistent throbbing in my head, my eyes renewed to a clarity that I had never before experienced.

The blood. Blood upon my hands, blood still wet. It should have dried, in that blistering heat it should have dried to a dark crust against my flesh, yet it remained wet, fresh, unctuous.

Horror overwhelmed me. My stomach heaved in roiling convulsions, bile rising up my throat to fill my mouth. My body shook, my muscles quivering beneath my taught skin as the terror filtered through every nerve ending. I rushed forward, hands plunging into the water, water splashing across my face, washing the horror away, scrubbing at the red that still clung to my skin until the water ran contaminated.

It swirled around the hammered metal basin, around and around, so much red, so much blood, *his* blood. I stared at it, transfixed, unable to tear my gaze away from that whirlpool of spilled life, of blood, inky red blood.

The blood is the life.

I wanted it. I could not stand the site of it just sitting there, swirling, tormenting me. My stomach squeezed and churned, moving inside me like some caged beast, and I felt a desire that I had never felt before, that I did not recognise, an excruciating need to feed, and I lifted the bowl to my lips.

It filled my mouth, flooding my throat as I gulped it down, mouthful after mouthful, never stopping for breath, swallowing the crimson water, taking it into my body, ingesting it. I wanted it all inside of me, every last drop of it. I needed it inside me as though my very life depended upon it. Higher and higher I lifted the basin, tipping its contents into my gorging mouth until nothing remained, not a drop of water or blood.

The basin flew from my hands and collided with the wall with a loud clang, the force of the impact crumpling the edge of the metal and gouging a dent into the wall.

I could not believe that I did that. The bowl left my hands with a power unbeknown to me and collided with the wall with such a force as to damage both.

Pain shot through my legs and devoured my bowels. I crumpled to the floor, agony ripping away at the lining of my stomach as spasm after excruciating spasm fired through my body. Everything inside me started to leech out, pouring out of my ass in a never-ending stream of shit and water. I felt urine pouring from the tip of my cock, pumping out of me in a continuous burning stream of piss. Sweat erupted from my pores and soaked through my clothes as I curled into a ball on the floor, agony silent upon my gaping lips, for I had no breath with which to scream. My bowel ripped as half-digested forms purged from my body, forcing their way through my anus in great indistinguishable lumps, ripping, tearing, bursting from my body in a never-ending surge of torture.

As I cowered there in a pool of my own life, I knew that I lay dying. The pain that fired through every bone in my shattered body, the blazing agony that set my nerves on fire, the unending torrent of fluids that poured from my every orifice, told me that I was dying, dying in a puddle of my own shit.

My heart raced inside my chest. It moved and juddered beneath my ribs, an animal thrashing in the last throes of life, and I wanted to rip that animal from my chest, to remove that failing organ from my failing body. The muscle shivered, slowed to a heavy, elongated thump as it convulsed inside me, screaming inside me, dying inside me. I opened my lips to cry out in agony, but the sound halted on the rim of my lips as my lack of breath refused to let my pain fly. I could not breathe out, I could not breathe in, and I convulsed upon the floor like a fish out of the water.

Through a cloud of exquisite death, I heard my body die. The sound of my heart, the pumping of my blood through my veins, I heard it lessen, I heard it falter, I felt it dying. My chest heaved as the muscle inside quivered one last time, as my blood froze between dying beats, and then my breath hissed from my lungs, pushing its way up through my throat and out of my mouth in one long, drawn out sigh.

Does one not see all that has transpired in one's life, at the point of death? As a soldier, I had killed many, some deserved, some not. Why did I not see their accusing faces as I died? As a man, I had slept with many men, a vessel for their desires and frustrations, a cum bucket for the wealthy. Why did I not see their faces then, as my bowels lay ruined before me?

To die alone, unwanted, I expected nothing else. The life of a soldier left no room for friends, and my path as a whore left no room for lovers. Friends were unnecessary and lovers unwanted. I chose my life, the killer, the cock sucker. I chose to be alone. What other outcome could such an outcast possibly expect?

And so I died alone, vanishing from the light into a world of darkness.

My body lay in a state of serene stillness. It felt wonderful to lie in such complete calm, without pain, without care, without the trappings of guilt or shame, for all thoughts of such things left me. I only felt the darkness and the knowledge that my life was over.

The black shell of oblivion that encased my mind exploded in a blaze of startling light, and I could see. My limbs unfurled, slowly, carefully, but they felt so strong, so powerful, and I felt so very different, renewed somehow. I lifted from the floor, one swift movement that saw my back lift off the tiles until I stood on my feet, and oh, the colours. I saw my room as I had never seen it before, a kaleidoscope of rich colour and detail that pulsed before my bulging eyes in a living, seething display of patterns and textures. Every detail, every crack, every speck of dust floating through the fading light, paraded itself before my disbelieving eyes, details that had, for so long, been lost to me. Never, even at the height of good health, had my eyesight been so sharp, and I marvelled at the seemingly limitless range of my new found, perfect eyesight.

Fuck, I felt good. For the first time since I could remember, no headache, no dull throbbing behind my eyes, and I felt so strong, unbelievably strong. I felt reborn, mind and spirit in new form, and I liked it. I looked at my hands, hands that glowed anew, smooth and beautiful, strong. Flesh so flawless and pearly white, unblemished in its perfection, and the arms to which they belonged felt so thick and muscular, bulging limbs of pure magnificence. My entire body felt so hard, tight, a rippling tower of power, of masculinity, it throbbed through me like a gift from the Gods — Adonis personified.

Death suited me.

Hunger. Never had I felt such hunger. The pain of it gurgled inside my stomach with indiscriminate fingers, fingers that dug deep into my bowels, ravenous fingers of unquenchable thirst. I could also smell it, blood, fresh and warm, pumping through the veins of the living, beckoning for me to feed, demanding that I drink, and drink deeply. If I closed my eyes I could hear it, whispering for me, calling my name, a desire of red that needed me to consume it, that demanded that I drink, and it drove me to distraction.

I wanted it. Above all else I had to have it, in my mouth, down my throat, all over my face, hot and sticky. I grabbed my spear, intent on using it, and as I burst from my little room into the courtyard, the desire to draw blood propelled me forward, and I didn't give a shit who saw me. The smell intensified, and I turned, allowing its coppery odour to fill my nose and inflame my senses. It drew me towards the bath house, a manly mixture of testosterone, spunk, and blood.

My new body flew across the courtyard in a single leap, but before I had time to marvel at the speed by which I moved, I burst through the door of the baths, standing amidst a throng of naked men.

"Fucking hell, Gaius, what the bloody hell is wrong with you? You look like shit!"

Marcus sat on the stone bench, looking at me as though I had just shit myself. His body glistened with sweat, highlighting the contours of his muscle bound physic, a dripping hulk of masculinity that only served to whet my appetite.

It all happened so quickly that I can barely conceive of the slaughter that took place in that small bath house. Five men died by my hand, and they did not die well.

My spear clattered to the ground, and I grabbed Marcus by the neck, lifting him off the bench, pulling him to my lips where my teeth exploded from my gums like two daggers. The sensation shocked me, but I felt so hungry, the impulse to drink so strong, that I did not stop to think about this new part of me. Within seconds I opened his flesh, ripping at his neck with my new teeth so that his blood pumped freely into my mouth.

I heard screaming and shouting around me, I felt frantic hands pounding at my back, my head, my arms, a desperate attempt to rip Marcus from my gorging lips, but I was drowning in the ecstasy of blood, consumed by the desire to drain him of every living drop. It hit my throat and slid down my neck in thick, pumping mouthfuls, making me swoon. The taste, the warm, coppery taste of life had me in its thrall, and I did not want it to stop. All of Marcus's life filled my mind, drowning me in red, and I lapped it up hungrily.

Nothing else remained. I threw his lifeless corpse to the floor and turned on my attackers. The horror on their faces ripped away their sanity, and as I reached out to grab a neck in each hand, I could see why. I did not recognise my own flesh. Hands, once so large and strong, now resembled claws, articulated talons that wrapped themselves around their necks with length to spare, ending in huge nails that sliced through skin and muscle as easily as my teeth. No wonder they screamed. I had turned into a monster.

I felt their necks snap between my fingers. One man tried to run from the bath, but I threw a lifeless body at him, and both fell to the floor in a crumpled heap. The other survivor lunged at me, a dagger grasped in his hand, but again my new found speed won out as I pulled the blade from his feeble fingers and ran its sharp edge across his throat. He crumpled to the ground in a gurgle of his own blood, a jet of red splashing across my chest, and I loved it, the feel of it, the warmth of it against my cold skin, and I realised then that my cock stood proud and erect.

The last man groaned as he pulled himself free of the corpse on top of him. His blood still pumped warm through his veins, I could hear his heart pounding furiously inside his chest, and it excited me. I reached down and pulled him up by the hair as he screamed. I turned his head towards me so that he could see my face, a face that felt twisted, inhuman, and as his eyes widened to look upon my true beauty, his scream turned into a low guttural moan as he pissed himself.

I wanted to enjoy him. I wanted to savour every drop that his bulging body had to offer, so I dragged him across the floor, through the blood and limbs, and I sat against the far wall with him between my legs. I wrapped one arm around his chest, pulling his massiveness against me, feeling my erection hard against his back, and I sank my teeth into the base of his veined neck. I began to work my dick with my free hand, long hard strokes that moved in time to the sound of his heart, his strong manly heart that pumped blood into my throat in a steady stream of orgasmic life.

All of him pumped inside of me. I could feel him moving through my veins, through my organs, through my cock. My hand jerked faster, moving up and down my shaft, rubbing against his back with an urgency that threatened to explode. I pressed my teeth in deeper, the flesh ripping against my lips, and all that he was, exploded from the wound in a great rush of blood that showered my face and ran down my back. With a cry of satisfaction, I ripped my teeth out of his neck, just as my ejaculate shot up his back, mixing with the blood that poured from the wound.

For a moment, I lay there panting, spent, and I felt my body, my face, my hands, rippling, claws retracting, teeth sliding back inside my gums, my human form returned to me once more. My tongue licked at the mixture of semen and blood, sliding across the dead man's back, devouring every drop, swallowing it deep until my body could take no more. I felt like a leech, swollen and bloated.

Caiaphas swept through the door wearing nothing but a loose cloth draped over his shoulder, his lithe body glistening with oil, and my new eyes saw for the first time, his full, magnificent beauty. It took seconds for him to register the carnage around him, and then his gaze found me.

He moved in a way that I found utterly shocking, eye blisteringly fast, lifting me up off the floor, slamming my body against the wall as though I weighed nothing.

Caiaphas' face, so sharp, so angular, so fucking lickable, pressed against the cold white skin of my neck, and he inhaled deeply, smelling me, breathing me in, and I felt my cock twitch between my legs again, aroused by his overwhelmingly sensual presence. He looked at me, his glowing, fascinating eyes regarding me with curiosity.

"What the fuck happened to you?"

"I don't know."

He moved closer, his groin pressed against my hardness, and then his tongue slipped out between his plump lips and traced a warm river down my neck.

For the first time, as he inhaled me, as he tasted me, I realised something about him that my old self could not detect, that Caiaphas was not human.

His tongue flickered around his lips, and his eyes widened, his huge golden eyes, and I almost laughed at the shock I saw reflected inside them.

"You're dead."

"No fucking shit."

"What the fuck are you?"

"I don't know. What the fuck are you?"

He flung me across the room with a strength of ten men, and I crashed into the opposite wall, but before I could slump to the floor, he flew at me, holding me up, his hands pinning my body against the cracked plaster, my feet dangling off the floor.

His face rippled, and for a moment I saw it, something hidden beneath the surface, something animalistic, something inhuman, and it frightened me.

Slowly he lowered my feet to the floor, his hand clamped around my neck, holding me firm. Again he inhaled, his nostrils huge, more an elongated snout than a nose.

115

"What... are... you?"

With a show of strength that shocked him, I pulled his hand away from my neck and held it against my stiffened cock.

"I don't know. What are you?"

"I asked you first."

My free hand reached out to search between his legs, and I found his cock, hard and throbbing beneath the cloth, and I wanted it inside me.

"Do you want to fuck me again, Caiaphas? It is Caiaphas, isn't it? Funny, you smell so different to me now, like rotten eggs."

"What have you done? I demand that you tell me! What are you?"

I kicked out against the wall with the soles of my feet, propelling us both towards the floor where we tumbled amidst the blood and the dead. I crouched over him, my cock grinding into his, my excitement building to the point of orgasm. Cumming two or three times in a row was never a problem for me, I could keep going until my dick dropped off, and fuck did I want him inside me.

"I thought you were human, I let you fuck me. Tell me what you are."

"I *know* you were human, Barbarian, but I don't know what you are now."

In a blur of twisting muscle, he lay suddenly on top of me, sitting astride me, pinning my hands above my head in his own, and I lay submissive beneath his exquisite weight, locked in his strong, immutable grip. He leaned into me, his face twisting, the animal beneath breaking through the human, and for a moment I thought I saw two long horns twisting out of his head.

"How is this possible? There is not a thing on this Earth that I do not know, and yet, here you are, new, original. Are you a creature of darkness, Gaius? If you are, then you belong to me. What are you, Gaius?"

I needed to taste him. Some irresistible desire, an insatiable hunger, grabbed me by my balls and squeezed until I could resist him no longer. My body changed, twisting beneath his frame, and I could feel my fingers growing, feel my nails ripping through my skin, my face distorting, cracking, and then something slid down from my gums, long and sharp over my lower lips, touching my chin. The look of astonishment on Caiaphas' face would have made me laugh, but I had no time for such hilarity, only for feeding.

"What the fuck?"

I reared up suddenly, tearing my elongated hands out of his tight grip with effortless ease, and I wrapped my arms around his firm torso, pulling him towards me, towards my mouth, and I sank my teeth into the soft flesh of his neck. A scream of shock escaped from between his lips as his blood pumped into my mouth.

His hot, rancid blood.

My teeth ripped away from his neck as I vomited my load across his face and chest, thick black clots of glutinous crap sliding down his skin.

"That's fucking rank!"

Caiaphas roared with rage, clutching at his neck with clawed talons as black blood pumped between his fingers.

"How fucking dare you! Don't you know who I am?"

"I don't give a fuck who you are, you taste fucking disgusting! What are you?"

With a roar of fetid breath and stampeding hooves, the Beast stood before me, a horned nightmare with black leathery wings and eyes that burned into my body to shatter my soul.

"Know my name, Barbarian, for I am your worst fucking nightmare, that's who I am."

We flew at each other, teeth and claws digging into flesh, into fur, writhing through the blood encrusted floor in a frenzy of destruction, a frenzy of passion that saw us ripping and shredding at each other's flesh. He was strong, but so was I, but he could fly, and he lifted us above the floor, his huge wings beating against my body, and then he threw me to the ground, the tiles shattering under the force of my impact. I felt my bones break, I felt pain, and for a moment I feared him.

"Is that fear I see upon your face, Barbarian? Good. Hear me, and hear me well. Whatever manner of beast you are, whatever manner of creature you have become, you belong to me, for all such dark things belong to me, I who was once held up above all others, loved above all others. I am the Fallen one, and you will obey me."

I didn't know what manner of creature I had become, what thing fate deemed to make of me, but one thing I did know for certain, I would obey no one.

I looked around, desperate for something to defend myself against the raging Beast, and I saw my spear, resting on the floor by the stone bench where I had dropped it. With a speed that thrummed through my limbs, I dived towards the bench, rolled over, picked up the spear and thrust it out towards the charging Beast.

The tip of the spear sliced into the side of the stampeding creature. He froze and looked down upon the wound in utter astonishment. His clawed fingers held together the gaping flaps of black flesh as blood pumped from the wound. Astonishment turned to fear as the Beast collapsed against the wall, his body diminishing, moving, body parts sliding like liquid across his transforming body until only the man remained, Caiaphas, looking at me in disbelief, and the spear in my hand.

"How is that possible? You can't hurt *me*, no one can."

I thrust the spear towards him, and he cowered away from its tip, terrified of the weapon that had so efficiently sliced through his arrogance.

"No? Really? Would you like to rethink that?"

"What is that? Tell me. What is it!"

I held the spear in my hand, its tip glistening black, and as I watched, the blood sank into the metal until nothing remained but the dried red stain of the man on the cross.

"It's a fucking spear! What the fuck does it look like?" The scathing anger that tainted my voice did nothing to disguise my growing fear. "I used it on him, I stabbed him with it, and then he bled, into my eyes, into my mouth. What am I, Caiaphas? Look at what I have done. I killed them. I drank from them. What am I!"

Caiaphas slithered across the floor on his knees, one hand clamping the bleeding wound in his side while his other hand reached out to brush my cheek. I flinched, because I did not expect him to touch me with such affection. It unnerved me.

"You are new, the first of your kind, the first occurrence. Don't be afraid, dear heart, let me help you."

"You just attacked me!"

"You bit me, bitch!"

"I couldn't help it. Something came out of me, took over me, something that needed to bite, to feed, to drink. And I'm so bloody hungry, I've just eaten them, and I'm still so fucking hungry!"

His fingers brushed my lips, parting them gently, examining the teeth inside, but they remained sheathed within my gums. He looked so inquisitive, gazing at me in such amazement, and I could see that he did not understand. Suddenly he flinched as his hand brushed against the tip of the spear resting in my hands.

"That thing. Keep it away from me, do you hear?"

"I'm sorry, I didn't mean to, I don't know what came over me."

"Makes a change from me."

"Very funny."

"Oh, I do try." Caiaphas slid away, clutching his side. He slumped against the far wall while I slid against the one opposite, and we looked at each other, two monsters regarding each other across a blood-splattered room.

A monster. Some had called me that in life, but death saw such insults made flesh.

As I watched, the wound in his side started to heal, fingers of flesh knitting across the raw muscle, pulling itself together. To see such a thing filled me with horror, yet more evidence of his bestial nature, and still I found it completely fascinating, and it made me a little horny.

"It has been a long time since anyone has damaged me. I would like to know how that is possible."

"I pierced his side, this blade entered his body."

"And slayed a God? How interesting." Something akin to darkness overshadowed his face, and I saw a look there, a faraway look, a thought that seemed to give him immense pleasure, because he smiled, a wide, lascivious smile

"A spear? Could it be? Is it that simple?"

"Caiaphas, I have had just about as much of this weird shit today as I can take, so will you please talk plain?"

When he looked at me, it felt as if he saw me for the first time, and his eyes glowed so bright, twinkling with excitement.

"Plain? Yes. Oh, I will talk plain, dear heart, and you will listen. I have a story to tell, and you, my strange new creature, you and that spear, may be just the answer I have been looking for."

Chapter Seven: A Long Conversation With The Devil

As Related By Melek

I was an Angel. No, really, I was an Angel, wings and everything. And yes, my father is God, it's a fact, get over it, move on. What is it with humans and their bloody labels? Father this, God that, gay this, straight that, really, get a fucking grip. I was an Angel, and I was beautiful — I was the most beautiful.

When Father created us, he did not create us equal. Oh no, let's just say that I stood in line twice for that little extra something special. So what was that *thing* that set me apart from the rest? Could it be my looks, my charm, my wit? My impossibly huge cock? No, what I had, in insufferable overabundance, was a huge capacity to love. Yes, you heard correctly, dear heart, my unending capacity for love, and compassion. Back in the day, I was one never-ending fountain of goody-two-shoes bull shit. It spouted from my mouth in a never-ending stream of piss. Everything I did, everything I said, everything I felt, all of it for the good of my kind, for the good of Father.

Heaven rang with the sound of fucking music. All of us so fucking happy. The thought of it now makes me want to choke on my own vomit. Or vomit down someone else's throat and make them choke. Maybe that's where I am going wrong?

The point is, everyone loved me. Everybody loved *me,* Lucifer the kind, Lucifer the generous, Lucifer the benevolent blah, blah, blah, and you know what? I loved them back.

Unconditional love. What the fuck's that all about? Really, sweetie, if you give out and you don't get it back, then you really do deserve a smack in the gob, with a fist full of rings, just after you have wiped your ass without washing your hands. Ah, but that's the new me, that was not me back then, high on the wings of fucking love. No, darling, we all went around patting each other on the wings and telling each other how wonderful we were, how lovely we were, how pretty we were. And I was pretty. I was fucking lush!

I did love Father. I loved Father unconditionally. I loved Father even though he could be a fucking asshole at times. Even when his actions hurt me so much that I had to hide away from him and all the others, in my own private place, where they could not see my face, and they could not hear me crying.

You see, Father dearest could be rather impetuous, prone to making snap decisions—and talk about impulsive. Regardless of the consequences or my feelings, Father did as Father wanted. Was I not his favourite? Did he not love me above all others? Was I not the most perfect of all his creations? And yet my point of view meant nothing to him, and therefore, sometimes, he made me feel like *I* meant nothing to him, despite my love, despite my adoration.

I had never seen him so excited as when he made Earth. He would stay inside his workshop for days on end, weeks. I would love to go inside that huge domed building that reached impossibly high and just sit there and watch him work, see his smile and hear his laughter as Father did what he did best, create.

So many wondrous things lay inside that workshop, and I barely understood a single one. It was a space filled with space, with swirling clouds of nebulous gas, stars twinkling from within their tenuous depths. A place filled with colours and smells that, as yet, remained un-named. A place where the building blocks of life danced to Father's touch, to a melody that only he knew, that only he understood. So I watched, and I marvelled, as Father danced amongst the stars, pulling from the clusters of creation long strands of life that moved and thrilled to his command. He brought them together, combining stone and dust until it formed a coalescent form of spinning matter. A process that took millions of years in human terms, but to us, sitting there on the brink of creation, took just a moment.

Over a period of weeks, Father gave the new planet a crust, and on that crust, he created the outlines of land, great swathing masses of land, indistinguishable from the crust from which they grew. I knew the moment approached, and I had to see it, because it never failed to thrill me, that moment when he would exhale new life into his creation.

Father breathed upon the surface of the Earth. I watched, transfixed, in awe of him, and I saw it happen, I saw him inhale, filling his huge lungs before exhaling across the craggy surface of the planet, an exhalation that lasted for days. Slowly the clouds began to form as the atmosphere grew, a billowing turbulence of chaos that spread across the surface of the Earth until it encased the orb with a shimmering film of air.

I wanted to move in closer to get a better look, to see for myself the miracle of life, up close and personal. But Father held me back, his face alive with such joy, and I shared that moment by his side, Father and son, and I felt his joy as the first drops of rain began to fall upon the dry crust.

Lightening flickered through the forming clouds, a fierce blaze of electricity that raged across the newborn planet. The atmosphere grew dark, black, coiling, and water fell upon the ground in a ceaseless downpour that made such a beautiful sound. We both dropped to the floor, lying on our backs hand in hand, Father and son listening to the sound of rain, laughing as the music of creation washed over us in a ceaseless wave of pleasure.

What an exquisitely beautiful moment. To witness the moment of creation, to witness the breath of new life, the creation of a new world. Father shared that moment with me. He shared his happiness with me, just the two of us, listening to the sound of the rain as it fell. His love for the new planet filled my heart, and I think in that moment, I could never have loved him more.

The rain stopped. We leapt to our feet, staring at the Earth in total wonder, because it was a planet transformed. Even as we watched, the great swathes of land, now surrounded by water, started to turn green as life established itself across its surface. Earth turned into a planet of sparkling blue water and green lands, and it looked fucking stunning.

Father danced. Father actually danced around the Earth, laughing and clapping, his cries of joy ringing around the dome in great peals of delight, and I could not help but join in.

What a load of fucking bollocks. Though, to be fair, it felt fantastic at the time. To watch him create the Earth, and to share in that joyous creation, yes, it felt good at the time. Yet, dear heart, true to form, it remained only a matter of time before Father's impetuous nature broke my heart.

I used to love soaring through the skies of Earth, my glorious wings buffeted by that pure sweet air, as yet untarnished by the pollution of man. How I loved the mountains, climbing into the Heavens to meet me. How I loved the vast emerald forests that swept across the surface in a lush crust of green that swayed in the wind. And how I loved the seas, the rivers, the lakes, the waterfalls that glittered like my wings against the sun. How I loved that virgin world, so sparkly and new, and barely a day went by that I didn't wallow in its splendour.

Only God knows how he used to like playing, and he just couldn't help himself, he could not resist populating his new toy with all sorts of strange and wonderful creatures, fucking huge creatures at that. Some of them walked on their back legs, enormous carnivorous monsters that devoured those unlucky enough to cross their paths. Some walked on all fours, huge bony plates running down the length of their muscular backs, gentle plant-eating creatures with big, adorable eyes. Then he made the ones who could fly, with huge leathery wings that captured the air to lift them higher, and he gave them massive beaks, long pointed snouts filled with needle sharp teeth. I loved them all, every giant, every monster, creatures of such incredible majesty, their tremendous footsteps thundering through the ground, their screeching roars bellowing through the forests, and I loved them.

One of my favourite spots lay surrounded by a ring of smoking mountains and thick twisted trees, a lake whose surface glittered so blue as to rival the sky itself, and lurking in its crystalline depths swam my favourite monster of them all.

Sometimes I would fly over that lake, my silver wings spread wide, fingers dragging through the surface of the water as I shot across its surface, and then I would rise into the air, hovering above its centre, and wait.

As I hovered there, giddy with excitement, the water below would start to boil, as though some vast thing moved up from its fathomless depths, heaving its bulk towards the glistening surface. Then the water would break in a tremendous foaming fountain as my monster broke through the surface, its huge grey head atop a long, proud neck, rising forever upwards until its head reached my feet. I would stand on that head, laughing at the sheer joy of it. The creature was so beautiful, its massive, heavy body just visible beneath the water, waves breaking across the occasional grey hump cascading down its long back towards a tail that seemed to go on forever. Oh, and its eyes, such huge black eyes filled with a gentleness, a soul, the most beautiful soul of all.

With a bark that echoed around the lagoon in great melodious howls, my monster would tear through the water at tremendous speed while I knelt on its head, riding the beast as we both cried out in pleasure. It was a simple act of playfulness, two of God's children playing in a garden of his creation. Nothing could have been more perfect.

Yet, Father's displeasure with his new creations reigned paramount. Nothing was ever fucking good enough for him. They weren't smart enough, not beautiful enough, not like us enough. He called them stupid mindless beasts. Yet, in my naiveté, I thought he would give them time, allow them to evolve, to become something more. At the very least I thought he would make some adjustments, tinker with them a bit, make them better somehow, even though I thought them perfect creatures in every way. They lived on Earth in perfect harmony with their environment, a balance of pure perfection that saw them flourish across the surface of that planet in so many wide and varied forms.

Heaven darkened. I saw the darkness form over Father's workshop, great coiling clouds of anger that spread out across Heaven, drowning us all in its wrath. We all felt it, the sadness that it carried, the weight of guilt that it shared, the profound sense of loss that rained down on all my brothers and me. And I knew. I knew what was happening, and as I ran towards the workshop, my heart shattered into pieces behind me.

I found Father in a rage. The workshop flashed with anger as his arms ripped great strands of insubstantial matter from the pockets of nebulous gas that surrounded him, his fingers manipulating the strands until they coalesced into a huge boulder of rock, a meteor of immense size that he sent hurtling towards the Earth with deadly intent.

I know I screamed, I heard it burst from my mouth in a cry of utter defiance and grief. He saw me then, and I think my presence there shocked him, angered him even, because he never allowed us into the workshop during an extinction event. His temper flashed from his glowing body as he stormed towards me in great thundering steps. But all I could see was the meteor hitting the surface of the Earth, and the tremendous fireball that spread across its surface. A blossoming flower of flame that consumed all in its path as its petals enveloped the planet in a swath of indiscriminate death. Pain exploded across my chest as I found myself flying backwards, evicted from the workshop with a simple swat of his immense hand, discarded like the creatures he had just murdered.

Hatred filled my heart, a terrible feeling so alien to me, so unfamiliar. I crawled from that place, away from the wrath of my father, away from that dome, and away from my brothers who watched so impassively as my beloved Earth burned. I crawled to my secret place, a place where Angels feared to tread, and I huddled inside that dark place, so filled with the voices of my long lost brothers, and I cried into that empty, dead space, drowning in the souls of the lost. My tears could not dampen the pain that ripped through my lips or the sorrow that tore at my heart. I felt a blackness that I had never known, a deep-seated loathing for the being that had given me life. How could he create something so beautiful, and then so callously destroy it? How could he be so cruel?

How could he be so evil?

Something else crept into my growing darkness, a feeling, a sensation that stirred me to defiance, a new emotion that frightened me, yet also offered solace. Anger.

The voices in the dark whispered to me, comforted me, loved me, Lucifer, their friend, the only Angel who ever talked to them. And I loved them back, with their voices soothing the fury that burned through my veins and bulged behind my eyes. We were brothers, lost together in our isolation.

I never really recovered from that loss. Earth just didn't hold the same fascination for me after that, too much ash, too many bones. I spent less time in the workshop. I could not stand the thought of Father creating anything else, for fear he would destroy that too. I started to feel disconnected from the Angelic Host, unable to be the loving sibling they expected of me. I found it... difficult. More and more I spent time in the dark place, listening to the weeping souls of those who had nowhere to go, because Heaven did not deem them worthy, and more and more I found myself identifying with their displacement, sympathetic to their cause.

Every soul belonged somewhere, be that soul good or bad. Who were we to judge otherwise?

Of course, now I know better. Every soul belongs to me, or at least it should, it will, but back then I was bat shit crazy, a burgeoning idealist on the verge of glorious revolution. Ah, the life of a rebel, so terribly delicious!

Then Father did the unforgivable. He created Adam and Eve. He created the Mother and Father of a new race.

The summons rang throughout Heaven, its deep, commanding tone demanding that Father's children present themselves before the towering dome of the workshop. And like the lambs to the slaughter, we obeyed, a flock of the faithful waiting with bated breath for our beloved Father to present his latest creation, and I stood there amongst a sea of feathered twats and waited.

I could not help but look upon the proceedings with an air of disdain. All around me my brothers looked on adoringly, faces so fucking serene and Angelic, blissful. I wanted to grab them by their shoulders and shake the apathy from their compliant bones, to instil some kind of reaction in their acquiescent manner. Yet I didn't. I just stood there, watching, seething, feeling my anger inflame my veins, trapped in my own black indignity.

Three figures walked through the wall of the workshop, hand in hand. Father stood in the middle. And didn't he look fucking pleased with himself, smiling at his adoring fans, soaking up the unconditional love that poured from his beguiled children towards him.

Father sent his new creations into the excited crowd, and my brothers swarmed around the two proto-humans, touching them, stroking them, admiring them. I looked into their smooth faces, one male, one female, and the minute I looked into their big round eyes I saw it there, lurking within their shiny new souls, and I remember how the shock of it radiated through every part of my body, and I wanted to cry.

Father used the souls of Angels to create the Mother and Father of a new race. I saw the Angel within, an unmistakable radiance that glowed with light and love. Those beings, Adam and Eve, Father made them out of us, and as such he had made them immortal. Father had created a new version of us to populate his Earth, immortal beings made from the stuff of Angels.

I ran. I threw myself through the throng of wings and eternal beauty, my outrage pouring from my mouth in a wail of unending pain. Was I the only one to see it? Was I the only one to understand? Was I the only one to feel the sting of Father's betrayal? The time of the Angels was over. He had replaced us.

Did extinction await us, too?

I cowered in my dark place, and I closed my eyes to block out the voices, the thoughts of my beloveds rushing around me in concerned whispers. However, I could only see Adam and Eve, hand in hand with Father, the three of them smiling so benevolently, and I wanted to be sick. The voices wanted me to talk to them, to explain the grief that poured through my body, but I could not. Father did not love the dark ones. He abandoned them to that dark place, alone and uncared for. Would that happen to us too, to the Angels?

I watched as Father remodelled the Earth, the bones of the past buried beneath oceans of time, while on the surface, he created a garden of such exquisite beauty as to rival Heaven itself. At its centre, he placed Adam and Eve, his new favourite children, and I watched as he took his love away from the Angels, away from me, and showered it upon *them*.

I felt so empty, lost, so alone. I tried to engage him. I tried to take an interest, but my efforts fell on deaf ears, and he brushed me aside as a leaf is swept away by the wind, and oh, how it hurt. Can you imagine how that felt? Can you imagine the torture of losing the love of one you have worshiped for all of eternity? How does anyone cope with the loss of a father's love?

I realise now that when he made us, he created us to love unreservedly. Father made us to love with every molecule of our bodies. Love powered our souls, he programmed our brains to demonstrate love, every action, every thought, all of it contrived towards him. Father *made* us to love him, and we had no way of turning it off.

I love him so fucking much that I want to rip his fucking head off and shit in the stump! But alas, dear heart, I digress.

Father thought his new creations so fucking perfect that he no longer created life. Instead, he spent most of his time watching Adam and Eve, sitting on the mountains observing his perfect little humans, laughing with them, loving with them, and we, his first born, he left to our own devices. Most of my brothers watched Father watching the humans, laughing when he laughed, loving when he loved, content in their sycophantic happiness, but not me. From the moment Father released his abominations upon the Earth, he forgot about me, his most beloved son, his favourite above all. He took his love away from me and broke my heart.

The forgotten remained my only friends. I could no longer stand to see the contented faces of my brainwashed brothers. I preferred instead to lie in the dark place amidst the whispering voices, enveloped by their adoration and bathing in their love. It sustained me. It made me stronger. It kept me alive and gave me purpose.

I wanted to do something for them. I wanted to give them a demonstration of my love, of my gratitude for their continued support. I wanted to show them that someone *did* care, that they mattered, that they belonged, and that gave me an idea.

The workshop lay abandoned. As I moved through the wall of the dome, as I felt the particles of the universe part at my touch, I felt exhilarated, but also terrified. What I was about to do had never been attempted, not by an Angel. Father would deem it blasphemy, so the thought of it excited me beyond reason. I would show him that he was not the only one who could create something beautiful, that he was not the only *God*. I knew my actions to be nothing more than a rebellious child crying for help, for attention, for love, for a father to be proud of his son.

"Look at me Father, look what I did! Am I not clever? Am I not like you? Am I not a creator too?"

Did I know how angry it would make him? Fuck yes, of course I did, and the more it pissed him off, the better. If I made him angry, if I pissed him off enough, then at least he would have to come down off his pinnacle and face me. Was that not the natural order of things between father and son, to test one another's love to the point of breaking so that love may be made stronger? Should a father not respect his son?

Everything that a child does throughout its life is at the behest of the parent. We grow up with their beliefs, we assimilate their behaviour, and we mimic their actions. Is that not how we learn? So are we not just another version of our parents? Do we not, ultimately, want the same things?

I wanted Father to be happy. So why did he not want the same thing for me?

I had lived an eternity of happiness in my father's arms. It only took one moment of pain to rip me away from them.

So many times I stood in that vast space, amongst the stars, and watched in fascinated awe as Father created new worlds, new life, and now it was my turn. I saw everything, an unending vista of creation spreading out into infinity with star dust and planets and suns, life in all its diversity spreading out to touch the void. All of it in Father's name. An entire universe set out before my astonished gaze, and I faltered, suddenly terrified of the daunting task ahead. Then I saw my dark place, an area outside of space and time, a hole in the fabric of creation where my beloved voices whispered, alone, abandoned, and it gave me the strength to continue.

My beautiful wings spread out into the void, the mists of creation swirling around their silver tips, and I shivered as the power filled me, as my hands crackled with electric life. Concentration broke my brow in thick beads of fear that trickled down my immaculate flesh in rivers of strain. But I held back my fear, I controlled my beating heart as I thought of them lost in the dark place — my whispering friends longing so much for a place to belong.

Time and space enveloped me as I flew through creation. I felt the Universe pour through me, all of my father's creations pricking at my skin, existence pulling at my wings, pushing me back, screaming at me to leave the dark place outside of reality. But I reached out and grabbed it, tearing through the bubble of creation, and pulled the void into existence.

I held in my hand the dark place, a black hole of infinite emptiness, while all around me the Universe screamed in complaint, but I did not care. The Universe convulsed in agony, but I ignored its pain, its anger, its fear, and I reached out and plucked the Earth from the Heavens.

In the one hand, I held the dark place, while in the other, I cradled the Earth. All around me, creation trembled in torment, but it's power, the power of life and death, thrummed through my body and set me on fire. I felt like a God. I was God!

So much fucking power. It radiated from every part of me, flowed through every part of me, streaming towards me from stars and planets and things as yet unmade. The entire workshop thrummed with the power of God, and I knew in that one moment how he felt as he stood in that place and performed his miracles, because I felt it too. No wonder he kept it all to himself. It felt intoxicating.

Above it all I could hear my heart beating inside of my chest, and the Universe pulsed in sympathy to its beat, the two of us in perfect synchronicity. As the power coursed through my veins, I began to bring my hands together, bringing the Earth and the dark place closer. Creation in my hands, *my* hands, not Father's, life at *my* fingertips.

Something started to happen. The two orbs pushed against each other in a howl of agony as the Universe repelled the two realities. The harder I tried, the more creation screamed, a pounding orgasm of anguish that tore at my flesh and ripped at my wings. I felt the torment in my limbs, in my chest, and I knew that it wanted to destroy me. Wanted to reject the unnatural act of two opposing worlds colliding. But I could hear the pleading whispers from the dark place, begging me not to give up, to give them a place in which to exist, and I would not, I could not give up. I would not allow the Universe to reject my creation as my father rejected me.

I held in my hand two worlds, one natural, one an abomination, and I needed to combine them, the light and the dark. I, Lucifer, first amongst Angels, first born of my brothers, would bend creation to my command.

Father did it. He stood in that very same spot. I saw him. I saw creation move to his whim. Planets and stars, a whole Universe born out of his fucking ass. I saw him create the Earth, and then I saw him burn it, wipe away my monsters from its surface until nothing remained but bone and ash. And yet he just abandoned my dark friends, he left them out in the cold, alone, forgotten, and unwanted.

It pissed me off.

It began to fill me, the rage, the anger, something primal, bestial, and I felt my body transform to accommodate it. My hands grew huge and clawed, vicious taloned extensions of my fury, my feet cloven hooves that bit into the ground of the workshop, and even my wings transformed into immense black, leathery appendages that filled the Universe with their glory.

Lucifer stood reborn, renewed — beautiful. I felt so strong. Muscles bulged beneath my fur-clad skin, and I knew that I could do it. I knew that I could create the impossible, because I was the impossible, the first amongst the Angels to defy God, to make myself something other than he intended, and I loved it.

A roar, feral and bestial, ripped through my maw. I pushed the two worlds together, the dark and the light. The Universe groaned, but the new me, the strong me, the defiant me, pushed on, forcing them together, and with an eruption of black fire, the dark place fell into the centre of the Earth. Whispers exploded through my head as my body trembled, the Earth spinning out of my hand back into the cradle of creation as the voices cried out with joy. I made them a home, and finally, they could belong somewhere.

I fell to the ground exhausted, the raw energy of creation leaving my body to re-join the tenuous clouds that roiled around me, ripping the power from the very depths of my soul until nothing remained. My new form rippled and melted, folding back into my flesh until I became my beautiful self once again. Yet, I was different. I felt different.

My wings. No longer did they shine that wondrous, silky silver of my brothers, but instead they glistened black, a glossy black that flowed and writhed across my feathers as I moved them. So fucking beautiful.

A cloud of frozen gas flowed past, a glittering miasma awaiting formation, and it was then that I noticed the second change in the reflection staring back at me from the cloud, staring back at me with different eyes. Yellow, and so full of depth, as though they saw everything within their infinite, golden pools. My hair, once golden and lustrous, now lay a deep jet black and slicked back tight across my scalp. My beauty almost took my breath away.

My hands slid down my body, enjoying the feel of the muscles beneath the tight skin, so lithe, so sinuous, and I felt a thrum of erotic excitement, another new sensation, an electric tingle that swelled between my legs.

Fuck, that thing between my legs felt huge.

I heard the noise coming from outside the workshop, the sound of raised voices, and that really surprised me, because my brothers never raised their voices.

The Universe parted before me as I ploughed through the workshop, but I noted that it did so with disgust, treating me like some foreign body invading its space. I felt its disapproval, but I didn't give a shit—what the fuck did I care how the Universe felt about me? I, who had just created life?

Lucifer one, Universe zero.

As I moved through the wall of the workshop, I walked into chaos. Thousands of Angels surrounded the dome, staring into the sky, their voices a gaggle of whispered outrage at the scene unfolding in the skies above them.

They filled the Heavens. My friends, the lost souls, they filled the air, their black shapes moving in an excited whirl above the dome, pouring out of the dark place into existence, a jubilant host of the disenchanted.

"Brother, what have you done?" Daniyyel stepped forward, and I almost laughed at his oh so earnest face, so full of concern and disapproval. He reached out and touched my black wings, removing his hand quickly as though burned.

"I have created something wonderful, brother. Look at them, look at the lost, welcomed at last into our Father's Kingdom. Are they not beautiful?"

I lifted my arms towards the sky, and my host swept down and lifted me into their jubilant arms, high above the startled heads of my brothers. Their whispering voices drowned out the sky, their gratitude, their love, crying out across Heaven, calling out my name.

They loved me. It filled my body, my heart, my soul, love for me, and only for me, not for him, not for Father, for the one who left them in the dark, forgotten in the cold. Their love belonged to me, and I took it into myself and let it fill my heart.

"Welcome to *my* house, my friends, where all of you are welcome!"

Their bodies moved around me, pressing against me, touching me, loving me, all of them crowding in until I could see nothing but darkness as their writhing mass blocked out the sky. So beautiful, so magnificent, so wonderful. I felt as though I belonged to them, and they belonged to me, my host, my Dark Angels, my subjects.

"Go home, dear hearts, go home, to the place that I have made for you, only for you."

They poured out of the sky like a black storm, raining down upon the workshop to disappear through its wall, plunging towards their new home. I closed my eyes, and pictured them streaming towards the Earth, a black mass tearing through the atmosphere, ripping through the planet's crust towards the warm place I had made them, and it made me feel good.

Father's huge hand plucked me out of the sky with a scream of rage so terrible that Heaven shook. His fury blazed through the sky in great forks of light, and ripping the air apart with his anger.

I saw something in his face, something that caught in my throat. Disappointment. His favourite child had disappointed him. For a moment, that old compulsion of familial love tried to reassert itself, tried to make me beg for his forgiveness, for his love, but I thought better of it and spat in his fucking face.

"See, Father," I bellowed defiantly, "I can create, too. Maybe now you will notice me?"

Heaven shuddered as his voice boomed from between his lips.

"If you love them so much, then you can be with them! Be their King in that Hell you have created. You are no longer my child, and you are no longer welcome in my home. I cast you out Lucifer, never to return."

His arm reached back, my wings were trapped beneath his burning fingers, and then, before my brothers, before the entire Heavenly Host, Father cast me out.

* * * *

"So, you are a Fallen Angel." More than just a little sarcasm laced my voice, but I could not help it.

"And you are a bloodsucking monster! Is that really too difficult to believe? That I once sat in Heaven, at Gods side? You have seen the real me, you know what I look like."

"So what do I call you? Really. Lucifer?"

Caiaphas laughed, a sound that still managed to send a tingle of excitement down my spine. Despite our little rough and tumble, I still could not help but fancy the horny fucker.

"What is it with you lot and names? Really. Lucifer bores me, it was who I was then, not who I am now. So you may call me Melek, I am, after all, King of all Angels."

"Okay then, Melek, King of all Angels, what the fuck are you doing here?"

Again he laughed, a slippery, sly sound, both chilling and erotic. Charisma positively oozed from every pore of his perfect body, a magnetism that drew me to him, and I just wanted to swim in it.

"I like you, dear heart. You are so refreshingly blunt. I came here to deal with that Messianic twat that you so kindly speared. He was making waves, and I don't do waves. I had thought that if I disposed of him, it would be enough to bring Father down to face me."

"And how is that working out for you?"

"Fucking shit, to be honest with you, and I'm not honest often. Anyone would think he wanted his son to die! Ah well, dear heart, never mind, I have you now."

I didn't like the sound of that, and yet, it thrilled me all the same. He wanted me.

"Meaning?"

"Meaning, sweetie, that I think you may be the answer to all my prayers, you and that charming little spear of yours."

"Run that by me again?"

"You may be a bulging mass of muscle my friend, but you really are rather stupid. We are going to build an army, an army unlike anything this world, or Father, has seen before. We are going to create creatures like you, lots of them. You are my Black Messiah, Gaius, and the means by which Heaven shall fall. When his beloved humans lie consumed by the feral force we shall unleash, he will have no choice but to face me, and I will ram that spear so far up his fucking ass he will be able to pick his teeth with it!"

For the first time, I saw the hatred burning behind his eyes, the unquenchable flame of patricide that drove him insanely towards the edge of his own personal cliff, and I have to admit, as ashamed as I am, it excited me. He excited me. To know that God existed, and Heaven, Hell, my poor brain could barely conceive of such a thing. Could I help him kill his father? I could barely come to terms with my own state of being, never mind getting involved in a war between Heaven and Hell.

"Listen, Melek, I don't understand how this has happened to me, never mind how to create more. How are you going to build this army of yours?"

"*Ours*, dear heart, ours. And it all began with blood, as it will end with blood. The blood is the life. You are this way because you ingested his blood. So you, my friend, are going to get me more of it."

Chapter Eight: I Am The Resurrection

As Related By Gideon

I saw the world through new eyes. As the sun set over the fields of Golgotha, I saw a range of colour explode across the sky that I could never have perceived with my failing, human eyes. Inky reds and burnt, fiery oranges, bled across wispy clouds so that it looked as though Heaven itself lay bleeding, and the colours flowed down to the ground where they merged with sand and rock in an indistinguishable shamble of pigment. My eyes were finally open, and I saw a world so beautiful that it filled my heart with joy.

Olive trees, so stunted and ugly in life, now took on a sculptural property that my new eyes found fascinating. Every detail, every dried leaf, every shrivelled fruit clinging to their branches found a place in my heart, and for a moment, I forgot the horror of the monster lurking within me.

Monster. I heard the word, and yet I did not feel it. The thing, the creature that inhabited my body, it did not repulse me. If anything, it fascinated me. My monster helped me see again. To see the world so crystal clear, and without pain, that had to be worth it. The strength, the speed, the incredible power that I felt surging through my limbs, all wonders of my new existence that I could not ignore, and I had my monster to thank for that.

Neither could I ignore the five men that lay dead in the bath house. I slaughtered them, I ripped them apart with my hands and my teeth, and I drank from them to satiate the craving that my body demanded. It was by far the most erotic thing I had ever experienced in my life. Just the thought of warm, viscous blood pumping down my throat made me hard.

What had I done? What was I doing? Nausea made my head spin as a wave of anxiety tore through my heart. I murdered five men, without thought, without mercy, and I fucking enjoyed doing it. It felt as though another person committed the crime, a beast outside of my body. I could feel its desire, I could feel the urgency of it creeping out of my flesh, but above all, I could feel its need to feed. Nothing could have stopped it. When the deed lay done, when those bodies lay scattered around me, broken and empty, I felt strangely complete – at peace.

Caiaphas, or Melek, whatever the fuck he liked to call himself, told me not to worry. He promised to take care of the bodies, discreetly of course, that my secret was safe. I just had to bring him blood, *his* blood, the blood of a God.

I agreed. Not because I felt that I had to, not because he promised to hide the bodies, but because I wanted to. I wanted to do it for him. I wanted to please him. I wanted to make him happy, and that surprised me more than anything, that I should care that much.

Every time his lips touched me, my body throbbed with excitement. He was a dirty, teasing, hard bastard, and he fucked like the Devil, because he was the fucking Devil, and every time I saw him, I just wanted to walk into him backwards. Had I fallen that hard?

Is that love? Is that how it should feel? To be completely and utterly infatuated? Or the sex, maybe? Good fucking, hard fucking, mind blowing sex. He knew how to make my body work, and no man had done that to me before. He touched me in a way that meant more than just sex – the stroking of my cheek, his fingers tracing my muscles bulging through my skin, the look on his face as he regarded my hard, sweaty body. He saw me as no other had ever seen me before.

However, he hurt Mary.

The sudden appearance of my best friend at the Pavement had taken me by surprise, and the look of pain that tortured her pretty face as I whipped that man haunted me. Did she see my own despair bleeding from my eyes? Yes, I think she did, she saw my reluctance, she saw my agony as I delivered each flesh tearing blow. Did she see the friend she had loved so very long ago? Yes, how could she not? Our childhood together, our deep understanding of each other, it had to count for something. Would she see the monster lurking behind my eyes?

Yes.

Mary always understood me, but now I found that I did not understand her. What the fuck was she doing in Judea? How the hell did she end up with those fanatics? Mary always thought of herself as a rebel, she never did follow convention, so to end up in the ranks of a bunch of perceived lawbreakers should not have surprised me. Yet, to see her again in Judea, at the moment of my greatest need, could it all just be a coincidence? Or was God trying to tell me something? Or the Devil. It seemed that I had both to blame for my current position.

So much grief on her sweet face, so much pain. What the hell had Mary got herself into? Why was Caiaphas so intent on discrediting her? My head buzzed with so many questions. It ached with doubt and uncertainty. I needed to see Mary, to talk to my friend, to feel normal again.

Normal again. What did that even mean? No man should have to contend with so much, but then I was no longer a man.

One thing at a time, that's what I told myself, deal with one thing at a time.

A huge round stone blocked the cave in which the corpse lay, but my new body moved it without effort, as though a mere pebble in my hand. Strength poured through my arms as stone grated against stone, and it felt sensational.

I could smell nothing, and that struck me as profoundly odd. In that heat, in such a confined space, the cave should have stunk of corruption, burst guts and rotting flesh. But my incredibly sensitive nostrils detected nothing foul, neither the stench of death nor the reek of decomposition. It should have been dark inside the cave, yet, curiously, the interior glowed. The setting sun did not have the strength left to illuminate its interior, but the cave glowed with an inner light as though it contained its very own sun, and it shimmered with an unearthly quality that made my skin tingle.

I paused, not so much out of fear, although I felt a fair amount of that—no it was apprehension. Inside that hole lay the son of God, a being so far removed from my comprehension that it hurt my head. The idea of real Gods and real Demons fucked with my head, it felt so surreal, and I could not help but feel completely disconnected from the situation, which was probably just as well, considering my grisly intentions.

I moved into the cave, my body poised for action, tense and alert, my spear held before me ready to stick whatever fucker appeared before me. The stance made my arms bulge beautifully, and I could not help but feel proud of my enhanced physique. If someone attacked me inside that cave, at least I would look fucking good as I shoved my spear up their ass.

His body lay on a stone shelf hewn out of the rock, his huge form shrouded in a cloth upon whose surface blossomed flowers of blood. Fresh blood. The sight of it made me shiver, partly out of hunger, but mostly out of fear. My hand hesitated over the corpse, afraid to touch him, afraid of what I might find. I had never touched a God before.

Slowly, I peeled the shroud away from his body, peeling the cloth back with a respectful reverence, expecting to see a bloated, gas filled corpse beneath the material, but nothing could have prepared me for what I found.

Someone had washed him, and his body lay in a state of such serene tranquillity that it made me gasp. He looked so calm, so perfectly still, and so fucking beautiful. No longer did I see the wretched creature marred by blood and filth. His skin glowed with a purity that I could only describe as Heavenly, and although his brow bore the cruel scratches of the crown inflicted upon him, his face remained so perfect, so peaceful, so handsome, that for one moment, I thought him still alive.

The thick beard that covered his face did nothing to disguise the supreme beauty of his features. A strong nose, plump, luscious lips, high strong cheekbones, those slight crinkles around the eyes that told me he smiled a lot in life, and his body looked to be sculpted from stone by the hands of a master, so defined, so... hard. He lay there, dead, a lump of inanimate meat upon a stone shelf, and yet he radiated a manly beauty that I had never seen in the living. As I looked down upon his Heavenly form, I felt moved somehow, a rush of emotion that took me by surprise as it stung the backs of my eyes. He moved me.

My fingers hovered over the flesh of his torso, trembling fingers, and I realised then—perhaps for the first time—that I had no breath. My heart did not beat inside my chest. My blood did not pump furiously through my veins. My breath did not pant from between my lips. At that moment, the epiphany hit me like a boulder upon my head that I was as dead as that corpse lying on the shelf.

I touched his flesh, flesh so supple, flesh that moved so easily beneath my finger. It felt so alive. My finger moved across the valley of his chest, across and down his bulging arm, tracing the veins so prominent beneath the tight skin, and it felt so erotic, so sensual, so wrong, but I could not help but touch him. I had to touch him.

With a slicing sting, my teeth slid out.

My hand felt the flesh of a God, the being responsible for my transformation, a creature beyond the scope of my understanding, as alien to me as my new condition. Yet I loved him. I felt it, without question, a love without bounds, a love beyond comprehension. It overwhelmed me in a swoon of utter devotion that filled me with a peace so profound that I wept, silent tears pouring down my face to splash upon his bare chest in little explosions of love. He made me. He healed me. He loved me. He died for me.

My teeth slid into the underside of his wrist without resistance, and his blood burst into my mouth in a torrent of ecstasy. I felt his innate goodness flood my very soul, fill my very heart in a moment of clarity, and I understood him, I knew him, and for a moment, I became him.

I had to pull away, to stop that flood of love from hitting the back of my throat, before it consumed me in a blaze of piety. I could feel myself drowning in his sanctity. His blood coated my lips, my tongue, my throat, it coated my heart with a layer of understanding, and I felt at peace, my troubles drowned in a red river of empathy. It took a supreme effort to pull myself out of that swoon, to drag my conscious mind back into that cave and my purpose. I could so easily have lost myself in that feeling because it felt so wonderful, and it hurt my heart to pull myself out of his soul.

Blood. It dripped from the wound in his wrist to the sandy ground at my feet, and I felt a sudden sorrow at its loss. To fall wasted to the floor—it horrified me. I fell to my knees, grief rendering my muscles useless, the feeling of loss so acute that I felt my stomach wretch. I moved within a daydream, pulling out the golden flask from beneath my robe, a gift from Caiaphas to contain the blood of a God, and I unscrewed the lid and allowed the blood to drip into the golden container, watching in fascinated awe as the container filled.

Her scream shook me from my reverie, echoing around the confined space with a shrillness that set my nerves on fire. I looked up, horrified to see Mary in the entrance with her fists rammed into her mouth to stifle the cry of horror that rang around the cavern.

I moved in a blur of instinct, replacing the stopper and secreting the flask back into my robes as I flew across the cave. Mary tried to back away, but I scooped her into my arms and pulled her into the interior, placing her down upon the ground in one, gentle movement, a graceful show of agility and strength that sent a thrill of excitement through my dead body.

She met my gaze in silence, and I saw within her green eyes not fear, not even terror, but confusion, and the need to understand what manner of man crouched before her.

"It's me Mary, Gaius, your old friend Gaius. I won't hurt you, Mary, please, you must believe that."

Her gaze flashed towards the body on the shelf, blood still seeping from the wound in his wrist, and I felt her confusion as surely as I saw the pain flash across her pretty features.

"I can explain if you will let me, what I understand at least."

Her hand reached out to my face, slowly, cautiously, but it did not falter, and it did not tremble. The tip of her index finger touched something sharp at my lip, and I realised with horror that she could see my monstrous teeth. I shrank away in shame, covering my mouth with my hand as I shuffled away from her, crouching in the dust and cowering from my old friend.

"No, Gaius, let me see?" I shook my head, deeply ashamed. Mary scuttled forward and pulled my hand away from my mouth. Before her astonished gaze, I felt my teeth slide back inside my gums.

"Does that hurt?"

"Is that all you can say? *Does that hurt?* Mary, we haven't seen each other for years, and the first thing out of your mouth is does it hurt?" For some reason, I found her question very funny, and I could not help but laugh, a slight edge of hysteria tinging my fumbled words.

"What the hell do you want me to say, Gaius? My, what big teeth you have?"

I laughed out loud, the sound strangely odd inside the small cave. Mary lashed out and thumped me on the shoulder.

"Are you a Demon?"

I must have looked surprised, because her face wrinkled up, the way it used to when we were children when I told her she couldn't do something because she was a girl.

"Yes, I know about Demons, I have seen enough of them." Her gaze settled on the corpse once more, her voice laden with a deep-seated sadness that visibly ripped its way from the depths of her soul "I have seen many things since I met him. He was quite a man."

"Were you in love with him?" Considering the depths of her sorrow, it seemed like a perfectly logical question to me, but her sour face told me otherwise.

"Since when did I need the love of a man to justify my existence? There is more than one kind of love, Gaius, and not all of it involves that flaccid thing between your bloody legs."

"Same old M, you never change."

"But you have. I was there, remember? I saw what you did to him, how you beat him."

That wiped the smile away from my face.

"What has happened to you, Gaius? What kind of thing have you become?"

My story poured from between my lips in a never-ending stream of confession, and true to form, Mary just sat there and listened, just like the old days. As children growing up together on the banks of Galilee, I was always the one that talked, and Mary always listened, never judging, never reproving, she just listened, her head resting on my shoulder as my words tumbled out of my mouth. That cave might have been the rocks upon which we sat so long ago, looking out across the bay, and we were children again, trying to understand the ways of the world, trying to understand ourselves and the adults that shaped us.

As I told her how the disease ravaged my body, how my eyes failed, Mary gripped my hand in hers, holding it tight, comforting me as she did so long ago. It was a moment of such stillness, such calm, a stolen moment that belonged to words, to grief, and to a sadness shared by old friends. Tears trickled down her face as I recounted my horror at the Pavement, and again her gaze fell upon his corpse, her own, painful story bubbling just beneath the surface of her pain. Mary closed her eyes when I told her about that moment in Golgotha, as I speared his side, as his blood entered my body, and the painful transformation that followed. But it wasn't until I explained about Caiaphas that her demeanour changed. She took her hand away from me, and she gazed at me so fiercely that it made me wither.

"You cannot love this man, Gaius, you cannot. You know what he is, who he is. You must promise me that you will not see him again, that you will not give him this thing that he asks of you."

I scooped up a handful of dust in my fist and watched with fascination as it spilled between the gaps of my clenched fist, my new eyes picking out every particle as it drifted to the ground.

"Gaius?"

"Yes, I know, I hear you. I just don't know if I agree with you. Look at me, I'm a monster now, who else could love me but another monster?"

Mary shimmied forward and took both my hands in hers, gazing at me in such earnestness that it silenced the denials perched upon my lips.

"Is that what you think? That you are a monster? Is that what you think he made of you? No Gaius, no. He healed you, he made you anew, something more, something better."

"Something that feeds upon the blood of the living!"

"You are seeing this all wrong old friend. His blood is in you now. He is a part of you, and you are a part of him. It is up to you as to what you do with it. You can be a monster, or you can be something different, something that can bring hope. If his blood healed you, if his blood brought you back from the brink of death, then what can your blood do? I refuse to believe that this transformation is without purpose—he has given it to *you*. It wasn't some Demon, some Devil, no, it was him, *he* gave it to you. Be more, Gaius, be more than you are, believe."

"Mary, my lovely Mary, always willing to see the good in people."

"No." She pulled her hands away sharply, cringing against the stone wall of the cave, suddenly very sad. "Did you ever wonder what happened to Leonidus? After you left?"

"I tried to find him."

"Your father told you to leave, and for good reason. Those assholes, they took Leonidus and they tortured him, they cut off his balls and made him eat them, Gaius, and your father was there, watching. He did nothing to stop it. I tried, I did, but what good was I, a mere woman in a world ruled by men convinced of their own bloody superiority? I saw a side to our village after you went, and there was no good in it, believe me."

"They killed him?" It horrified me, the thought of my beautiful soldier, mutilated because of me, because we loved each other. Yet more blood to taint my hands.

"No, your father killed him. He used Leonidus' own sword, and he ran it through his heart as the others held him down. I hated them, all of them, I hated everyone after that. It took another man to help me see the good in the world again." She reached out a hand towards the corpse, but withdrew it before her fingers made contact with him. "He saved me, Gaius. He made me realise that while mankind may be flawed, it was also worth loving. If you could have seen him, the outpouring of love that he instilled in everyone he met, the hope and the faith that he gave to all whom he touched. I saw so many things with him, miracles, things that go beyond our simple human understanding. I met so many wonderful people because of him, people and friends that I love, and he did that. He helped me to forgive, he helped me to love mankind again, to find the love that was dying in my heart. And you must do the same, Gaius. You must learn to forgive yourself."

"What do you mean?"

"Nothing that has happened here is without purpose. He wanted to die. He thought I didn't know, but I did, I always know. He believed it the only way to save us, to give us all hope, that in his death, we could all find life. And I believe that, Gaius, I really do, and you must too."

"Mary is correct, Gaius."

I spun around so fast that my ass nearly caught fire.

My eyes saw him, and yet later, I could barely remember what he looked like. It was the strangest feeling to stare into those pale blue eyes that sparkled with flecks of gold, eyes that saw straight through me, bored through me. His boyish face, his tightly curled hair that glittered golden like his eyes, the perfection of his slender body bulging through white linen, all details that would disappear in a fog of evaporating memory the moment he left. However, at that moment, as I looked up at him from the floor of that cave, he was the most wondrous thing I had ever seen, a vision of perfection that radiated an inner power that I felt sure would burn me if I touched him.

"Who the fuck are you?" I think Mary already knew, because she cursed me under her breath as she pulled me back gently.

His wings unfurled from his back and filled the cave with their silvery splendour, refracting light in every colour across the rough stone interior.

"My name is Daniyyel, and as you can see, I am an Angel. Mary, please, you do not need to kneel, not before me."

"You are most beautiful." Her mouth dropped open in awe, and I nearly laughed. Seldom had I seen Mary lost for words. "That brain and mouth thing still not working then?" I quipped.

"You're a fine one to talk. Look at the trouble your mouth has got you into."

"My mouth is perfectly capable..."

"As amusing as this human interaction is to you, I do not have the inclination to listen to your banter."

"Are all you Angels so rude?"

"No, some of us are positively witty."

"Mary is right, though, you are beautiful." I felt her elbow hit me in the ribs. "Well, he is, look at him."

"All of my brothers are beautiful, something I think you already know, Gaius?"

Was that a blush I felt throbbing beneath my cheeks? I certainly felt warm all of a sudden.

"Stand up, Gaius."

I stood up, and suddenly his hand wrapped around my throat and he slammed my back into the stone with such tremendous force that I felt the rock itself shudder. I heard Mary scream, but the Angel held me powerless in his immense grasp. My teeth slid down across my lips, and I felt them slicing into my skin as I thrashed and screamed in his grip. But the Angel stood impassively against my claws, his flesh unblemished, and regarded me with curiosity.

"Ah, I see. Well, that's different." He dropped me to the floor, not ungently, and I knelt spluttering at his feet.

"I'm sorry, Gaius, I needed to see what you are, no offence."

"None... taken," I coughed as Mary patted my back.

"Was that really necessary?" snapped Mary angrily, and I could not help but feel a sense of pride at her fearlessness.

"I had to bring out the monster. I needed to see what he has become."

"So is that what I am? A monster?"

"Only if you want to be, Gaius."

"For fuck's sakes, if you are from up there, then you know what I am! He was one of you after all, wasn't he?"

"One of us? No, he was so much more than that, and he still will be. As for you, well, that was unexpected. As for what you are—who can say? Are you a creature of God? Or are you a creature of the Devil? Mary is right, my new friend, only your deeds may determine such a thing. If you want to be a monster, then you will be a monster, or, you will be more. "

"Great, cheers, that helps a lot."

Daniyyel chuckled softly, a sound like music that sent a ripple of forbidden pleasure down my spine.

"Help? No, sadly we have rules against that. But, if I may, I would like to offer a bit of advice, with regards to your love life?"

I shot him a look, but the Angel did not flinch.

"Be careful," he said, smiling genially.

"Is that it?"

"Yes, but I will say this. Caiaphas is not the man you hope he is. There is a reason why men call him the great deceiver."

"He hasn't lied to me. He's told me everything."

"Has he? Has he told you what he did to Adam and Eve? Have you asked yourself why he did not come here himself to procure the blood? No?"

I searched for something to say, but I couldn't think of anything, because he was right, and he knew it. So I picked up my spear, and I shook it in his superior face, and then he did flinch.

"He likes my spear, though. Do you like my spear? He said that this is the only thing that can hurt him. Would it hurt you, Angel?"

Daniyyel stepped forward and gripped the tip of my spear with his hand, fingers clenched tightly around its sharp edge. The sudden, unexpected move took me by surprise, but it shocked him even more, because the superior smile that creased his superior face melted at the sight of his own blood running down the blade. He pulled his hand away quickly, staring at the gash across his palm in disbelief. When his gaze fell back on me, I saw the fear lurking behind his eyes, and for some reason, I felt a stab of guilt pierce my chest for hurting something so beautiful.

"You must not let that spear fall into his hands. Gaius, you must promise me this, please. You have no idea what he could do with it."

"He could kill God." Astonishment blossomed across his face, but I felt no pleasure in my petty victory. "See, he does tell me things."

"Then monster it is, then." His words slammed against me like a rock slide crushing my bones, and I felt deeply ashamed, and more than a little embarrassed. I dropped the spear to the ground, suddenly afraid of it, of what I was becoming, and again I questioned him, my words desperate upon my inhuman lips.

"Please, Daniyyel, what am I? I don't want to be a monster. Don't let me be a monster."

Daniyyel held out his bloodied palm towards me, and I could see the wound knitting back together.

"No wound cuts so deep that it cannot heal."

Tears sprang to my eyes, sudden and unwanted, but they tumbled down my cheeks never the less.

"I don't understand."

"No, Gaius, I know. All you understand is the raw passions of desire. Real love is something that you have yet to comprehend, because you think you do not deserve it, because of what you are."

"I don't know what I am!"

"I do not talk of your lust for blood."

I looked at him, at the pale blue of his eyes, and my anger faded, because there was so much kindness there, so much love, and I felt it, I believed it.

"Is it so wrong?"

"No, my friend, how can anything made by God be wrong?"

"So does that mean he is in Heaven?" asked Mary hopefully, indicating the corpse.

"He will be." To my dismay, Mary broke, falling to the floor sobbing, her entire body shivering with grief. "Dearest Mary, you have suffered much through this, and I fear that your suffering has yet to end. The Sanhedrin wanted him dead, and Caiaphas wanted him dead. What hope did he have in a world that wanted him dead? Caiaphas thought that to destroy him so completely would be enough to bring Father down to face him. He did not consider this to be planned, that death, that sacrifice should be the intention, planned from the start, known only by two in love. The repercussions of his death will ripple through history for the rest of eternity, and his name will give hope to generations to come, and all will know his name because of his self-sacrifice, for his name will mean love, to all men."

His words hit me with tremendous force, and I felt so moved by his sincerity that my own lips barely gave voice to my thoughts. "Love to all men?"

"Yes. All men. Love is never the problem, only those who interpret it."

"Is he using me?"

"I cannot interfere, and I have said too much already. You know all the questions, Gaius, now you must find your answers."

"I think I love him."

"Yes, Gaius, I know. When all you crave is love, real unconditional love, it is difficult to see the truth lurking behind a lover's intentions. I think that he does love you, in his own way. My brother has always been very good at love, but sadly, it is something he usually reserves for himself. I believe you are here for a purpose. What purpose I do not know, but nothing happens without a reason, it's just that your reason has yet to manifest. Be better than he wants you to be, be more than he wants you to be, and love will find you."

He bent down then, taking both of Mary's hands in his. I felt his wings brush against my flesh, and my flesh tingled in response to his touch, wanting him, loving him.

"Mary, listen to me Mary, for your work is not yet over. You must go to the others, and you must leave this place, all of you. There is danger here for you if you should stay."

"They don't frighten me." Again with the defiance.

"Then if you will not listen to me, maybe you will listen to him."

When Daniyyel moved out of the way we saw *him,* no longer lying on the shelf, but standing before it, the stained shroud draped around his muscular frame. A sound escaped from Mary's lips, a pained cry that caught in her throat as she gazed upon that beautiful man.

When he suffered, he suffered with dignity, but in death, he looked serene. The man that stood before us went beyond description, beyond explanation, a transcendent being of such exquisite beauty that even my new, improved eyes had difficulty believing what they saw. His hair, his beard, so glossy, a dark seductive brown that glistened against skin so unblemished, so smooth that it glowed like marble, exuding an inner light that extended to his eyes, his magnificent round eyes. Emerald eyes.

Nothing remained of the torture inflicted upon him prior to death. And when he looked at us, oh, I felt him inside me, I felt him touch my heart, and I thought I would never again look upon something so perfect, that I would never again know peace.

Mary scuttled forward and began to kiss his feet. The sight of her prostrating herself before him shocked me to the core, embarrassed me even. Yet, when I looked at him, I could understand such devotion.

"No, Mary," he said, his voice so full of kindness that I felt my own emotions fill my chest once more. "No man, or God, shall see you at his feet my friend."

Mary lifted her face to look into his, and tears poured fiercely down her cheeks. So obviously full was she with emotion that she could hardly speak.

"I never thought to see you again. You live! You have come back to us!"

"No, this is not life, it is just a transition. You must go on without me, Mary. You must all go on without me. Our work, there is still so much left to be done, so much left unsaid, and the world must hear it, from you, my dear friend, it must come from you."

It pained me to see such happiness melt from her face in that instant, to see the heart-breaking sadness that replaced it. While I did not understand his words, I understood her pain. He was telling her that he was leaving her again, and my heart broke for her.

"But how? Who will listen to me? I am a woman in a world ruled by men..."

"And you are the dearest of all my disciples Mary, and the strongest of us. If anyone can make our message heard, it is you. So you must tell the others — leave this place, and don't ever look back."

"Will I ever see you again?"

He touched her with such tenderness that I felt it in my gut. He lifted her to her feet and wrapped his big arms around her, pulling her into his embrace, and they held each other in silence, and I recognised that embrace because it was the same one I gave Mary when I left home. He was saying goodbye, and I could almost hear Mary's heart shatter within her chest.

"What about me?" I asked.

His emerald green gaze fell upon me, and I felt a weight lift from around my shoulders from the kindness they gave me. In life, I hurt him. In death, I hurt him. And yet he gazed upon my supplicant soul with a kindness that crept into my devastated heart and filled it with love.

"I forgive you, Gaius, that much I can give you. As for anything else, I do not know. You are new, a creature born of my suffering, whose purpose is unclear. You are Vampire, the first of your kind, and I fear that your path will not be an easy one. My advice to you would be the same, leave this place, go with Mary and the others, live as they live, and maybe that will be enough to heal your broken soul."

Vampire. He called me Vampire. It was a new word, unfamiliar to me, and yet, it seemed to fit.

"Vampire." The word felt so strange upon my lips, but my maker gave the name to me, and I took it, together with his forgiveness, gratefully.

He pulled himself away from Mary, and she let go reluctantly, falling into my arms where I held her close. Her tears poured down my chest, mixed with my own, for I was crying with her, our pain combined in friendship.

"Daniyyel, is he there? Is he waiting for me?" he asked the Angel.

"Yes, he is there, he is forgiven. Are you ready my friend? Are you ready for the question?"

"Yes, I am, take me to him, Daniyyel, take me back to his loving arms."

The Angel filled the cave with light as his wings once more unfurled, and I thought I saw him smile at me, a small kind smile, and maybe a nod, a small promise of friendship that comforted me in my grief. The light blazed, so bright, so very white, and then they vanished from existence.

We sat in silence for a moment as I rocked my friend back and forth in my arms until our tears dried upon our faces. I wiped her face with my robe, and she gave me one of her famous smiles, and I knew that somehow, everything would work out just fine.

"I hate crying, I never cry!"

"You cried when you father pulled that baby dolphin out of his nets. You wanted him to throw it back into the water, do you remember?"

"Yes," she laughed gently. "It died, too."

"Mary, what did he mean? Who is waiting for him in Heaven?"

"Oh, Gaius, you never could see what was right before your face. You saw him that day, at the Pavement. Judas, he is going home to Judas. They were lovers."

Chapter Nine: A Break With History

As Related By Eli

I exploded from my chair in a fit of blinding rage, no longer able to stand the sight of Gideon's fucking mouth, or listen to the bullshit that poured from his gaping hole. The constant drone of his voice was getting on my tits.

"This is fucking bollocks! All of it! How do you expect me to believe a single word that comes out of that gob of yours?"

Gideon shot me a look of pure exasperation. "I just revealed one of history's best kept secrets, and all you can say is bollocks? Have you no respect, Eli?"

"I'll tell you what I have, a numb ass from sitting here listening to your sob story."

There it was, that look, the look of a killer, the murderer I knew him to be, cold, unsympathetic, and it was all I could do to stop myself from smacking him in the fucking face.

"You need to hear this. I don't have time for any more of your crap, and you need to hear this."

I used to love it when he got all hard like that, all butch and demanding, but I could no longer contain my temper than I could my Vampire squirming beneath my skin, so desperate was I to rip his throat out and shut him the fuck up.

I looked around at the others, with their stunned, solemn faces. Daniyyel stood away from the main group, leaning his lithe frame against the staircase, all wings and chiselled cock

160

rest chin. I could see the disappointment shadowing his face, aimed at me, of course, for he never could tolerate my outbursts. The shitty crinkle of his lips told me that much.

Isaiah just stared at the floor, and I could almost hear the cogs turning in his head. History lay shattered before him, and I could not help but wonder if it was proving too much for the old man to bear, because it was certainly proving too much for me. All that he knew, all that he believed, came from a book, and now, to hear it from someone who actually lived it? Poor sod. Ethan, however — he looked at me with those huge emerald eyes of his, and what I saw reflected in them cut me to the bone more than the Angel's insipid disapproval. I saw pity. He pitied me, and he was right, I deserved it. How could I live with a man, love a man, for so very many years, and know nothing of the things spoken in that room? So pity the fool, the twat who knew no better.

Flesh, warm and exciting, brushed against my clenched fist as Ethan took my hand in his. It felt so good to touch him. His hand, resting in my hand, one belonging in the other. Yet I pulled away, suddenly embarrassed by his sympathy, unworthy of his compassion, and I regretted it immediately because it caused him pain, disappointment and rejection flashing behind those beautiful green eyes.

Eli the fucking twat.

"Why? Why do I need to hear your shit?" My stupid words flew from my stupid mouth.

Gideon started to stand up, but suddenly his hand flashed to his chest and his face twisted with pain, sending his massive frame crashing back down into the chair. He looked ill, and I thought of that splinter, the piece of the one true cross, burrowing its way through his body towards his heart.

I never thought that such a little prick could cause him so much pain.

Daniyyel started forward, but Gideon motioned for him to stay back. I could see the concern upon the Angel's face, and it unnerved me.

Gideon spoke through gritted teeth. "To understand the present, you must first understand the past."

"Does that include Mary?"

Gideon froze, the shit fest that was London once again in the room. The bloodbath that was London was once again laid bare before our eyes. The killer, the butcher from London, once again sitting before me.

"It's not what it seems Eli, I promise you, just hear me out."

"Hear you out? All I have done is hear you out, for fucking hours! And what has any of this got to do with me? You fucking made me! When are we going to get to that?"

Yet again I saw him glance towards Ethan, a look of awe, of disbelief, of adoration. It burned behind Gideon's eyes, in every stolen glance, and it infuriated me.

I hated him at that moment, Gideon, or Gaius, or whatever his fucking name was. Hell had come knocking at my door, and he could do nothing but spout fairy tales.

"You?" Gideon shot to his feet and stood in my face. "It's always about you, isn't it?"

"Funny that," I spat right back at him, "because the only thing I have heard in this room is about you."

He grinned, yet no humour lay in that bestial snarl, just hostility.

I felt Daniyyel's arms pulling me away from the tower of muscle that bore down on me, and I tried to resist, but the Angel had strong hands, very strong hands.

"Hear him out, Eli, listen to what he has to say, it is important."

"Listen to him?" I turned on Daniyyel, my fury blazing from my lips in a shower of spittle. "And you can piss off as well! You could have told me that he made me! You could have warned me!"

"No Eli, you know I couldn't do that, Father forbade it."

"Then you can shove your God up your fucking ass, for all I care!" I felt the itch between my shoulder blades, pulling me skywards, and then I lifted above their heads, looking down upon them, just the fucking way it should be. How dare they look at me with such pity in their eyes. I didn't need their sympathy, and I certainly couldn't give a shit about their disapproval. I turned and pointed my ass in their faces, and I rose up and up, and I didn't stop.

The view from the roof always managed to soothe my aching soul. The icy cold wind howled against my skin, and I closed my eyes to better feel the slap of God against my flesh. The smell of pine, water, snow, and ice filled my nostrils. I could almost taste it, my home, my sanctuary. I opened my eyes, and I saw how the dark, bitter edge of the clouds caressed the tops of the mountains, smothering their peaks from existence, and I knew how they felt. I was losing myself. I was losing my home. Soon, there would be nothing left of me.

Winter fell from the sky in a last, defiant flurry, soft against my Vampire skin, cold and icy like my heart. It would not last long, it never did at that time of the year, and I had seen enough years at Alte to know. Suddenly I found myself gripping the edge of the parapet, my world a dizzying fuck around my head, my stomach churning in a storm of fear and dread, and I felt bereft. I felt Alte slipping away from me, lost to the maw of my own mistakes, leaving me, as Malachi left me, and it was all my fault.

No, his fault, not mine, he lied, not me, Gideon the God breaker.

"Eli?" Speak of the Devil.

"Fuck off, Gideon, I want to be alone."

"Tough shit, Garbo. You don't fool me. You've never wanted to be alone in your life. Suck it up, fella, wake up and smell the shit."

I turned around, slowly, giving him my very best *you are a fucking twat* look.

"Yeah, I can smell the shit all right, and it's standing right before me."

"Hate me as much as you like Eli, I deserve it, I know that. But find out why I lied to you first, before you make up your mind about me. Let me fill in the gaps."

He stepped forward, and I should have stopped him, but he was there, right in my face, all six foot of him, all muscle and sinew, there, in my face. His hand, his great big manly hand reached out and touched my face, brushing my cheek, sliding over my perfection, and I could feel the roughness of his skin, and it made me moist.

"Don't touch me. You don't get to touch me. I don't want you to touch me." Now who lied? Once upon a time, that was all I wanted, for him to touch me, much as he touched me then, with kindness, with affection, with tenderness. I could feel my skin blossoming beneath his touch, and I hated him for it.

"It was all for you, you know? All the lies, all the secrets, all to keep you safe. I had to keep you hidden from their eyes."

I no longer felt the cold of a desperate winter, just a rising heat that ebbed through my loins.

"I don't want you to touch me." I thought that if I said it enough, it would be true.

"I missed you."

"I don't want to hear it."

"You must hear it. I missed you."

His fingers reached my neck, tracing the outline of my collarbone, and I nearly cried out at the sensation, so fucking familiar, so fucking erotic, and I closed my eyes against the world to block out the lust that crept upon my raging thoughts.

"Hear what?" My voice sounded painfully quiet, a timid squeak that barely pierced my lips. My trembling lips. "What do you want me to hear, Gideon? More lies?"

"My love for you was never a lie. It still isn't."

"Bullshit. Love is a deed, not a word, words are just hollow things."

His hand fell to his side, but he stepped closer, his huge body pressing against my own, and with my back pressed against the parapet, I had nowhere left to go than over the edge, a pain I had no intention of repeating.

My body thrummed to his touch, to the massiveness of him pressed against me. He felt like some huge magnet, and I felt irrevocably drawn towards him, an inevitable clash of opposites destined to stick together.

"All those years, trapped within a block of ice, to protect you. Is that not deed enough?"

"All those years lying to me. All those years refusing me. Those are the only deeds I know. Oh, not to mention what you did in London."

"There are things about London that you do not know. Hear me out, listen to what I have to say, then maybe you will understand."

"Mary?"

"Damn you, Eli."

Gideon turned away from me, a pained snarl fracturing his sculptured face. I felt my body sigh as his body left my proximity, and my nipples were not the only thing that could cut glass.

"Damn me?" I was shouting again, annoyed as much by my own arousal as his words. "How can you possibly justify what you did? What am I to think? All I saw was blood. There was nothing but blood! Don't you dare tell me that you did that for the greater good."

"Is that why you killed Malachi? Was that for the greater good?"

My fist flashed out towards his face, but he caught it in mid-flight before my claws could rip into his smug face. We stood there, two beasts, monsters in pain, snarling at each other as our Vampires flickered over our features. Every inch of my being wanted to rip his throat out with my teeth, to feel his blood spurt over me, to watch him wither away to dust before my uncaring gaze, because I didn't care anymore, I didn't love him, and I didn't want him.

His tongue smashed between my lips and entered my mouth as he pushed my back into the stone parapet behind me. Gideon pinned me in place, his huge body blocking out the world as his eager tongue explored my mouth and his voracious hunger reached down inside of me. My fists hit his shoulders, hammering against solid muscle and bone, but it felt like digging for gold with a toothpick for all the good it was doing me.

My body gave in to the familiar shape of him, moulding itself to his every familiar curve as my arms wrapped around his thick neck to pull his tongue deeper into my mouth. He ground his hips into me with such urgency, the hardness between his thick legs pressing against my own bulging desire, and I felt my own wetness weep from my swollen cock. I felt weak, useless as his mouth swallowed my face, tasting me, eating me, and for a moment, for just one divine moment, I was his again.

I jerked my head away, my words a panting whisper upon my throbbing lips.

"No."

"Yes," he grunted as he grabbed me by the hair, violently, pulling my head back to expose my neck, and then I felt my skin begin to rip at the touch of his sharp teeth. He paused, sliding the tips of his Vampire teeth along my pulsing artery, and I moaned at the divine pain that fired through my neck in anticipation of his feast. My fingers sought out the thick bulging muscles of his arms, so taut as they held me in place. As his teeth punctured my flesh, as my blood pumped hard and fierce into his mouth, my claws dug into the mass of his biceps, and we both moaned in exquisite agony.

I felt his muscles shred beneath my claws, and Gideon ripped his teeth out of my neck as he screamed, blood splattering across my throat, across his face, and I feared that he would throw me off the roof in a fit of rage. I grinned at him, enjoying his pain.

Hands and claws ripped at my pants, exposing my hardness to the bitter air, and suddenly, I was facing away from him, my upper body bent over the edge of Alte, staring down at the rocky ground beneath. Teeth pierced my shoulder, the pain of it excruciating, making me cry out, but the scream ended abruptly as another pain shot through my lower abdomen, a pain so sharp and so intense that the sound of my agony could not escape from my throat, the exquisite pain of penetration.

Gideon fucked me, and he fucked me hard, my body crashing against the stone with bone pounding power. I could not believe it. His cock, his huge, thick, throbbing cock lay inside me, inside my ass, pushing deeper and deeper, harder and harder, and I floated away on a wave of ecstasy. My hands clasped stone as I pushed myself against him, willing him deeper, feeling the whole of him enter me. All I could think of was all those wasted years, all those years of rejection, never wanting me, never fucking me, and there, on top of the world, Gideon was in me, hammering away at my ass as though his life depended upon it.

His teeth withdrew, just as his cock withdrew, and I felt every inch of it leave my body. He turned me around, and I saw my blood upon his lips, upon his face, but there was such a look upon him, such a sadness, a resignation that chilled me. I opened my mouth to speak, but he pressed his finger against my lips to silence me, while his other hand reached out to grip my own throbbing cock, his fingers tugging on my girth with painful urgency.

A single tear fell from his right eye. I watched it fall down the side of his nose to mingle with the blood around his lips, and that single tear filled me with a profound sadness that shot through my heart in a moment of pain.

Something happened in that moment, something passed between us, a stillness, an understanding, a calmness, and there existed a question on his face. Something pleading as he slowly turned around — his agonized gaze a thing of utter torture to my eyes. He pressed against me, his hand guiding my cock towards his ass, a feeble, pathetic gesture that broke my heart into so many more pieces, and then he spoke, one word, one haunting word that ripped my soul apart.

"Please."

I felt the sob reach up my throat, but I held it back, my pain, my grief, and I wrapped my arms around his magnificent chest as I pulled him onto me, my cock sliding inside him with the ease of a well-worn shoe. My head nestled into his, my lips tasting him as I moved in and out, feeling his tightness around my shaft, sensing his pleasure build as I felt my own. We were one, moving in unison, feeling each other inside each other, old, distant, angry monsters, connected by a love long lost, a love of betrayal and distrust, a love stirred by time. My hands moved down his body. A body that I once loved. A body that I once worshiped. Across a stomach that I once kissed, across the valleys I once licked, so hard and so rippled, until I gripped his manhood in both my hands, and manipulated it in time to my own slow, deliberate movements. I could hear the whimper upon his lips, that small sound he always made as he grew close, so I let myself loose within his body, my anger exploding inside him in great pumping streams as his own passions exploded through my fingers, shooting hard and fast to the ground.

I pulled out of him, slowly, yet we remained joined at the hip, my arms still clinging to his torso, and there remained a reluctance there, on both out parts, a reluctance to tear ourselves away from each other. It felt like an ending, a goodbye, and if we parted, we would never touch each other again.

My heart ached with sadness as I lifted my head from his broad shoulder, but when I looked up, I looked straight into the face of Ethan.

"I'm sorry... I didn't mean... Daniyyel said that I should find you..."

"Christ," mumbled Gideon as he hastily tried to buckle up his trousers. But I couldn't move, I stood frozen to the spot, turned to stone by the look of disappointment that shadowed Ethan's painfully handsome face. I met his gaze, but the emerald sparkle of his eyes dimmed, replaced by the darkness of betrayal. Ethan turned and walked away without another word.

"Shit." I couldn't pull my trousers up fast enough.

"I'm sorry, Eli. He should not have seen that."

"What the fuck have you got to be sorry for?" I found his contrition peculiar, and he made to speak. I could see the words forming on his hesitant lips, but a darkness fell upon him and extinguished the moment, replaced instead by the shadow of a man, a man in pain.

"Go to him."

"What?"

"Eli, go to him, don't let him think that this was anything more than it was."

"And what was it?"

"A goodbye." Gideon moved in a blur, leaping over the edge of the parapet, and I watched, awestruck, as he hit the ground below with a sublime grace that I could only dream of. I fell from that tower once, and there was nothing graceful about it. He looked up, a quick glance towards me, and with a shadow of a smile, he disappeared back into Alte.

I cleaned up before I went to find Ethan. It would not do for him to smell sex clinging to my clothes or see the blood so fresh upon my face. As I scrubbed my skin clean, I could not help but wonder what I would say to him, and as I threw on fresh linens, I wondered why it felt so important. We remained two strangers, Ethan and I, thrown together by circumstance, but Gideon and I, we shared centuries. Even so, I could not shake the feeling that I had betrayed Ethan somehow. Whatever connection existed between us — and it did connect us, that something bubbling just beneath the surface — we shared an attraction that went far deeper than the flesh, a feeling of knowing that reached into my soul, a feeling of belonging that went beyond my comprehension. I owed him an explanation, another slice of humble pie to make me choke. It was becoming a habit between us.

Ethan sat on the edge of the bed in Malachi's bedroom, his elbows on his knees, his beautiful head cradled in his hands, staring blankly at the floor between his feet. He had big feet.

"Can I come in?"

"It's your house to do with as you please."

A cold shiver trickled down my neck, I did so love his bluntness. I sat on the edge of the bed and looked down at the same piece of floor, at the same corner of a well-worn rug, its silk threads faded with time. It reminded me of me.

"It shouldn't bother me, but I find that it does. Can you explain that to me?" So bloody direct.

"It just happened, I..."

"Seriously? Are you seriously going to use that line? It just happened?"

Ouch. Perceptive as well as direct. I washed my face with the palms of my hands, and for once, I did not know what to say.

"You were together a long time, I get it. So what was that? Make up sex?"

"Shit, Ethan, no. It was goodbye sex." Goodbye sex? The moment I heard the words tumble out of my mouth, I knew they were a joke. They made Ethan laugh anyway, though I detected precious little humour in his chuckle.

"Why don't you just admit to yourself that you still love him, Eli? Save yourself all these endless arguments."

My mouth opened as I started to answer him, and I suddenly realised the truth of the words forming upon my lips, and it felt like a release, one that, up until that moment, I had not wanted to admit to myself. All those years of mourning his loss, all those years of pain eating me away from the inside, and all those years of hating him for all the lies. I kept the pain, it defined me, it kept me locked away from the world around me, because it was all I had left of him. While I wallowed in my own self-pity, Gideon was never far from my heart, but I no longer loved him.

"I... I will always love him Ethan, but I'm no longer in love with him." The words tumbled out of my mouth, and I believed them. The realisation of it hit me with a cold shiver of truth. I could barely grasp that I could say, and mean, such a thing. But I did mean it. I loved him once, I loved him with every fibre of my body, and a part of me would always love him, but my heart no longer belonged to Gideon.

Ethan lifted his gaze from the floor and looked at me. His eyes searched my face, seeking the truth of my words, and I think he saw it there, in my eyes. He saw the weight of my burden lift from my countenance, and for the first time in very many years, I felt my pain release me.

Ethan hesitated, reluctant to speak, but when he did, I could hear how carefully he chose his words.

"Do you have any room left inside you to love, Eli?"

"You know, maybe I do after all. If the right man came along." I looked into those green eyes of his, and I saw it again, that twinkle, that spark of something, reignited in the depths of that green, and not for the first time, I wanted to press my lips against his. I walked into darkness for Ethan. I faced my worse fear for him. Was that love? Whatever it was, whatever I felt, whatever thing drew me so inexplicably towards him, I would take the time to find out.

"Come on," I said, rising from the bed, extending my hand towards him. He looked at it and he smiled, and then he took it, and I pulled him off the mattress. "Let's go find out what else history has in store for us, shall we?"

Chapter Ten: Run From The Devil

As Related By Gideon

Mary's words echoed through my head as I made my way back to the Palace. Love. They died for love. Love for each other, love for mankind, love that defied convention, defied the law. Two men, just men, standing up for what they believed in, in a world that would silence them and erase their names from history. Yet, despite everything, death remained their only thanks, and I could not help but wonder if it was worth it.

When I thought of Judas, the moment before he hung himself, the pain of betrayal and loss etched so deeply into his beautiful face, I could not help but feel sorry for him the most. His remained the heaviest burden, to condemn the man he loved, a burden he could not hope to survive. Only Mary knew their secret, as she once knew my own, and my respect for that amazing woman only intensified in my heart.

Could I have done such a thing? Betray the man I loved? No matter that they planned it between them. Could I watch as they dragged him away? As they beat him? As I beat him. As they sentenced him to death? It happened as they planned it, but could I do it?

No wonder Judas lost his mind. It was a love doomed, and from the moment they shared that fatal kiss in the Garden of Gethsemane, they condemned themselves both to death. Judas sentenced the man he loved to the cruellest and most undignified death of all, and it left him with a guilt that no man should ever have to endure.

I held within my hand the spear that pierced the flesh of a God. I kept, strapped to my hip, a flask of blood from the body of a God. A God made me. Gods and monsters walked amongst us, of that, I had no doubt. And if God was real, then the Devil was real, and I was on my way to meet him.

All that Caiaphas told me, all of it was true, his eviction from Heaven, his vendetta against God, and that left me with a choice to make. Mary had decided to go to Rome with the others, and she wanted me to go with her. Caiaphas also wanted me to go with him, to stand at his side, hand in hand. I had to choose between the love of a friend and her mission to continue the work started in Judea, or the love of the Devil and his mission to bring God to his knees.

I did not believe for one minute that Caiaphas loved me, but he did want me, and he touched me as no other man had touched me, made me feel as no other man had made me feel. After all the things that I had witnessed, after I had seen true love die on the cross and at the end of a rope, did I deserve to expect any more? I thought love never died, but I had seen it, I had been a part of it, so should I not grasp what little happiness I could, no matter how tenuous?

God or the Devil? A question that would resonate throughout history, but at that moment, as the Palace reared up before me, I knew precious little about either, yet both had extended the hand of friendship towards me.

As soon as I stepped into the courtyard, it felt wrong, and a creeping sensation of dread trickled up my spine — irritation, a flicker of warning that brushed against my skin alerting me to a threat as yet unseen. I looked towards the bath house, the memory of blood and semen rising in the back of my throat. But the danger did not seem to come from there, more that it came from all around me, a feeling of oppression that pushed against the hardness of my body from all directions.

My body burned with anticipation, a coiled spring ready to strike at the slightest provocation, moving with a deathly silence through the columns and balustrades of the Palace, towards the Pavement. My teeth slid down, brushing against my lower lip. The sensation still felt so unreal. My inner monster so new to me—my Vampire still untested. But my hearing, my eyesight, my senses, all worked together in a way that I had never before experienced, acting on a higher level of alertness that allowed me to pick up the slightest sound, the smallest speck of dust, the faintest odour.

Blood. I could smell blood. It had a staleness about it, a sour aftertaste that stung the back of my throat as I inhaled. And as I moved towards the marble colonnade that led to the Pavement, I felt a pricking of my skin, a dread that pressed against my chest, but I had to go on. Before me, out there in the world of the living, lay choices, and for some strange reason, I had the distinct feeling that some of those choices had already been made for me.

The smell hit my nose like a fist, the rank, putrescent stench of death. The human side of me wanted to turn tail, to find Mary and run from that place without looking back, but the monster side of me, my burgeoning Vampire, pushed me on with a curiosity that bordered on the edge of insanity.

I stood at the end of a colonnade of statues, huge busts of Emperors atop marble columns bearing down either side of me, their dead, painted eyes watching in that haunted silence. It was so dark, but the arch at the end of the corridor blazed with light, the Prefect's throne silhouetted black against the sun, and I moved towards that silhouette, the smell of corruption growing with each careful footstep.

The sun hit my skin as I stepped out of the shadows, but it was a cold thing against my dead flesh and offered me no comfort against the terrible sight that met my gaze. I saw nothing else, the world disappeared in a red blaze of outrage that crept around my horrified eyes in a gauze of sickening guilt.

Limbs jutted out from the pile of cadavers, as though some obscene sculptor had placed them there deliberately, every angle an offence to the sanctity of life. Raw flesh, already crawling with maggots in the intense heat, glistened from twisted torso and neck, from wounds ripped into skin, puncture marks around which blood dried, puncture marks from which I fed.

My head reeled from the shock of seeing them, my victims from the bath house, a composition of my birth pains laid out to bask in the sun. Shame, my shame, shivered through my limbs, and I knew then how it felt to be betrayed.

"Exsanguination. It is an interesting form of execution. I'm impressed."

I spun around, my spear held out against that voice, the voice of my Prefect.

Pilate sat slouched in his throne, his white robes wrapped tightly around his nose, so his voice sounded slightly muffled. "Though I must say that the smell is beginning to turn my stomach. You are full of surprises, Gaius."

I did not know what to say. The sight of my victims displayed so cruelly before me numbed my brain and froze my lips.

"When Caiaphas told me what you did, what you have become, I did not believe him. Now that I see you, and what you have done, there can be little doubt."

Pilate lifted himself from his throne, and as he started to move down the steps towards me, a horde of Praetorian guards streamed out of the Palace behind him, surrounding me with shield and spear. I felt the beast within me rise, the urge to lash out with tooth and claw, but I held my Vampire back, for I had spilt enough blood that day already. The evidence of that lay in a putrid heap behind my back.

Pilate moved towards me, and his guard parted before him so that he stepped into the circle of men, but his eyes, his focus never left me, or the object which I held raised at my side.

"Is that it? Is that what you used to spear his side?"

"Yes."

"Can I see it?"

I pulled the spear away from his inquisitive hand, and I saw a flash of fury flicker across his face.

"I am told that you speared the side of a God with that thing. A God, no less. Who would believe such a thing? But I have seen much today that has opened my eyes to such possibilities, and I find that I now have an appetite for the impossible."

Pilate reached out a tentative hand, and I flinched away from it. He stepped forward, unafraid, and laid his warm, slightly clammy hand against my cheek. He snatched it away in surprise.

"Cold, you feel cold, dead. What manner of man are you?"

"That is still something I am trying to find out myself."

"Then show me, show me what you are, Gaius, let me see this thing inside of you that would make such meat of your fellow men."

I stood my ground, defiant against the man who once stuck his cock up my ass. He smirked, and nodded towards the guard nearest to me. The Praetorian moved with the speed and accuracy of someone well versed in defence of his master, his own spear lashing out to dig in my side in a flash of precision. My skin ripped just above my hip, but my monster appeared before the metal left my flesh.

My body did not feel like my own. I felt the curve of my face transform beneath the skin, I felt my teeth fly out and slice into my lower lip and my claws slice through my fingertips in an agony of transformation. Before the guard could react, I had his spear in my hands, breaking the wooden shaft into matchsticks in a second. My mouth curled into a vicious snarl, and I wanted nothing more than to rip the fucker's neck open and gorge on his pumping blood.

Pilate pushed past the guards that surrounded him, clapping.

"Bravo! How wonderful! You are a monster indeed. Magnificent. Do you think that you could take them? All of them? Do you think that you could take on the entire Empire?"

I pulled back, calming the rage that powered my transformation. The wound in my side knitted together, a strange itching sensation that saw it healed in an instant, and Pilate saw that I remained unharmed. Was that alarm I saw behind his eyes, or something else? Desire?

"I have no quarrel with you, Prefect, or the Empire." My voice growled over my teeth with a deep, menacing resonance that rumbled through the ground. Pilate stepped back.

"Well then, there we have a problem. You see, if you are not with us, if you are not part of the great Roman Empire, then you are against us. What do you think Tiberius would say if he knew that a monster roamed his world? A monster not of our control. Do you think that he would just let you go? And what could I do with such a creature as you? Could you bring me the Empire? Could you make me like you? Could you make me an army like you? I think you could."

"To be quite honest Pilate, I couldn't give a fuck what your Emperor thinks. As for letting me go? I would like to know how you intend to stop me—go on, I would like to see you try."

"Why, dear heart, really, it's not Pilate that will stop you, my beloved, but me."

His voice crept across my skin in a wave of purring malevolence, and when I saw what he held in his arms, I felt sick. My defiance fell away from me in a sigh of bitter resignation, because he held Mary in his grasp, and she looked at me with such terror in her eyes that I felt instantly impotent beneath her gaze.

"Not so ebullient now, are we, Barbarian?"

"Don't give it to him, Gaius!"

Caiaphas grabbed Mary's hair and pulled her head back with a vicious snap, and she fell to her knees screaming.

"One more word from you, sweetie, and you will be wearing your cunt for a moustache. Do I make myself quite clear?"

"Harm her, and I will rip your fucking wings off with my teeth!"

Caiaphas turned his head towards me, a slow, calculated movement that sent a chill down my back. His eyes glowed golden, and his mouth split so wide as he laughed that I could glimpse the evil squirming inside of him.

"You are welcome to try. I think we have yet to see the true nature of your monster, but do not ever forget mine. Give Pilate the spear, dear heart, do be a good chap now won't you?"

I did not know if I could take him, the Fallen Angel, the Devil, but for her, I would try if it meant saving her, if it meant saving Mary. I handed over the spear to Pilate. I would not risk Mary's life for the sake of a piece of metal.

Caiaphas looked down on Pilate, who held the spear in his hands with a trembling reverence. The spear both transfixed and fascinated him.

"Ever fancied ruling the world, Pilate? And not just the Empire, we will make bloodsucking monsters of them. With that spear, touched by a God, you may control the hearts of men, all men — you will make them *want* to be monsters. How does that feel?"

"Yes, all men, they will... obey me?"

"Oh, dear heart, trust me, they will do whatever you want, and when man is but a broken memory upon the face of the Earth, then God will come down to face me. Then, and only then, will you give the spear to me, and I will run it through my Father's heart and sit on his throne in Heaven. Oh, I do so love it when a plan comes together, it makes me feel so.... fruity."

"Coward!" The word exploded from my lips without thought.

With a violent shove, Caiaphas threw Mary down the steps, where she landed at Pilate's feet. I started forward, but the Praetorian Guard closed ranks around me, their spears pressed against my back and my chest. Caiaphas laughed.

"What's the matter, Barbarian? You want to rip them apart, don't you? I can see it in your eyes, the blood lust. Wouldn't you just love to suck them dry? Don't let me stop you."

"I'm not a fucking killer."

"Ha! That pile of decomposing shit behind you says otherwise. Oh, have I hurt your feelings? Did you think that I cared about you?"

I felt my skin flush with anger and shame, because that was exactly what I thought. I wanted him to care about me.

"Ha! You did, didn't you? Don't get me wrong, you were nice and tight, nothing like a tight hole around one's dick, but care about you? Really? As a Demon, well, you may have possibilities, but when you were human? Please! The only thing I want from you, dear heart, is something sharp and pointy, and now, I have it! Deep joy!"

"You are a fucking coward! Why else would you need us to do your fighting for you? Because you are a fucking coward."

The Devil shimmered across his face, a darkness that wriggled and crawled, and his eyes blazed with hatred.

"You, come here, boy."

One of the guards, a boy of no more than eighteen, moved to stand before the steps and looked up at Caiaphas, a look of pure love, of pure rapture emblazoned upon his pretty young face. He looked as though he wanted to fuck him there and then, on the spot.

"Kiss your Prefect, boy. Show him how much you love him."

Pilate made to protest, but Caiaphas pointed at him with a taloned finger.

"Stand your ground, Prefect, I am your master now."

Caiaphas froze, afraid to move beneath that terrible yellow gaze.

The guard turned around to face Pilate, and then he grabbed the Prefect by the hair and pulled him to his lips. Even from where I stood, surrounded by stunned Praetorians, I could see the boy's tongue burrow into the back of Pilate's head.

Caiaphas laughed. It stopped suddenly as another idea seemed to flash through his sick brain.

"All of you, turn around and kiss the man next to you."

Swords, spears, shields, all crashed to the floor in a rain of clashing metal. To my utter astonishment, the Pavement turned into an orgy of entwined limbs, as men threw themselves against men, tongues exploring mouths, hands exploring a plethora of erect dicks that twitched beneath a sea of loin cloth.

"Don't ever doubt the power I have over men. I do not need to use a spear to assert my will, I am there, in their hearts, lurking in the dark places of their sins. But you see, I am bound by rules, yes, I know, it's hard to believe, isn't it? If I do something, then they can do something, and one cancels out the other, and then on and on we go, the endless circle of pointlessness, so very exhausting. As God preaches to the hearts of men, so I whisper to the darkness in their souls, so it has always been. But... that spear, God made that spear, not me, I am blameless. See what plaything you have brought me? Is this not wonderful? Is this not art? And I cannot be blamed!"

I started as a hand brushed against my leg, and I looked down to see Mary cowering at my feet. I pulled her off the ground and held her close as the world around us exploded in a sigh of premature ejaculation. Even Pilate seemed lost as the youth suckled at his dick, the Prefect pulling the boy's mouth onto his erect penis with vigour.

"Oh, where is a scribe when you need one, dear heart? Would this not make the most wonderful entry into the annals of history? Porn for the modern day masses. Porn on demand! Now there's a thought. With this spear, I could wank the world to death! Ha!"

Mary ripped herself free of my arms and pointed a steady finger at Caiaphas.

"I know who you are. I know what you are! And *he* knew it, too. You think that he lies dead, that you have wiped the word of God from our lips? Well, you are wrong! The word of God is still alive, because he has risen, I saw it, I was there. The word of God is already out there, and I will spread it far and wide, so stick that up your pompous ass and suck it!"

Fuck. Mary never could keep her mouth shut. I pulled her back towards me, but she refused my hands, shrugging me off, her anger reaching new and impressive heights.

"You thought you could silence him, didn't you? You thought that by killing him, you would win. But you are wrong, Devil. He is stronger now than he ever was in life, and you have yourself to thank for that. He died for us, for all of us, and you did that, so thank you for making him stronger, thank you for giving him what he wanted."

"Stop! All of you." His sudden howl startled Mary, and she fell back against my chest. The groan of sexual desire ceased abruptly also, and all eyes fell upon Caiaphas, who looked out upon his captive audience with a calm that froze the sun in the sky.

"Why didn't I know this? Who checked the cave?"

"I did, sir." The young guard disengaged himself from Pilate's cock and stood to attention at the foot of the steps.

"Was the cave empty?"

"Yes sir, after I saw Mary and Gaius leave the cave, I went inside to check, and it was empty."

"And you did not think to tell me this little fact dear heart?"

For a moment the boy looked confused, and it pained me to see such desperation transform his pretty features.

"It was just an empty cave sir. I did not think it important."

"You did not think it... important? The son of God rises from the dead, and you do not think that important?"

I held Mary close, willing her to silence as a further outburst filled her lungs. Thankfully she kept her cool, but I could feel her anger trembling through her muscles at the sight of the squirming youngster. Poor bastard didn't have a clue, and an empty cave meant nothing to him. What did a mere boy know of Gods and Angels?

"Let's see, shall we? Let's see what this marvellous new toy is capable of. Pilate, you know what to do."

Pilate looked surprised and slightly stupid standing there, his erect cock still dripping as he hastily tucked it back inside his toga. He looked at the spear in his hand, and then at Caiaphas, a quizzical expression upon his flushed face.

"For fucks sakes, you stupid little man, use it, command someone! Show me that I have chosen wisely."

"Oh, right," muttered Pilate as he held the spear before him. "Right, here goes. You there, ugly fuck, come here."

Pilate certainly did not exaggerate his insult, for the man who walked forward looked repulsive, having lost half his face in a sword fight. His left eye, his left ear, and most of his left check contained nothing but scar tissue, giving him an oddly imbalanced countenance. Half face picked up his sword and moved to stand before Pilate.

"You, stupid boy who doesn't think, take ugly fuck's sword." The boy reached out and took the weapon from his comrade, and he did it thankfully, his desire to please blinding him to the horror yet to come, a horror I could do nothing to prevent, not with Mary there, so human, so vulnerable.

"Now, kneel."

The boy got down on his knees and smiled up into the face of his Prefect, and in that one moment of absolute horror, I hated Pilate with all my heart.

"Slit your throat."

The boy lifted the sword, and still smiling, he ran the blade across his own throat. I think Mary screamed, but I could not be certain because I could only see the red smile that split the boy's neck from ear to ear, and I could only hear the sound of his flesh splitting at the command of that sharp blade. The smile slowly widened into a kiss, and then his life gushed forth in a torrent of red that splashed onto the stone beneath him in a river of blood.

All the time the boy kept smiling, and then he simply fell forward, face down into his own blood where his body lay twitching.

My teeth exploded from my mouth, the smell of blood filling my nostrils in a frenzy of hunger that gripped the pit of my stomach with fingers of stabbing pain.

Caiaphas laughed. "Oh dear, does that turn you on, dear heart? Do you fancy a snack? Speaking of blood, give it to me Barbarian."

His words pounded against my ear drums, but I did not hear them, I could see only blood, I could hear only blood, pumping from the gash in the young boy's neck with every dying beat of his heart. I wanted to get on my knees and drink from that fountain of red, to gorge myself upon his dying light until my body felt bloated like a slug, to bathe in his death until it appeased my own insatiable hunger.

Maybe I was a monster after all.

"Gaius, the flask. Give it to me. Now."

I felt the Vampire ripple across my face. My body convulsed as the beast within erupted through my flesh, and I could not help but love the look of absolute panic that flittered upon the faces of the Praetorians as they leapt away from me.

Yeah. I was fucking badass.

"Mary, come here."

Fuck. The command in Pilate's voice hit Mary, and I felt her jerk in my arms, the pull of the spear too great for her to resist.

"No, Mary, no."

She tried to pull away from my hands, but my Vampire kept her in place. Immediately, I felt a dozen manly hands grab me from behind, from the sides, and I screamed my rage into their faces as Mary wrestled free.

"Good girl, now come here."

"Leave her alone, you fucker!"

I grabbed the nearest hand, ripping it away from my bicep, and I sank my teeth into its soft edge, tearing the flesh away from the bone in a splatter of warm blood. It tasted of fear and pain, and I loved it.

"Pick up the sword, Mary."

Fists beat at my body, and I felt the tips of metal slice into my flesh, sliding through muscle, grating against bone, but I didn't care. My head jerked forward and plucked a neck from amidst the sea of attackers, and I shook it in my mouth, artery, bone and gristle snapping, skin ripping in a fountain of red as my teeth sliced through his life. I felt a knife at my throat, but I snatched it out of his fingers in a blur of movement, plunging the blade into his eye with a pop of blood and liquid.

Even through the blood, through the raging tempest of muscle and limbs, I could see Mary reaching for the sword. Fingers reached towards my eyes, and I bit them off, blood filling my mouth, fingers filling my throat, and I spat them out into the face of the screaming man as my claws shot out to silence his agony.

"That's it, Mary, pick it up, there's a good girl."

The world turned red with blood. It exploded around me as my hands shot out against every moving thing, as my teeth bit into anything soft. Howls of agony rang into the oncoming darkness, blood shooting black against the dying sky, and I was a monster, a beast, ripping limb from the socket, and twisting heads off shoulders as I raged against the night.

"Now turn the blade to face you, Mary, that's it, good girl."

A blade entered just at the base of my spine, and pain exploded through my body and up my back. Any normal man would have died as the blade ground against bone, as the tip erupted through my stomach, but I was no normal man. I spun around, wrenching the sword from the surprised guard's hands, and I grabbed him by the shoulders, pulling him against me so that the blade sliced into his stomach. His lips opened to scream, but I covered his mouth with my own, my tongue searching for his, and then my teeth clamped over his tongue and ripped it from his mouth in a gorge of thick red. That stopped his fucking screaming.

"Now Mary, run the blade through your stomach."

"No!"

I threw the last man to the ground and ran towards Mary, pulling the blade from my back as I did. As fast as I moved, time seemed to slow down, the air itself resisting my charge, pulling my feet to the Earth with leaden insistence. Pilate loomed up before me, but I threw him aside, seeing only Mary and the blade held in her hands.

I saw the blade caress her stomach, the fabric denting at its touch. Blood blossomed across the cloth, a red bloom that unfurled with alarming speed as the blade sank deeper.

I slid towards her on my knees, skin peeling away from my knees, but I didn't feel it. I grabbed the end of the sword with one hand, and placed my other above the wound, and I pulled the metal from her stomach, pressing the palm of my hand against the bleeding hole.

"Fuck, Mary, no."

Mary looked at me, but her eyes dimmed as she slumped into my arms.

"Don't defy me Barbarian, you'll lose."

I lifted Mary into my arms, her head slumped against my shoulder, blood pouring from her stomach in a dark stain of approaching death. My friend, my childhood friend, dying in my arms, and it was all my fault.

"Though, fair play Barbarian, you really have put on the most wonderful show. Look how the place is littered with your dead. Impressive."

"If you ever come near me again, I'll kill you."

"Sticks and stones Barbarian, sticks and stones."

I ran from that place, I fled with Mary in my arms, dying in my arms, with the sound of the Devil laughing at my back.

Chapter Eleven: More Of Me

As Related By Gideon

I could not run any longer. Mary, my friend, I felt her life slipping away, dying in my arms, so I found a cave on the outskirts of the city, one with a high vantage point overlooking the sparse fields beneath. Nothing could approach me without my knowledge.

Her body felt so cold as I laid it upon the stony ground, her frail, broken soul clinging to life with every pained breath that pulled between her blue lips. So much death tainted my hands, and I could not stand to lose her, my friend, the sister I never had.

Desperation fuelled my actions. Mary had lost a lot of blood, and I had plenty to spare. I don't know what made me do it, or why I thought it would help. Some other force, some inner instinct driven by the Vampire inside of me, moved me to action, yet it felt like the most natural thing for me to do. My teeth sliced through the soft flesh of my wrist, and I held the wound over her lips, watching fascinated as my blood dripped into her mouth, willing her to drink, to swallow my red gift so that she may transform and live.

Mary's eyes snapped open, eyes so huge, blood tinging the whites as my life flooded her system. Her hands gripped my wrist, pulling it to her mouth with urgency, drawing the blood from my veins in great gulps, my blood, my blood inside her, filling her, healing her.

My head felt heavy, and I started to feel weak. Black was creeping around the edges of my eyesight. I pulled my hand away from her soiled lips, now ruddy and plump with blood, and I fell back onto the ground, exhausted.

Mary sat up abruptly. "I want more."

The flask. I pulled the flask out from beneath my bloodied robes, and I gave it to her pleading hands. The flask contained the blood of a God, the same blood that had transformed me, and she drank from that flask until it lay empty upon the ground before me.

Mary's eyes widened, and I saw in her face such a look, as though she saw something beautiful, something that only she could see, and then she smiled before slumping backwards, unconscious.

I picked up the empty flask. Caiaphas wanted to build an army with that blood, and I had just fed it to Mary, and she would rise from her slumber a monster like me, a Vampire. Did I have that right? Was it my choice to make? I chose for Mary another life, a different existence, because I could not stand to see her die. Would Mary know that I had no choice? Would she forgive me?

As I contemplated throwing the empty flask away into the depths of the cave, something extraordinary happened. Before my astonished gaze, the flask replenished, blood filling the interior to the brim. I knew without question that it was his blood, the same blood that ran through my veins, the same blood that even now, transformed Mary into a new breed of creature. Did God want me to create more Vampires? Was it a sign? Was it my purpose?

My own transformation, from one life into another, began with agonizing pain, and the eviction from my body of everything human. As I looked at Mary, as I waited to see the first signs of such agony start to rip through her changing body, no such humiliation occurred, and I could not help but feel the sting of jealousy at the ease of her transition. She squirmed slightly, her hands clasping her stomach, then, much to my surprise, she shot to her feet and ran to the back of the cave, and the privacy of darkness.

"Mary?" I heard a few uncomfortable noises, sounds that I would normally associate with a barrack full of men, and I had to clasp my hands across my mouth to stifle my laugh.

"Stay there! And close your ears!"

Tears stung my eyes as I shoved my laughter back down my throat. She would not thank me for laughing. Lady-like to the end. That was my Mary.

A couple of moments later, she emerged from the back of the cave, and of all things, she was frantically re-arranging her hair into a neat bun.

"Sorry, I wouldn't go back there for a while if I were you. Must have been something I ate."

"Mary, don't you remember? He made you run a sword through your own stomach, you were dying. I saved you, the only way I knew how."

"Yes, I know."

"Is that all you can say?" Her calm demeanour shocked me, I expected her to be a little upset at least, angry even.

"What do you expect me to say, Gaius? I was dying, and you saved me."

"But—I've made you a monster."

Mary rushed forward and grabbed me, and the strength by which she held onto my arms proved that she was no longer human.

"Is that what you think? That you are a monster? No, Gaius, no. His blood saved you. His blood has saved me. I refuse to believe that we are anything other than what God has made of us. Daniyyel was right. We make our own choices. I saw you, I saw you stand up to Caiaphas, I saw you fight to protect that which you love. I saw you fight for what you thought was right. You carried me from that place without a single thought for yourself. You saved me, Gaius, you saved me. Those are not the actions of a monster."

Mary embraced me, and I wrapped my arms around her body, feeling the power that throbbed through her new body, and I believed her, because nothing so beautiful as Mary could be a monster.

"Well fuck me sideways."

"Eeww," laughed Mary, slapping my shoulder playfully. "Do you mind? It would be like incest, eeww."

"Oh ha, ha, very funny."

"I know."

"I was in bloody agony when I changed, nothing but blood, piss, and shit, but look at you, you're glowing."

"Oh please, I'm a woman, I've been bleeding all my adult life! And how do you think we give birth? This was nothing, trust me."

"Mary, you never fail to amaze me."

"Yes, I know. I'm good like that."

Suddenly, I felt her arms around me again, holding me so very tight, as though her life depended on it. In the midst of so much death, we had that at least, a moment of affection and friendship that no Devil could take away from us. Whatever came next, whatever horror snapped at our heels, we would always have that moment in the cave, when the two of us loved each other again, the best of friends, safe in each other's arms for all of eternity.

"Thank you, Gaius."

"Always, my friend, always."

Mary pulled away, wiping the tears from her eyes, and I loved her then, as I had always loved her as a child. I felt closer to her somehow, as though we shared the same life, the same body. I felt her in my blood, in my heart, in my mind, and I knew that she felt the same way, because I felt it.

"What now?" Such simple words, but they carried with them so many complications.

"I need to get my spear back from that fucking cunt, and then I need to hide it, somewhere where no one will ever find it. What about you?"

"I need to find the others. Peter is desperate to leave for Rome, and none of them are safe here, so I need to get them out of the city."

"I would do that now if I were you, before the shit really hits."

"Gaius, I love you for what you have done, never forget that, okay?"

"The world is not ready to lose you Mary, and neither am I."

Mary nodded, and with a sad little smile, she headed towards the cave entrance. She looked so beautiful, framed there against the dark of the sky, the stars twinkling so brightly behind her, and I could not help but think that the Vampire condition suited her. She paused then and looked back at me, a thought resting upon her red lips.

"Gaius? Can we die?"

It had never even occurred to me. The wounds inflicted on me by the Praetorian had completely healed, and so had Mary's. Normal weapons did not seem to harm us. I did not know what could harm us. Did that mean we would live forever? I shrugged, unable to offer an answer.

"That's okay," she said, smiling sweetly, "it was just a thought. Be careful, Gaius, I will come back as soon as I can." Then Mary walked out into the night, and for the first time since I first left my home, the outcast, I felt truly alone.

I sat down in the dust, staring at the stars outside. Such a beautiful sight, blackness pierced by light. What manner of things lived in such a place? Creatures with wings of the purest silver, or so I had come to understand. Up there, in the Heavens, another world so unfathomable, an existence beyond my comprehension, and I was a part of it, moved by a hand in ways I could not, as yet, conceive. A creature of light, or a monster of circumstance? Time alone would tell.

As I looked into the heart of the night, I realised that I had not slept for days, and yet I did not feel the need to close my eyes. Yet another new facet of my Vampire condition.

I saw something move against the dark, a figure black against the stars, moving towards the opening of the cave. Surely it could not be Mary, not so soon, but as I watched, the figure, now obviously that of a man silhouetted against the stars, began to change. The outline blurred, bleeding outwards, and then it moved and pulsed, diminished, coalescing into a form that moved on all fours, a beast of such enormity that I shot backwards into the cave, terror gripping my heart as the thing entered the mouth of the cave.

I recognised the creature, I had seen Lions before in the Gladiatorial ring, but the monster that padded towards me looked unlike any of the golden beasts I had seen. Its paws were huge things with massive claws splayed across the ground as it moved, and its mane swayed from side to side as though with a life of its own. It's mouth, filled with teeth that glittered even in that darkness, spilled thick rivulets of drool that dripped to the rocky ground, smoke issuing from each point of contact. But it was the colour of the thing that shocked me the most, black, and glistening, its fur radiating a rainbow of blue and purple hues that seemed to ripple across its immense form with each lithe movement of the muscles beneath the black skin.

The beast reared up before me, its front paws almost reaching the ceiling of the cave. It had a huge erect cock, a massive thing that pulsed and twitched, the cock of a man, and the Lion thrust the engorged dick towards me with a roar that shook the ancient stone that entombed us.

I became teeth and claw, my own beast rising to the challenge, and I lashed out with every ounce of strength that my new body could muster. My fingers brushed the underside of the creature's belly, flesh opening at the touch of my talons, but the wounds healed over before my fingers withdrew from the flesh. I kicked out, my foot aiming for the engorged organ that it thrust towards me, and the monster reared back with a howl, just as a thundering paw raked across my shoulders and down my chest, tearing through skin and fabric in a shower of shredded flesh and blood.

I fell backwards, my back cracking against stone, blood pouring from my broken body, bone glistening through muscle and sinew. I scuttled backwards, my chest on fire, my scream a muffled cry upon my agonized lips, my one arm hanging loosely at my side. I felt the wall of the cave hit my back, and I could go no further.

The black Lion padded towards me on all fours, and I feared another swipe of its lethal claws. But the creature stopped, towering over my broken body, and it lowered its massive head, its hot breath putrid against my skin. I felt the chill of its black nose as it touched me, felt the wetness of its bloated tongue slide across my wounds, and I screamed as it sent a whole new wave of agony tearing through my body.

The creature stepped back, and it looked at me with eyes that burned yellow, and it watched me as my muscles started to twitch, as torn tendons and skin began to knit together, pulling my broken arm back into place, and weaving my chest and my shoulders together. I felt it all, muscle and vein, flesh and skin, move and twist inside me in a ballet of pain, wiping every gash, every scar from the surface of my perfect body. It hurt like a fucking bitch.

The Lion saw all this, and then, with a slight nod of its enormous black head, it moved back out of the cave, its yellow eyed gaze never leaving my shaken form, until it reached the mouth of the cave and turned, lumbering out into the night.

The Lion merged with the black of the sky, its huge bulk blocking out the stars. Then the form twisted and changed, exploding out against the night before snapping back into itself, a collapsing mass of writhing black that transformed into the shape of a man. The man paused and turned his head back towards the mouth of the cave, and I saw his eyes, yellow eyes, burning in the night before he faded from my sight.

My entire body throbbed. My shoulders, my chest, my right arm. That beast nearly tore me apart with a single swipe of its huge paw, and yet my body pulled itself back together and healed. Fatigue washed over me in a crashing wave of exhaustion. I felt a hunger coil inside me, a yearning that demanded satisfaction, but the darkness pressed against my eyes, it pressed against my soul, and I had no choice but to give in to it, to succumb to the sleep that had so wanted to devour me.

I walked through an endless field of dying trees, their stems twisted and gnarled, arthritic fingers pointing into a sky that bled. Dark clouds haemorrhaged against the crimson, heavy, billowing pillows that threatened to empty their loads upon the desolation bellow in a torrent of savage anger.

In the middle of that twisted field of skeletal branches, one tree stood out from the rest, its boughs laden with deep green leaves, glossy and dark, with olives glinting like emeralds throughout its spreading canopy. That single beacon of tenuous life drew me inexorably towards it, and I found myself picking my way through the rocky ground, ground that crunched beneath my sandaled feet. When I looked down to see why the ground crunched so, I found that I walked upon skulls, skulls mixed with tiny bone fragments that resembled complex finger joints, and scattered liberally through these remains lay the desiccated remnants of feathers that crumbled to dust as I touched them.

I felt sick. I could not reach the tree without trampling across the dead, and with every hesitant foot that I placed before me, another skull lay crushed, and every footstep became a nightmare of noise. I tried to block out the sound, to think of anything other than the dead I walked on. And I found to my relief, that as I reached the tree, the area around its canopy remained clear, almost as if the remains had rained down from the sky, with the spread of the tree offering the only sanctuary beneath its spreading branches.

Something hung from the tree, swinging gently from a thick lower branch. Dread tied my stomach into a heavy, coiling knot as I rounded the thick base of the tree because I knew what hung there, who hung there, and I felt my heart wail at the thought of witnessing his grief once more.

His gaze followed me as I moved around the thick, knotted trunk, such startling eyes staring out of such a startlingly beautiful face. I felt my heart heave as I saw the pain etched into that face. I wanted to take him into my arms, to wrap him in my heart, to love him as he deserved to be loved, without question, without prejudice, without fear. I felt his pain, I felt his yearning, the gaping chasm of his heart, a heart that just wanted love, a heart that needed to love, and every part of me wanted to give that to him, to take him away from the burden of his guilt and just love him. When his lips cracked open, and his words whispered from that dry throat, I thought my heart would explode within my weeping chest.

"So many dead. It's all my fault."

"They died for God?"

"Not for God's sake, you stupid twat, for my sake!"

I saw the bleeding sun reflected in the watery depths of his incredible eyes, eyes devoid of hope, devoid of life, devoid of reason. My own eyes wept for him.

"You do not deserve this. You only did what was asked of you. This torture, this self-inflicted misery, you don't deserve it, you deserve to live, you deserve to love. Please, leave this behind you, put away your pain and your suffering, and let me show you another way."

"What do you know of my suffering, of my pain?"

"I know what they asked of you. I know the love that you had to betray. I know the price you paid."

Suddenly his body exploded into movement, his arms outstretched across the darkening sky, a cruciform shape silhouetted against red, and he threw his head back, bellowing into the angry Heavens.

"Let me die! Why won't you let me die, you fucking cunt!"

"No, please, don't die, not like this."

His arms were wrapped around his chest, and tears fell from his sad eyes in a river of sorrow that dripped to the dry ground beneath his feet. As the tears soaked into the dust, green saplings sprouted from the specks of moisture. I looked into his face, and I saw my own loneliness looking back at me, my own need for love. His lips trembled, the words struggling to form, and when he spoke, my heart shattered.

"Death is just the beginning. Love is the end."

I awoke from my nightmare to the sound of voices, a dawn chorus outside the cave, so I crept forward, the morning sun streaming through the opening, fingers of light pushing me back into the darkness, trying to shield my eyes from the sight that awaited me. As I blinked away the glare and looked out over the fields, my asshole exploded with shock.

Bellow me, in neat groups of lines, sat a classic formation of Roman soldiers, a Legion of men, camped at the base of my cave.

Chapter Twelve: Gaius Cassius Longinus, Superstar

As Related By Gideon

I passed down the middle of two rows of sweaty Roman soldiers, their chests bare in the morning sun, the air filled with their thick, musky scent. Under normal circumstances, I would have considered my situation a horny one, a sea of pert nipples awaiting my eager tongue, but I knew they wanted to kill me, not fuck me.

So much for the sanctity of my hiding place. Caiaphas, the conniving bastard, had given me away. So I decided to face them, head on. An idea formed in my head, that maybe, just maybe, I could use my new Vampire abilities to my advantage, to frighten the Roman Empire into leaving me alone. Risky? Fuck yes. I had no idea how much damage my body could withstand, but with the entire Legion parked in my front garden, I had precious little choice. I also wanted my fucking spear back.

I felt their gaze upon me, one hundred pairs of eyes as I walked through that sea of hard, rippling men, and I felt the heavy weight of their gaze, their hatred and revulsion pressing against me, but I did not let that intimidate me. I walked with my head held high on my magnificently broad shoulders, and I kept my gaze firmly ahead at the bastard sitting on his throne at the front. They would not see the fear that pumped through my body, and I would not give him the satisfaction of seeing the dread that lurked behind my eyes.

Pilate lay draped across his throne, with one leg hanging casually over the golden armrest, a white toga wrapped loosely around his bronzed body against the sun, and on his lap sat my spear. Caiaphas stood behind him, a supercilious grin splitting his cunt of a face in two. He wore a shimmering black gown with a huge fur-lined collar that framed his stunning face, and his eyes glowed yellow in the sun.

"That's quite far enough Gaius."

"What's the matter Pilate? Are you scared?"

Pilate picked up the spear and wafted it in front of his face. "Afraid? Of you? Do I look afraid."

"Be afraid. Be very afraid."

Pilate leapt off his throne, possessed with a fervour that I had never seen in him before, a passion that seemed to radiate through his sinuous body. He seemed possessed of confidence, a self-assurance that poured unfettered from his mouth as he addressed the Legion of soldiers.

"This man is a murderer! A killer! He butchered innocent men, men like you, your comrades, your friends, and he did it without mercy."

An angry murmur rippled across the muscled battalion like a stone thrown into water. The air felt charged with power as if every word that spilled from Pilate's mouth energized the unsettled crowd. It had to be the spear, imbuing him with a charismatic edge that never existed in his day to day life.

"Are you afraid of me Pilate? Are you afraid of what I know, what I have seen?"

"I am afraid of no one."

"Is that why you brought an entire army with you then?"

His face twisted with anger as my words hit home. I had belittled him before his army, and he knew it.

"They are here so that each and every one of them may have a piece of you. You killed your own, and your own will punish you accordingly."

Pilate offered me an opening that I could not resist, and I would take full advantage of it, so I turned my back on Pilate, to face the throng of pert nipples and hard abs.

"You were there, most of you, you lined the streets as that man dragged his cross through the shit and the dust. You saw him hang on that cross, and you saw him die on that cross. Pilate, and this Devil in disguise would have you believe that he was a man, just a man, but I was there, I saw him rise from the dead. Does that sound like a man to you? Do you know who it was that you killed? Do you know *what* it was that you killed?"

Black words slithered from between the Devil's black lips. "And what is it that you are, Gaius? Man? Or monster?"

"You're a fine one to talk, Caiaphas, how about showing them your true face? You have two of them, after all."

"Bravo, Barbarian, so clever, so droll, but really, dear heart, they are words, just words."

I lunged at the nearest soldier and ripped his dagger from his belt.

"Men do not resurrect, Gods do! His blood, the blood of a God, it runs through my veins, *my* veins!"

I plunged the dagger into my chest, right up to the hilt. Pain, sharp and intense, burned through my body as the metal blade hit a rib, and I felt, and heard, the rib snap beneath its penetration tip. But I did not flinch, and I did not let the agony show on my face. I left the dagger inside my chest, and I opened my arms out to my shocked audience.

"See! Am I not a God, too? His blood is in me, and I am him. I saw the Angels come down from Heaven and embrace him. All that he was, all that he said, it was true, all of it. Who are you to doubt a God?"

I had them. I could see it in their faces. Fear. I had literally put the fear of God into them. Slowly, deliberately, and grinding my teeth against the searing agony that accompanied it, I pulled the dagger out of my chest, and let it tumble to the floor, blood dripping into the hungry earth at me feet.

"Everything is about to change. Your world, your life as you know it, all of it will change. The old Gods are dead."

Pilate seethed forward, the spear, my spear, held out towards me with a trembling hand.

"Kill him! Do you hear me? I am your commander, and you *will* obey me. Kill him!"

I felt the command pour from Pilates body, from his every fibre and surge across the unsettled crowd in a tidal wave of compulsion. Yet it did not touch me.

I felt the need to kill, the desire to kill, rise in the soldiers, I saw it on their faces, in their eyes, a lust to see my flesh opened to the bone, but I also felt their resistance. I could smell their fear. I could taste it on my tongue.

"Is that it? Is that all you have? You shake your magic stick, and what? Nothing?" I cried as I smeared my own blood across my toga. "Killing. Always with the killing. Have we learned nothing these last few days?"

"Kill him!" Pilate's voice raised to a hysterical pitch, but his terrified army remained unmoved. The victory belonged to me, and Pilate knew it.

The horror of what came next has haunted me my entire existence because I only have myself to blame. Should I feel guilty for the senseless slaughter that followed? It is a question that time has refused to answer, and one I fear will always remain unanswered. They came to that field, to that cave, to kill me, but instead, they killed themselves. Guilt is not the go-to mode of a monster, and yet it pulls at my heart every time I think back to that day.

"Groups of ten, now!"

I could not stand by that bastard's side and watch. So I turned to him, my monster flickering over my face as my anger simmered beneath the surface.

"So who's the fucking killer now?" I growled.

Pilate sneered back at me. "I'm not the one doing this, you are."

I sought the sanctuary of my cave from which to watch, unable to stomach the massacre about to unfold from up close. Decimation is a cruel punishment, used only in cases of mutiny or extreme insubordination. The Legion, consisting of one hundred men, would divide into groups of ten. Each man within that group had to draw a straw or a piece of string, and the one with the shortest length would then suffer a terrible death at the hands of his comrades. Literally at their hands, for only fists and stones were permitted, to maximise the horrific nature of the punishment.

No matter how much the sight repulsed me, I felt compelled to watch. The brutality of men never failed to surprise me, and in a sick, fucked up kind of way, it also aroused me. As a Legionnaire, I, myself had committed such horrific acts and thought nothing of it. Duty took precedence over morals. As a Legionnaire, I belonged to something far bigger than myself, and to obey orders without question became a way of life, a drug even, an addiction. As an outsider, as a Vampire, it fascinated me. To watch death uncoil at the hands of man, to watch them beat the living shit out of each other, sweat, muscle, and blood, it appealed to the animal within, and I felt the shameful ripple of excitement trickle down my spine.

Each group of ten men pulled their straws in turn, and I could smell their fear, taste their terror, and hear the pounding of their hearts inside their chests. Even from my high vantage point, looking down upon them, I could smell the shit that filled their pants.

Yet, despite the aphrodisiac of fear that enriched my senses, I could not help but feel drawn to the look on Pilate's face. The man looked so enraptured, so filled with the power that flowed through him from the spear, that he resembled a man possessed. His eyes were huge and round, saliva bubbling at the corners of his mouth, and as he raised the spear above his head, his cold, hard voice rang out across the field with inhuman power, with a single word of death.

"Decimation!"

The monster lurking behind my eyes erupted through my flesh, my long nails slicing through the hard muscle of my thighs as I watched the ten victims fall helplessly to the floor, cowering from the onslaught of fist and boot. Their comrades — their friends — kicked and punched the living shit out of them in a brutal expression of violence.

I had to close my eyes, to still the creature inside, to stop myself from flying down that hill to rip, and tear, and feed. The compulsion to drink, the desire to kill, it rendered me helpless, and for a moment, I became nothing but a ball of instinct, the killer in me desperate to snuff out the human. So many hearts, banging in time to each sickening thud of boot against body, so many hearts pounding as rib and cheekbone shattered. I heard every snap, every crack, and my monster liked it. I heard the sound of agony, of torture, and every snap of bone, every rip and tear of flesh. It enticed my Vampire with a song of torture that saw my bloodlust rise as my teeth chewed into my bottom lip, filling my mouth with my own blood.

The agony of man played out to the bitter end until ten men lay in broken pieces at the feet of their Prefect. Heartbeats stuttered, and heartbeats failed, but even as they buried their dead in a hastily dug hole at the base of my hill, I knew that some of them yet lived. I could hear the whispering of their blood pumping weakly through their veins, the stutter of their hearts inside their shattered ribs, beings barely alive, thrown into that ignominious hole like so much meat thrown out for the carrion. That, more than anything, moved my monster to the brink of insanity. A hunger unlike anything I had ever felt devoured me from the inside, demanding to be heard, to satiate myself upon those discarded bodies, and there was something else, too. Something new to me, something irresistible, the desire to breathe new life into those ruined forms and take them under my wing.

I ran into my cave and cowered in the dust, fighting the thing inside me that wanted to feed, that wanted to breed, to rage against the living, and in that cave, alone in the dark, hungry, confused, and frightened, I cried. My tears did not belong to those men, beaten and buried alive, my tears belonged to me, to my own despair that raged inside of me, that ripped out my heart and blackened my soul. I felt so lost, so alone, surrounded by death. Where was Mary? I needed her, I needed the guiding hand of my friend to take me away from all that death.

Daniyyel said that I could choose my own path. The Angel said that I could be good. Yet I only felt darkness, the lust for blood, and death. As I made Mary, I would make another, I needed to make another, Vampires like me. I could not love Mary, not with my body at least. I wanted a man, the comfort of a man, the love of a man, the man hanging in the tree, and that made me weep all the more.

Time seemed to know no end, and the night, my black friend, arrived with a sighing reluctance that brought with it a darkness more profound than its own inky depths.

The huge black Lion stood framed in the mouth of the cave—Caiaphas, with his huge fur collar rippling black blue in the breeze.

"You feel it, don't you, Barbarian?"

"I feel nothing, fuck off."

"Come now, I know you do." He slithered into the cave, tall, handsome, deadly. "You want nothing more than to go out there and rip their throats out. You want to go out there and drink of them, to feel their blood pumping into your mouth, down your throat. I feel it, sweetie, your desires, burning inside of you. You forget, I was once an Angel too, I know these things. And there is something else too, something that tortures you... well fuck me seven ways to Sunday, you want to make more, don't you?"

"No!" The word felt meaningless, without conviction, and he knew it.

"Don't lie to me, I can feel the need writhing inside you like a dick up your ass, it's filling you. Do it, Gaius, is that not what we planned? Give yourself over to the dark side, Gaius, be beautiful like me. Fuck God, come and fuck me instead."

"I will never do anything for you. Ever. You lied to me, you made me feel wanted, you made me think that you loved me, when all you wanted was that fucking spear and my blood."

"Oh, dear heart, love is so subjective, don't you think? And as for helping me, well, you already have done that, have you not? Look at what you have achieved in but so short a time! Today you have set man against man. Today you caused the death of ten innocents. I must congratulate you, I couldn't have done it better myself."

I felt my body lift from the floor, and I saw my clawed hands reach out for that bastard's throat, my teeth snapping for his slender neck. I wanted to feel my lips against his skin, to feel my teeth penetrate his flesh, to rip his fucking life out of him. Instead, I found myself flat on my back, pinned to the ground by an immense paw as the black lion stood over me. Rows of sharp teeth clamped around my arm, and I heard muscle and sinew twang, and I felt the strings of flesh rip and snap inside the beast's mouth as it wrenched my limb from my shoulder.

I thought the pain would never end as my agony echoed around the small cave, a monstrous howl that flew into the night on wings of torture. Red filled my eyes, red inflamed my nerves, red pain that burned, and I thought I should die in red as my blood pumped thick and fast from the ragged stump.

My teeth slid into the thick hide of its massive paw, and I shook my head savagely, tearing a bloodied wound across the limb. Black blood pumped hot and rancid across my face, in my eyes, down my throat, but I kept tearing and ripping, my own bile vomiting from between my clamped lips. The lion roared with fury, and with a toss of its enormous head, my severed limb flew into the depths of the cave. Claws, huge and sharp, raked down my stomach, and I felt my skin part at their kiss, my intestines bursting through layers of ruptured muscle. No words could describe the white agony that flashed through my shattered mind. Even the scream that formed on my cold dead lips froze in disbelief. My brain could not conceive of such agony, could not feel every nuance of the devastation that broke me. The cave began to spin, blackness creeping across my eyes as the lion stood upright, Caiaphas glaring down at me through yellow eyes.

"See if you can heal from that you fucking bitch."

Caiaphas laughed, the sound infused with derision, and the sound moved around my head as my world spiralled out of focus. The cave started to fold in on me, black wave after black wave, smothering me, suffocating me, and all I could hear was his laughter as the darkness consumed me.

It might have been a dream. It should have been a dream, because the moments that followed felt like a living nightmare. In my delirium of pain, I felt my intestines squirming on my stomach like a pack of glistening grey worms, coiling and twisting as they slithered back into the gaping wound, which itself twitched and rippled with a life of its own. Fingers of muscle and skin reached across the divide, pulling and knitting my stomach together. I can only liken it to an infant in the womb, the feeling a woman experiences when the unborn child kicks and punches inside of her. It was me, and yet not me, another part of me, alive and independent of myself.

Something brushed across my shoulder, just behind my head, and through a cloud of pain and disbelief, I saw my dismembered limb pull itself towards the stump of my shoulder, bloodied fingers pulling itself into position. The arm flexed and rolled, strands of sinew, shattered fragments of bone, pulling itself onto my body, and I screamed in terror at the sight of my own limb moving, living, walking, and all disappeared in a howl of disconnection as my mind snapped, and I allowed oblivion to smother me.

My eyes snapped open. The cave remained dark, but I saw everything clearly, a string of crystal clear thoughts that pushed all other concerns out of the equation. I had to get the spear back, no matter how, and no matter the cost.

Through the bloodied remnants of my clothes, my stomach glistened hard, its rippled ridges defined against the dark of the night, whole and unblemished. Not even the faintest scar remained of the devastating wound inflicted upon it. I ran my hands down my stomach, both hands, for my arm remained once again attached to my body, and I enjoyed the feel of myself beneath my fingers, the slipperiness of my skin, the hardness of my body, the shape of each muscle. My body, whole again, strong, hard, and indestructible. I ripped the remains of my clothes from my body, feeling the warmth of the night against my skin in a breath of invigorating heat, and I moved out of the cave with a singular purpose.

I slithered down the steep slope in complete silence, starlight bouncing off the smooth contour of my body. Blood and dirt smeared my skin, masking my body against the blackness of the sky and the stars that frowned down upon me.

The bodies lay buried beneath a layer of loosely compacted dirt, barely a foot deep, and I pulled those wretched corpses from their grave with ease, lining them up around the edge of the pit. Ten bodies lay exposed to the night, but two hearts continued to beat, just two weak traces of life amidst ten discarded souls.

I cannot explain how I knew what to do. Much like my experience with Mary, instinct, deep and carnal, seemed to take over as the Vampire inside of me moved me to my knees. The arm of the dying man felt so weak in my hands, and I tried to think whether I knew him in life, but his rugged features meant nothing to me, only the faint sound of his fluttering heart bore any recognition for my monster, for it meant food.

The twin points of my long teeth pierced the skin of his limp wrist, brittle skin giving away with a slight pop. Blood trickled weakly into my mouth, his heart too weak to push it through his veins, and I had to suck hard to draw out the coppery liquid, swallowing it gratefully. The heart stuttered, its life almost extinguished, and I withdrew my teeth, biting into my own wrist in a haze of excitement, blood gushing from the ragged wound. Before the wound had time to heal, I pressed the gash against his lips and allowed my blood to pump into his mouth.

For a moment, I thought my actions too late, that his body lay ruined beyond resurrection, but suddenly, his hands shot out and grabbed my wrist and jammed it to his bloodied lips, gulping down big mouthfuls of my red gift.

As his body began to spasm, I pulled my wrist away, and quickly moved to the second survivor, performing the same ritual until both men writhed in pain in the dirt. Weak, and desperately hungry, I lifted a cold, stiffening corpse to my lips, my teeth sliding into his neck, and I sucked on the blood of that corpse, cold, dead, stale blood that tasted foul inside my mouth, making my stomach twist into painful knots. The blood of the dead felt wrong, it felt corrupted, sour, and I threw the corpse to the ground in frustration, just as the first of the newly converted struggled to his trembling feet.

The man looked at me, and I saw reflected back at me my own insatiable hunger. It burned behind his eyes, a fierce need to feed, to tear at living flesh, to drink warm, living blood. Yet, as I looked at him, he seemed different to me somehow, savage, lacking the humanity that seemed to persist within myself, and Mary. I gave the man my blood, the diluted blood of a God, a subtle difference, but one that my Vampire self remained acutely aware of.

"How do you feel?"

"Hungry. I feel hungry, and strong, yes, strong." His new condition did nothing to disguise the ruggedness of his appearance.

"I want to rip those cunts apart for what they did to us!" The other soldier pulled himself to his unsteady feet, and he smiled at me, his teeth glinting over his lower lip, and he was beautiful. "You did this to us? You brought us back from death?"

"Yes."

"Then you truly are a God," said the rugged one. His new teeth sliced into his lower lip as he talked, and he brought his fingers to his bloodied lip in surprise. "This is going to take some getting used to. But I like it."

"Can we kill them? Now?" asked the pretty one enthusiastically.

I thought about it. It would be nothing to kill the remaining men as they slept, to feed on their blood, to quell the hunger that burned so fiercely inside us. Ninety men. To Pilate, to the Empire, it would mean nothing. More men than that had died while building the roads and aqueducts that stretched across that barbaric land. No, I had to teach the Roman Empire a lesson, one that would ensure my safety, and my privacy, one that would ensure the return of my spear.

"No, not yet. I need to put the fear of God into them, I need to make sure that they never challenge me again. Tomorrow, they will call for reinforcements, and I will go down onto the field to face them."

"But we are hungry."

"Yeah, and I want to see those pricks torn to shreds for what they did to us."

"Not yet."

"But why?"

"Because I fucking say so! You will do as I fucking want, is that understood?" The command belched from my throat with a rumbling growl. It did not sound like my voice, and yet it rolled across my vocal chords with such power, with such authority, that it pulsed through my body and issued from my throat with a conviction that took me by surprise.

My command had a startling effect upon my newborns, for they stood to attention like the soldiers they were, soldiers held within my thrall.

"There is a chasm at the back of the cave at the top of this hill, dump the bodies in there." Without hesitation, my new soldiers picked up a body under each arm and sprinted up the hill towards my cave in an impressive show of obedience and strength. It made me shiver, a cold trickle of pleasure, rather than the guilt I should have felt.

I carried two bodies into the cave and dumped them unceremoniously into the deep hole at the rear, and when the final two disappeared into the chasm, I sat just inside the entrance to the cave, overlooking the field destined to become my battlefield.

I felt the gaze of my newborns bore into my back, and I could almost feel their questions burning into my skull, and with a small gesture of my hands, I indicated for them to sit. They hunkered down either side of me, the muscles of their bulging arms brushing against my nakedness, and for some reason, as I contemplated my existence, and the battle to come, I found their touch intensely erotic.

"What are we?" asked the beautiful one. I answered without looking at him, staring straight ahead at the dying night in an effort to control the growing erection between my legs.

"We are called Vampires. We were created by a God, and named by an Angel."

"For what purpose are we made?" asked the rugged one, his voice a low growl that made my cock twitch.

"I have yet to fully understand our purpose. One would have us rage against the Heavens, while the other would have us do God's work. Light or dark. What we do here, what will happen tomorrow is dark, and yet we do it for the light."

"You brought us back to kill, didn't you?"

I looked at the pretty one, with his bright blue eyes and his pouty, full lips. Desire flooded my cock as I gazed into his beautiful eyes, and I found that I wanted him.

"Yes. I brought you back to kill them. It is a fight that Pilate started, but I will fucking finish it."

"And what happens to us, then?"

The rugged one asked me something that I had not considered, and it made me feel ashamed. Heavy eyebrows encased deep set eyes that looked so black in that half-light, and he had a smashed, asymmetrical beauty about his rough face that I just wanted to fuck.

Hunger and desperation, a heady mix that toyed with my libido most effectively.

"You move on. Take your revenge. Rip those cunts from limb to limb for what they did, and then go. Leave this place. Live your life however you see fit. That is all I can offer you."

"Is it?"

He took my hand in his, the muscles of my huge arms bulging, tense, and he lifted my hand to his face and placed my index finger between his lips. The moisture of his mouth tingled across the tip of my finger as his tongue wrapped and curled itself around its length, and all the time his gaze never left me, the blackness of his eyes fucking me where I sat.

Something wet enveloped my throbbing cock, and I glanced down to see the beautiful one leaning over, his lips surrounding my pulsing head, sliding down the length until my cock hit the back of his throat. I gasped at the sensation, but as the sound sighed from between my surprised lips, the rugged one pulled my head back to face him and inserted his tongue into my mouth.

The three of us were filthy, covered in dirt, in blood, but the moment didn't care about the filth, about the grit in our mouths, the filth that clung to my cock. All that mattered was flesh, tasting, licking, swallowing. The three of us moved as one body, as hands, lips, and mouths entangled into a single orgasmic being, drawn together by need, bound together by death.

The rugged one's cock sprang from beneath his loin cloth, a thick, veined organ that glistened wetly in the starlight, and it filled my mouth as my lips moved down his hard, rippled body to receive it. As the beautiful one swallowed me, so I swallowed the other, my teeth scraping along its girth, my tongue lapping around the head, tasting the pre-cum saltiness that seeped from within. He moaned, and in a flash of pain, I felt his teeth slide into my shoulder blade. I felt his mouth suckle at the wound, sucking away my body fluids as I sucked away his, and I felt my own release pump hard into the mouth that fed so eagerly upon my very hard cock.

Arms wrapped around my chest, strong arms that pulled me on top of him, the rugged one sliding me into a position over his body, the thick cock, still wet from my mouth, sliding against the cheeks of my ass, searching and fighting for a way in. I brought my hand underneath me, guiding him inside, feeling his length slip into my tight space, filling me with his rough manliness in a blur of pain and pleasure. His arms wrapped around my chest, pulling me to his chest, a grip so hard as to shatter the ribs of any normal man. He bent his knees, his feet flat against the floor, and then he started to move inside me, the entire length of his thick cock grinding in and out, from head to base, deep and hard, with a rhythm that slapped flesh against flesh.

The beautiful one straddled me, his hand holding my cock that throbbed with new life, and slowly he lowered himself onto me, my massiveness sliding into him with a cry of satisfaction.

I felt my own orgasm rising yet again, building inexorably, desperate to release itself, but the beautiful one reached behind him and pulled on my balls, so tight within their sack, an explosion of pain calming the eruption that threatened to end my pleasure. His own cock, slender and smooth, slapped against the base of my belly as he moved up and down on my cock, his movements perfectly timed to the hard thrust of the other, and my vision exploded in a vista of stars as my body shivered with the pleasure inflicted upon it.

The beautiful one leaned over to kiss the rugged one, sandwiching me between them, my body at their mercy as their tongues flickered inside each other's mouth. His cock lay so close to me, and I leaned in further, straining my back, ignoring the ripping pain that shot down my spine, and I took the head of his long slender cock into my mouth, my tongue flicking around the head, sucking that beautiful cock that tasted of youth.

The two men separated as the thrusts became more urgent, and I grabbed the youth's dick, my fingers sliding around its length, manipulating his shaft as the sounds of desire filled the cave in a roar of pleasure. Just as my own cock exploded inside the beautiful one, his own semen shot across my chest and face, sliding down over my lips, my tongue flicking out to lick it, tasting him, swallowing him. The rugged one grunted as his own need reached a crescendo inside me, and slowly, the thrusts subsided, until we three lay upon each other, spent.

"That was unexpected and most welcome," I said, in an effort to break the silence.

"You know what they say, when in Rome," laughed the rugged one as he pulled himself from underneath me. The three of us sat in silence, staring out into the growing morn, to watch as the field below filled with men.

Below us, as the sun broke the dark, a cresting halo of light that cracked over the far horizon, two hundred men gathered on the field.

Chapter Thirteen: Into The Realm Of Legend

As Related By Gideon

Fear. The smell of it rolled across the morning sunshine like shit running down a leg, in uncontrollable spurts of anxiety. My little stratagem from the night before seemed to be working like a treat, the empty grave sending ripples of panic through the army of men gaping down into the empty hole. Horror passed between them with a whisper, moving from man to man, ear to ear with deadly effectiveness. The smell of it filled my nostrils, a heady mixture of nervous perspiration and skid marks. I wanted them afraid, so afraid that their bowels would fall out of their squeaking assholes. I wanted them to think that the dead had left their hole and that at any moment, white pallid hands could pull the flesh from their bones.

As I moved down the hill, they parted before me, a sea of two hundred men, two Legions of fit, brave warriors, two Legions of men afraid of *me*. Even Pilate looked at me with fear glistening in his eyes, and I breathed in the scent of his unease with satisfaction.

"Give me the spear Pilate. Then, and only then, will I leave."

Caiaphas once again stood behind Pilate's throne, and he wore a look of sly approval in his tight little smile as I stood there, defiant against the Prefect. He wanted me by his side, to be his lover in darkness, his cohort in sin, but I had other plans.

Pilate leapt off of his throne, his sweaty face pressed against my own, his spittle flying across my cheeks, and sliding down my neck as he screamed.

"Who the fuck, do you think you are? Who the fuck, do you think you are to defy me, to defy Rome?"

I moved my head slightly so that my mouth whispered against his ear. "I am your worst fucking nightmare, and neither you nor Rome can stand against me."

Pilate shivered, my words slithering down his spine in a current of fear, and he reeked of it. My teeth slid down, my monster enticed by the appetizer, and Pilate fell back in horror, his eyes as wide as shields.

"You will never get the spear back..." he stuttered, "never."

"Then I cannot be held responsible for what happens here today. Do not say that I didn't warn you."

Not one man touched me as I made my way back to my cave, despite Pilate's insane cries for my death. Instead, men went down on one knee as I walked through them, bowing their heads in deference, and it infuriated Pilate. No matter what he did, no matter that he carried the spear with its unfathomable power over men, they refused to touch me.

Yet again, Pilate invoked Decimation, and twenty men went to their deaths, beaten to a pulp at the hands of their Legion brothers. I watched from the entrance to my cave, and I beckoned to the others to watch with me, but the sight sickened them, and I felt their pain as they remembered their own brutal deaths. As bodies filled the field with every sickening thud, I felt their need for revenge, for justice, and I could feel the heat of anger swell within their veins, and they would need it for what lay ahead.

The sun burned high and hot, beating down upon our naked bodies without mercy. But as I watched, I noticed the arm of the rugged one start to blister, faint wisps of black smoke billowing from his bubbling flesh.

"Your arm! What the fuck is wrong with your arm?"

Suddenly, the pretty one began to scream as his face burst into flame, flesh melting down his pretty features in sizzling chunks. He collapsed to the ground, his hands in the flames of his burning face, his arms igniting, his screams tortured through the thick mass of fatty smoke that poured from his blazing body.

To my dismay, the rugged one collapsed to the ground too, a trickle of flame running up his arms and across his shoulders, until he too burst into a screaming ball of pain. In my panic, I grabbed him around the waist, ignoring the searing heat of flame that licked and blistered my own skin, and I dragged him kicking and screaming into the cave, into the dark, cooling shadow of rock. No sooner did his body hit the shade than the fire died and sucked back into his blistered body with a loud hiss.

The beautiful one stopped screaming, his agony dying behind a lipless mouth, but his body lay twitching in the sun, flames covering the entirety of his blackened body. I pulled him into the cave, grabbing his feet and sliding him across the sharp ground, my hands melting into the flesh of his ankles as chunks of his flesh left a burning trail behind him. My own scream of agony echoed around the cave interior as I finally pulled him into the shade, and as the flames died, I pulled my hands off of his liquid flesh with a sickening rip of ruined skin.

I sank to my knees, my hands before my incredulous eyes, unable to comprehend what had happened, but as I watched, my hands started to heal, skin and muscle sliding over bone, until they looked like my hands again, and I wiggled my fingers with relief.

As for the other two, it took them longer to heal. I thought the pretty one finished because his body resembled a lump of charcoal, black and encrusted from head to foot, exhibiting no sign of life. The other one writhed on the ground, his suffering all the more profound for his silence.

In my rage against Rome, I had made them, and now hubris saw them broken at my feet, and I did not know what to do. Was my blood not strong enough? The sun did not affect me, and yet just a short exposure caused them to burst into flame. Was Mary safe? Like me, she had consumed the blood of a God, raw, undiluted power, and it was that, I felt sure, which made all the difference. So much of my new existence remained a mystery to me, and my newborn offspring bore the brunt of my ignorance.

The hard, blistered shell around the pretty boy began to crack, and to my relief, the crust started to fall away from his body in an ashen cloud as he struggled into an upright position. His body glistened with sweat, rivulets of perspiration tumbling down his beautiful body, dripping from his pert nipples, and I could not help but wonder at the perfection of him. I saw how the flames consumed his flesh, I saw how the meat had melted from his bones, charred muscle falling to the ground in black lumps, and yet he emerged from his ashen cocoon unscathed.

The rugged one felt his own face, his chest, his gaze darting in fear across his bulging arms, but he too looked like new, though his regeneration did nothing to improve the squashed appearance of his battle-worn face.

"What the fuck was that all about?" he growled.

"I don't think sunshine is a good idea."

"No fucking kidding!"

"It didn't affect you, why?" The pretty one looked so disturbed, and I felt sorry for him.

"Because you are not the same as me, not exactly. I made you, but I was made by a God."

"I'm nobody's fucking bitch!"

I spun around to face the rugged one, my own anger spitting from between my lips.

"And nobody is fucking asking you to be!" He cowered away from me, and a part of me felt deeply satisfied by the power I seemed to hold over them, how they cowered as my voice trembled over my vocal chords. "Look, all I'm saying is that we have to rethink this. We will take them by night, that's all."

They both nodded and skulked into the darkness to lick their wounds, or their pride at least. I, however, couldn't give a fuck. I didn't need them to love me. I didn't even need them to like me. I just needed them to obey me.

A smell started to fill my nostrils, burning flesh and ashes. I rushed to the mouth of the cave and looked down into the field to see a huge funeral pyre blazing at the base of the hill, and those who survived the Decimation loaded their dead comrades into the flames. Cloth and flesh ignited, black, fatty clouds billowing into the sky, which wept red at the travesty of human carnage beneath its weeping canopy, skull and muscle and bone exposed to a crying Heaven.

Well, I wanted them to fear me, and it worked—I had put the fear of God into them. They burned their dead rather than risk my claiming their bodies. How very astute of them. One more push, one more act of terror, would bring them to their knees, then maybe they would leave me the hell alone.

There was nothing left to do but sit and watch those bodies burn. Flames leapt into the sky, kissing the sun, indiscriminate tongues of heat that consumed everything with a voracious greed. The pyre burned as one huge human candle, a flickering beacon of hate, and it smelled like Hell. The monster inside of me growled, hunger ripping at the edges of my sanity, but I calmed my beast. I watched the sun as it made its way across the sky in a slow, graceful arc, until finally, it kissed the edge of the horizon and turned the sky the same colour as the smouldering heap of human remains beneath it.

As the first stars pierced the Heavens, we moved. Our limbs slithered down the slope in silence, and as we approached the pyre, with its twisted, melted sculpture of humanity, we allowed our Vampire selves to blossom, our teeth glinting by firelight, our faces transformed into the beast like countenance of the true Vampire. I felt their hunger, their excitement, rising to almost euphoric levels as they moved around me, their hard bodies sparkling in the firelight, but there was nothing sparkly about us. We moved as monsters, hungry fiends about to tear the heart out of that Roman Empire.

The command arose in my throat, a deep, guttural sound that rumbled from between my lips, making my cock twitch with excitement between my legs. Death, blood and sex, an irresistible combination that spoke to my inner Devil, and I answered it with mounting pleasure.

"Feed on the fuckers, show no mercy!"

We fanned out into the night, a three-pronged trident of death, and I felt an insane pride as my children—for I knew nothing else to call them—sprinted ahead of me, their limbs close to the ground, skimming the rough terrain in utter silence. As the first cry of terror ripped into the darkness, I felt my own thrill of satisfaction as I pulled a soldier into my arms. My teeth slid into the back of his neck, my cock stiff against his back as I sucked the life out of his veins and threw his dead body into the night.

His short, brief life filled my body as I fell onto the next, landing on his chest like some feral beast, howling into his terrified face, loving the fear that exploded from his every hole. I bent my face towards him, my tongue licking at his trembling lips, and all around me, the night screamed in terror, a shriek of agony that rivalled the stars with its piercing brightness.

My hand groped between his legs, feeling the bulge that nestled between them, and as I sank my teeth into that soft spot beneath his chin, I felt his dick stiffen in my hand, engorged by the ecstasy of death that suckled at his neck. His blood pumped strong and hard into my mouth, hitting the back of my throat, sliding down my gullet, and I sucked until his cock exploded in my hand, thick, warm semen exploding across my back as the last of his life hissed between his blue lips.

My head reared back as I screamed into the sky, my own frenzy of blood adding to the music of the night, and never, ever had I felt so powerful, so in control, and I loved it. As the blood that swelled my body fuelled me onto the next victim, and the next, I felt the pleasure of the others. I could smell their desires, their excitement, mixing with the blood that soiled the ground, adding its own heady mix to the ash that filled the air, and I revelled in it.

Something else pulled on my instincts and tickled my senses, the presence of something else, of others, of monsters born in that frenzy of carnage. I could feel them—I could hear them. My eyes scanned the area, alerted by their excitement, their thirst, their unbridled need to feed, their primal, animal instincts filling my mind, and then I saw one.

The creature that scampered towards me looked so unlike the human that birthed it, a thing out of a nightmare, a creature as far removed from mankind as the God who made me. His body, so terribly thin and emaciated, glistened grey and pallid in the moonlight, his long limbs painfully thin, ending in talons that dripped fresh blood. He hunkered down, sniffing the air, the gaze of his huge black eyes never leaving me, and slowly he edged forward, wary of me, frightened of me.

I stood up, my body strong and muscular, my veins, engorged with blood, bulging through my skin, and the thing faltered, scuttling backwards away from me. Yet he was unmistakably a Vampire, his fierce teeth two sharp pins, hung so low as to pierce his chin, his head devoid of hair, and his ears pointed like that of a bat. He held his longs arms before him, one hand draped across the other, long twig-like fingers twitching below the wrists. The twisted parody of a man represented but a shadow of a Vampire, and yet I knew him to be one of us, a child of my child, his being lessened by the lack of that one element which retained the humanity in the others, my blood.

"Come to me." My command rumbled across the ground to smother the creature, and a sound like a whimper hissed through his thin, pale lips. He moved a little closer, wary, cautious, his big black eyes darting around, afraid to look at me, and I could not help but feel pity for him, that thing so irrevocably entwined with my bloodline.

"Come here!" The newborn monster could not resist my voice, and he rushed to my side, his long, cold hands enveloping my waist, his head brushing against my bulging legs in a surprising show of affection. I felt his love fill me, a devotion without question, and to my surprise, I felt the same overwhelming emotion for him, a strange, instinctual love that made me feel protective towards him. Something ran down my cheek, and my hand flew up to my face, and to my surprise, I felt a tear upon my skin.

Other newborn Vampires started to approach, so many of them that I lost count, and pretty soon they surrounded me, a sea of Feral Vampires, their adoration drowning me in a tidal wave of love. Hands reached out to touch me, so many of them, all around me, crawling at my feet, bodies slithering over bodies to get at me, pleading with me to love them, eyes imploring me to feel their need. I held my hands out to touch their desperate fingers, but their emotion overwhelmed me as my tears spilled thick and fast down my cheeks.

"No, there are too many of you... don't push me. There's too little of me... don't crowd me. Feed yourselves!"

My words cracked across the grey mass like an explosion, and they scattered before me, fear gestating in the blackness of their eyes, and I felt so guilty for hurting them. I felt their pain, their anguish, and I just wanted to envelop them in my arms, to love them all.

The scream came from somewhere before me, a cry not born of terror, but of defiance. The Feral moved as one, turning towards the direction of the sound, their noses sniffing the air hungrily, their dripping fingers twitching beneath their hands in anticipation. I knew that voice, and he belonged to me. Pilate was mine.

"Follow me," I bellowed to the hungry mass, "but do not touch him." The throng of grey scurried around me as I moved towards the sound, my ears deafened by the pounding of his heartbeat. My senses were overwhelmed by the stench of fear radiating from the only human left alive in the camp. I sensed the other two, my children, their hunger as yet unappeased, their fury palpable upon the bloodied night air, and as I reached the base of the camp, I found them before the cowering Prefect, waving the spear defiantly in their faces as he screamed.

"Cock sucking cunts! Do you think that I'm afraid of you? Do you think that the whole of Rome will not hunt you down and grind your bones into dust?"

As his gaze fell upon me and the wall of grey, hungry teeth that followed in my footsteps, his face changed, his smug countenance wiped away by the grim realisation that I had beaten him.

"Back off, you two, he belongs to me." My offspring turned on me, snarling, spitting, and their claws flashed through the air in their need to feed. It made the Feral nervous, and I felt their collective tremble of unease.

"You will obey me! Leave him!" They pulled their monsters back, an effort of supreme willpower, considering the frenzy that possessed them, but they did back away, their human faces shimmering into place as they waded into the sea of grey at my heels.

"You would do well to call off your creatures, *slave.*"

"Slave?" I stepped forward, my body glistening by starlight, my inner monster manifest in all its terrible glory. There, in the dark, before the Prefect of Judea, I was beautiful, surrounded by my children, enveloped in love, powerful, indomitable, and for the first time in my life, I felt I was worth something.

"I will never be your slave, or the slave of Rome again. Is that understood?"

"I will bring more... more men, by their thousands, we will hunt you, we will destroy you."

"And how is that working out for you so far?"

"But I have this!" He lifted the spear before his wide eyes, and I saw behind them the glint of madness, and I knew I had broken him.

"I am death, and I am life! Death is just the beginning. One hundred, two hundred, a thousand, it makes no difference. You may be able to control man with that piece of metal in your hand, but man will never turn against me, and do you know why? Because I am a God! Listen to me Pilate, and hear my words, for they are the most important words that you will ever hear. You see behind me, this army, *my* army. I control them. Take him."

As the last syllable of the command left my lips, a writhing mass of grey limbs and gnashing teeth exploded into the air, talons extended, black eyes bulging with desire, burning with hunger, and Pilate fell back shrieking.

"Stop! Back off." As one, the mass surged backwards, a growling horde of hunger that slithered around my ankles. Pilate whimpered on the ground, urine spreading beneath his cowering body.

"One word, just one word Pilate, that's all it will take for me to destroy Judea, to destroy you, to devour every last

Roman, and as your army diminishes, so mine shall grow. Do you understand?"

"Yes." His voice sounded so pathetic that it barely escaped his lips, so I hunkered down beside him and ran my teeth along the length of his arm, towards his neck, until my lips brushed his ear.

"I didn't quite hear you."

"Yes!"

"Then, my work here is done." I turned to my children, and I felt their anger, their disappointment that I should leave Pilate live, but if Pilate died at my hands, Rome would never stop hunting me, and I would never be free.

"Take them back to the cave, it will be light soon." My children started to herd the Feral before them as a flock of sheep, and as I looked up towards a cliff top to my right, I saw a figure silhouetted by the moonlight, watching the proceedings with keen interest. Caiaphas.

"Oh, and one more thing," I continued, turning back to Pilate, who still lay in a pool of his own piss. "Tomorrow morning, you will bring the spear to me, do you understand?" One more show of power, one more devastating demonstration to assure his compliance, and then it would be over. Such a demonstration required an equally devastating sacrifice, and it ate away at my conscience with insistent teeth. I saw a man, a God, sacrifice himself for the greater good of his beliefs, but did I have the right to sacrifice someone else for mine?

"Here, take it, it has brought me nothing but death." Pilate held out the blade towards me, and I hesitated, temptation there at my fingertips, but I had to see it through, to the bitter end.

"No, you will *bring* it to me! By the light of the morning sun, before God himself, you will submit."

I walked away from Pilate, a lone figure wandering through a field of death. Many bodies lay sprawled in the dust, white, bloodless corpses, drained of their life in a fight for my freedom. It seemed to me, as I picked my way through limb and torso, that freedom remained just another word for war, and war another word for indiscriminate killing. Not all those on the field became Vampire, Feral, and I thought the quiet dead to be the lucky ones. What would become of my army of Vampires? I had not thought that far, I could not see past the next morning, and it plagued me as I followed the path of spilled blood to the cave.

Caiaphas stepped out of the darkness like a shadow, but the man standing before me looked unlike the Caiaphas of old. Gone were his robes of feather and silk, replaced instead by black cotton cloth that clung to his body, seemingly painted onto his slim, fit body. His hair looked so short, slicked back across his scalp to reveal a high, intelligent brow, smooth and glistening in the fading moonlight. Only his eyes remained the same, a deep, penetrating yellow that radiated from within his skull.

"Caiaphas."

"Melek. It's time you called me by my real name, dear heart, one of so many, I might add, but Melek will do."

"I don't give a shit what your name is. What do you want?"

"Oh, my dear Barbarian, feeling a bit dejected, are we? Look, it was good, I give you that, but really? A relationship? Darling, I'm not the settling down type."

"Oh piss off, don't flatter yourself."

Melek moved so fast that even my Vampire eyes could not see him. And before I could react, his tongue was in my mouth, pushing deep down my throat, his lips so soft and wet against my own lips. I grabbed the back of his head, a fist full of slick hair in my fist, and I pushed my tongue deep inside of him. His hand moved down between my legs, feeling my growing excitement, and then he laughed.

"Whatever, dear heart, whatever. You and I both know the truth, don't we?"

Melek pulled away from me, and a part of me died as his hands left my naked flesh, and I hated myself for wanting him, but fuck, that tongue of his was a Demon.

"I must congratulate you. You played quite a marvellous game. To humiliate Rome, wow, I must hand it to you, I didn't think you had it in you."

"And your point is?"

"And my point is this, dear heart. I'm impressed, and it takes a lot to impress me. You have passed every test I have thrown at you..."

"Test?"

"Why yes, of course. You are new, my wonderfully undead Barbarian. I had to see how far you could go, how tough you are beneath that undead skin—gorgeous as it is— I needed to see what you are capable of. And now I know."

"I still don't see your point."

"Oh dear, you may be beautiful, but you are not the brightest muscle in the bunch are you? I'm offering you a job."

"Shove it up your fucking ass."

"Gaius, please, wash that mouth out. Oh, sorry, I've already done that haven't I?"

"You are not getting me, the blood, or the spear."

He walked around me, his long, slender hands clasped behind his back, and he made me nervous.

"The spear is no good to me, not at the moment, but time will tell Gaius, time will tell. And when I'm ready, well, I will just come back and take it from you. You so know I can. When I'm ready. Until then, keep your little trinket safe. As for the blood, well dear heart, I don't need it. Look at what you did here tonight! You made more monsters in the last few hours than I have made in years! Your plague will spread across this planet for me — why do I need to make an army when you have already done it for me?"

My head reeled around my asshole as my world spun in a dizzying whirl of fuck. He was right, I had made an army, an army of Feral Vampires that knew only how to feed, monsters driven by pure instinct, with no respect for the lives they consumed. The dark closed in around me, and I seemed helpless in its thrall.

"I see by your silence that you had not considered such a thing, no? Well, my Barbarian, I shall leave you with that thought. Battle with the dark if you will, but the dark always banishes the light. Until we meet again, Barbarian."

To my utter astonishment, the ground beneath him burst into a scorching column of red flame and smoke, and with a smile that froze the blood inside my throbbing veins, Melek descended into the ground, the rock healing over him until nothing remained but the stench of sulphur.

My mind failed to function as I approached the cave. So many thoughts fought for my attention, and my temples throbbed with the weight of my actions.

My actions. I sat on the ground, just inside the entrance to the cave, and stared at a mass of grey limbs and twisted bodies. Lying entwined in each other's arms were my children. The results of my actions. Was it a thing of evil I did that day, or was I acting for God? Fuck, nothing was ever black and white, just grey, so many fucking shades of grey. What had I done, and why had I done it? To protect myself? To stop Pilate? To save mankind from the spear?

Both. I did it for both. A little bit of black, and a little bit of white. Damn those fucking shades of grey.

Melek's words wormed their way around my head, the inevitability of them stinging my eyes. Before me, curled around each other like a mass of bloated worms, lay an army of my own making, a sea of Vampires that could exist only to feed, and they would feed. They would sweep across the land in a swath of teeth and blood, as indiscriminate as any hunting animal. My children, blood of my blood, what would become of them? Deep down I knew, I felt it coiling around my guts, a growing dread that blinded me with pain. I knew even if I could not admit it to myself. It hurt too much. On the field of battle, beneath the stars, knee deep in shit and blood, I felt their love, unconditional, and I felt their obedience, absolute, but what's more, I felt love for them too. In life, they represented my enemy, the face of oppression that I so needed to escape, and yet, in death, they became my brothers, my children, my eternal lovers, and I felt them all within my heart.

I would not take my eyes off of them until the sun blinked above the distant horizon. I owed them that much. So I sat, and I watched, and I allowed the tears to stream down my mud caked cheeks unchecked, owing them every single tear that spilled from my eyes. Pain crept across my chest, sharp and insistent as my heart broke, but I did not take my eyes off them.

Light exploded behind me, I could feel the heat upon my back, and I knew that the moment had come. A strange calm seemed to settle over the Feral as the sun began its journey into the Heavens, and their squirming movements stopped. They seemed like statues, an intricate carving of grey stone, so still in the safety of the cave, and my heart broke just that little bit more.

My ears picked out his footsteps as he approached the cave mouth, so I stood up to meet him. Pilate stood before the entrance, his gaze darting behind me, a question perched upon his lips, and I knew what he was thinking.

"Yes, they are sleeping."

His shoulders slumped in relief.

"Come in here for a moment. No, they will not harm you, have no fear."

Pilate stepped inside the cave, hesitantly, every trembling footstep a battle of will. Once he stood inside, safe in the embrace of darkness, I picked up the nearest Feral. The creature lay limp and lifeless in my arms, and for a moment I clutched him close to my chest, and I could not help but kiss that grey flesh as my tears fell cold and fast down my face. I turned to Pilate and offered him the grey corpse. Pilate backed away, shaking his head in horror.

"You will take him, and you will carry him into the light."

Pilate trembled so much that I thought his arms would break, but he took the body from me, and slowly, he walked into the light.

It happened so fast. As the sun kissed the Feral's skin, his skin erupted with black veins that pulsed to the surface of his flesh. The veins hardened, and then they cracked, and flakes of grey skin began to drift away from the body. Pilate's face transformed into sheer horror as the body literally disintegrated in his arms, and for a moment, just a fleeting second, I saw the human beneath the ash, the soldier, and then the body crumbled to nothing.

Pilate backed away from me, his own terror dripping down his legs. The man looked as pale as one of the Feral, and I knew that I had won, that it was over.

"That will happen to you, to all of Rome, if you do not leave me, and my friends, alone. Do I make myself understood?"

Pilate could barely speak. Dribble bubbled from the corner of his mouth, and he just stood there, broken. He delved into his soiled toga and pulled out the spear, holding it towards me.

"Take it, please, just take it and go."

I snatched the spear from his weak fingers, and he shrank away from me.

230

As Pilate walked away, I turned back to the cave. There was just one thing left for me to do.

Darkness claimed the land once more by the time Mary appeared. I sat in a mound of ash, a pile so high that it covered my legs, and when I saw her sweet face, my tears fell thick and fast.

"Gaius, what happened?" I must have looked a sight, sitting waist deep in grey ash, my body, my face, grey with the remains of the dead, flesh streaked by the unending grief that ripped at my heart.

"I killed them... I killed them all Mary, all of them. I carried their bodies into the light, and I watched them burn."

The words tumbled from between my lips in a never-ending stream of pain. To prevent evil, I created evil, and my only way out was the greatest evil of all. When I had finished, and I could bring myself to look into my friend's face, I saw my own pain reflected back at me. I knew then, in that one moment, that I would always be a monster, because to cause such pain, to be the architect of such devastation, I could be nothing else.

"Can you forgive me?"

"It is not for me to offer forgiveness, Gaius. It is not for me to judge. What we are, what we do now, how we act now, that is what will make us, that is what matters. You had no choice here, and sometimes we have to fight evil with evil."

"Would *he* have done that?" Mary couldn't answer because there was no answer. There was no excuse for what I did that day, for the lives I destroyed, and I would pay for that crime for all of eternity.

"The spear, Gaius, do you have the spear?"

I pulled the shaft of metal out from beneath the ash.

"I have to hide it, Mary. I have to hide it somewhere he will never think to look for it, because he will come for it. No matter where I go, he will come for it."

"Then let me take it to Rome with me."

"I have an idea Mary, somewhere to hide it where he will never think to look, hidden from him, and hidden from men. But you are not going to like it."

"Tell me."

I told her about Melek, and how he came for me in the night, how he would torment me, how he would mutilate me. I told Mary how the Lion ripped open my stomach so that my insides littered the floor, and how my body healed without even so much as a scar.

"I don't understand. How can that help?"

"Because we can hide the spear, inside me."

Chapter Fourteen: It's All About The Truth

As Related By Eli

Isaiah shuffled with excitement, his fingers recording every word that Gideon spoke. Part of me wanted to rip that fucking diary out of his wrinkled hands and shred it, with my teeth, and wipe my twitching ass with it, but I felt too lost in Gideon's painful history to move. I saw Ethan watching me, his gaze so full of concern, and I had to look away. *Fuck me, don't pity me.* Something was coming, some great big fucking twat of a *thing*, I could feel it, just there out of reach, waiting for me to see it, waiting for me to recognise it, to recognise me, and it wanted to suffer.

Gideon did not take his gaze from me, and when I finally plucked up the courage to look at him, the tears that poured down his face shattered my already broken heart. Whatever truth perched precariously upon his trembling lips, it broke him, it killed him. I could see it in his face, in his eyes, the moment when he would finally tell me who I was, and I thought that I could die.

Don't tell me.

I don't want to know.

Let me live my lie.

Bollocks. I had to know, of course I had to know, after all those years of torment, all of it leading up to that point, I had to fucking know. The truth. Everything leading up to that one mind fuck, that one crucifying moment when I would cease to exist, and the real me would come alive.

233

Ethan, Isaiah, Gideon, Daniyyel. All of them looked at me, and I wanted them to fuck off. I wanted them to leave me alone. I just wanted Malachi back. I just wanted to be alone, in my castle, with my best friend.

No. I could see it, the *thing* beckoning to me, taunting me with my identity, and I had nowhere left to hide.

My mouth felt dry, and my voice sounded hoarse as it forced its way through my cracked lips.

"The spear, is it still inside you?"

Gideon shook his head. "No."

"So Mary... London..."

"Yes."

Damn him. My grief burst from between my lips in a howl of agony, years of torment and pain, of lies and secrets, of hate. I hated him for so long because of what he did, and even that turned out to be just another lie.

I felt Ethan's hand brush against me, a gesture of comfort, but I did not want it because *it* arrived, that *thing*, and now I had to face it.

"Who am I, Gideon?"

A shower of silver coins tinkled at my feet.

"Really, dear heart? Are you really that stupid?"

I heard Melek's voice, but I could not tear my eyes away from those coins, silver coins at my feet.

Everything that happened at that moment seemed to unfold in slow motion. Gideon flew out of his seat, his Vampire exploding across his features as his claws grabbed Melek by the neck and slammed him against the wall. Isaiah and Ethan shot to their feet, But Daniyyel moved in to keep the humans away from the monsters.

"You fucking cunt! How fucking dare you be here!"

"Oh, my dear Barbarian, I wouldn't dream of missing the party."

I bent down, my fingers swirling through the silver coins, my mind disconnected from reality, because in that moment I knew, I knew my real identity.

Melek didn't lift a finger against Gideon, he just smiled at him with that sickly grin that revealed the Demon within. With a scream of rage, Gideon threw Melek to the floor, and then Gideon flew on top of him, his long teeth snapping at his slender neck.

"You don't get to tell him! You don't get to be here!"

Melek laughed, a cold sound that vibrated through the floor.

"Careful, sweet cheeks, you'll do yourself an injury."

Suddenly Gideon screamed, pure agony that ripped from his mouth in a shriek of absolute terror. His clawed hands ripped at his own chest, and I saw the fear that twisted his face as his Vampire melted away, and he became the man again, a man in pain, a man afraid.

Isaiah pushed past Daniyyel and rushed to Gideon's side, pulling that immense body away from the Devil on the floor.

"Isaiah, it hurts, for the love of God Isaiah it hurts so much, I can feel it."

Isaiah cradled Gideon's head to his chest, and the old man's gaze found mine, and I felt the cold of his terror trickle down my spine, the terror of helplessness.

"For the love of God, Gideon? Well, how apt, considering that little prick is seeking out your heart." Melek picked himself up off the floor and dusted down his black suit. "Really, Eli, your floor could do with a clean, now I'll have to get a new suit, how rude."

"Melek," gasped Gideon, his lips a thin line of pain, "don't."

"Don't what? Tell Eli how he is one of the most despised figures in history? I think he has already come around to that little fact, haven't you dear heart?"

235

It was there. The *thing* was there, fucking me in the ass. Silver coins trickled between my fingers, blood money, and I knew. Even as I looked at my bastard ex-boyfriend, as I saw the truth of it written all over his pained face, I knew.

"Gideon? Is it true?"

"Yes, but let me explain."

* * * *

When we first built the Apostolic Palace, the Cappella Magna stood an unassuming chapel of unremarkable stone and marble, but Pope Sixtus IV had a profound love for the renaissance movement, and his restoration work saw the chapel transformed with paintings of the most exquisite beauty. Botticelli, Perugini, Roselli, I met them all. Such was the profound impact of that Pope's unrelenting search for artistic perfection that the faithful renamed the chapel in his honour, and history would forever know it as the Sistine Chapel.

Nothing, however, could compare to the genius of its most famed artist, brought to add his unique touch to the chapel in 1508 by the then Pope, Pope Julius II.

Michelangelo had a knack for making me laugh, and he turned out to be one hell of a good lover, passionate when I needed him to be, rough when I demanded it. He called me his muse, and there is much of me, or at least parts of me, scattered throughout his work. I used to stand and watch him paint for hours. I never tired of the sight of his muscles twitching beneath the fine olive skin of his arms as his brush danced across a canvas or caressed stone. He was a true Master, in every way that I needed him to be, but as with all those who crossed my path and dared to love me, I broke his heart, too.

I walked into the Sistine Chapel — the last time I would do so for many years — to the sound of whistling from the top of the huge scaffolding standing in the middle of the space. My Maestro lay up there, painting his magic onto the ceiling, creating a blaze of exquisite colour with every stroke of his brush. I smiled and climbed up the wooden structure with ease.

Michelangelo lay flat on his back, brush in one hand, and a wooden palette in the other.

"What are you so fucking cheerful about painter man?" He liked it when I called him that. It never failed to make him smirk, and he really did have one hell of a sexy smirk.

"I'm doing it, Gideon, I said I would."

"You little fucking shit, let me see." I crawled onto the platform and shimmied over to lie beside him. Above me, flesh already vividly realised, I saw two fingers painted with such perfection, two fingers reaching out across the void with the germ of a spark between them.

"The creation of Adam."

I started to laugh—I really couldn't help myself. That's what I loved about him the most, his insane ability to make me laugh, a pleasure long forgotten in my bitter past.

"You fucking shit, why would you paint that cunt on the ceiling of the Sistine Chapel?"

"Language, Gideon, what would God say?"

"Fuck God, he's fucked me over enough, thank you very much."

Michelangelo laughed, and I turned over and rammed my tongue down his throat, pushing my length into his open mouth until his own wet organ embraced my tongue.

"Do you kiss God with that foul mouth of yours?"

"Shut the fuck up, painter man, and answer my question."

"Well, you see that finger there? Well that's my finger, and originally the other finger was going to be your ass hole, but somehow I didn't think his Holiness would approve."

My laughter shook the platform, and I couldn't help slapping the wood surface with my hand, it made me laugh so hard.

"Hey, muscles, do you mind? You might be immortal, but if this bloody thing collapses I'm screwed."

I turned to face him, my handsome, rugged painter.

"Then I would have to turn you."

"Hey, the only thing I want to see turned is your ass. Stay still, I want to try something."

Before I could say anything, Michelangelo shimmed down the deck and started to pull my already stiffening cock from my bulging linen trousers.

"What the fuck... ahh!"

His mouth wrapped around the girth of my cock, and his tongue flicked across its throbbing head, and I brought both of my hands to grip the top of his head, ramming my length deep into his throat.

Michelangelo took my hands away from the top of his head, holding them either side of my waist as he continued to swallow me, his warm, wet mouth moving up and down my shaft in long, deliberate strokes that made me gasp. His movement began to gain momentum, his tongue frantic against my head, licking, sucking, spit running thick down my cock, but he didn't relent as I felt my balls tighten. I tried to move my hands, to stop him from bringing me to a climax, but he held my arms firm. I could have stopped him, easily, but already I felt my cock swell, and I gave in to his insatiable hunger. With a cry, I felt my spunk shoot from my cock, filling his throat and his mouth in great pumping waves of passion until I emptied myself completely into him.

"Fuck in hell, someone was keen."

Michelangelo shimmied back up the platform, his mouth tightly closed, and then he spat my load onto his wooden palette and began to mix it into his oil pigments. As I watched, he coated his brush and continued to paint the fresco with the spunk and paint concoction.

"What the fuck are you doing?"

"Adding you to my masterpiece, of course. Now you will forever be a part of this space! If I can't have your asshole up here, I can have your semen. Now, when I am long gone, every time you walk in here, you will think of me and this moment."

"You are off your fucking head."

"Yeah, maybe, but you love me anyway."

Clapping echoed around the chapel, and then a voice bellowed upwards towards me, one that I had hoped never to hear again.

"Bravo, Barbarian, nice to see that you can still entertain."

Before the last syllable left his filthy fucking lips, I fell from the top of the platform to land at his feet.

The bastard looked good, standing there in tightly fitted black leather pants that clung to his bulge and a white see through shirt that accentuated his erect nipples. He wore thigh length black boots, and his black hair lay slicked back across his magnificent head. I never thought to see those eyes again, to feel their yellow fire burning into my soul, but there they were, fucking me over yet again.

"I must say, Gaius, eternity suits you. Looking good!"

"It's Gideon, you prick, what the fuck are you doing here? How did you find me?" I glanced up towards the platform and saw Michelangelo looking down on us. I shook my head at him, an urgent little gesture, praying that he would stay out of the way.

"Oh don't stress out, *Gideon,* your little play thing means nothing to me, though I must admit, I have always fancied having my portrait done. What do you think? My left side? I always fancied that my left side is best, don't you?"

"How did you find me, Melek?"

"Oh please, have you forgotten who I am? Really, dear heart, you're not exactly discreet, are you?" He brushed the side of my face with a long index finger, and I could not help but shiver at his touch. "Don't trouble yourself, Barbarian, I'm not here for the spear, not yet."

"Then what the fuck do you want?"

"Something has... come up, something that I thought you should see. Come with me, there is someone I would like you to meet."

Melek led the way, and the last I saw of Michelangelo was his confused face hanging over the edge of the platform. Yet another regret to add to my long, long list. I never said goodbye.

As we walked through the marble halls of the Vatican, I felt the chill of the stone permeate my hard flesh, or it may have been the presence of that creature walking next to me.

"What the fuck is all this about Melek? Where are you taking me?"

"Somewhere where Angels fear to tread, my strapping Barbarian, to meet an old friend."

"I'm surprised you don't wither away in here, or that God doesn't shit on your head from a great height."

Melek skidded to a stop, his yellow eyes blazing into my cold flesh. That had touched a nerve.

"Have you forgotten who I was? I was an Angel once, remember?"

"Thrown out by your own father."

"Yes," he boomed as he stormed ahead. "And I wasn't the only one. Keep up, Barbarian."

I had to wonder why he chose that direction. Every bit of stone, every step, every piece of marble ransacked from Rome, I knew them all, I had helped build it, so I knew exactly where his footsteps led, towards the Apostolic Palace.

"Why are you taking me to the Stanze?"

"Patience, dear heart. I must say, it's so nice to be back. You know, I could tell you a story or two about this place. My, the Borgia's knew how to party! The things that went on in that..."

"Raphael is working up there."

Melek turned and grinned. "I gave him the day off. Come on."

The apartments, like much of the Vatican at that time, felt the loving caress of skilled craftsmen during an extensive renovation programme. Pope Julius II was a wonderful man, but like all men, he could not help his vanity, and he remained determined to out-decorate the works of his predecessor, and rival, Pope Alexander VI. As a result, artists of the greatest renown added their unique skills to the walls of the Vatican. Julius had tasked Raphael with the renovation of his private apartments, and the smell of pigment and medium filled my nostrils as Melek barged into the Popes rooms.

Huge swathes of cloth covered the walls and floors, draped across tables and trestles in a cob-web of billowing white. A huge, glistening mahogany desk, enriched with gold decoration, seemed to grow out of the centre of the room, and standing behind it was Pope Julius II. He smiled at me as I rushed in to take his hand, my lips brushing his fingers as a show of respect. I liked him. He had a very kind, very old face. He also understood me, and he didn't judge me, he just listened, the two of us sharing many an hour steeped in history and conversation.

"I do hope you don't expect *me* to kiss your ring?"

"Melek, I would rather you kissed my ass!"

I could not help but stifle a laugh at the Pope's quip. He was known for his sharp wit, and his acid tongue, and I liked that most about him.

"Oh how terribly droll, how terribly clever, moving on."

"Gaius... I mean Gideon, sorry, sometimes I forget, don't you know. I'm so sorry about this, really I am. You don't have to go through with this you know."

Poor Julius, he looked so concerned, but I didn't have a fucking clue what he meant.

"It would help old friend, if I knew what was going on."

Julius shot Melek a look that could wilt an erection at fifty feet.

"You haven't told him?"

"Now, dear heart, and spoil your sanctimonious apologies? And why would I deny myself that little pleasure? Do go on."

Julius lifted the gold Pectoral Cross from his chest, the red of the Rubies set into its heart sparkling like fresh blood.

"We built the Vatican as a doorway to God so that we may be close to him..."

"And show off your obscene wealth and live in the lap of luxury..."

"Melek, if you have nothing good to say, just shut the fuck up!"

"Do you speak to your congregation with that mouth? Now there is something that I would like to see!"

"Do you always have to be such a twat?"

Melek smirked at me, and it made me flush with heat despite myself. How could I forget the underlying monster that squirmed beneath that smile?

"It is an art form, Barbarian, one honed over centuries of abandonment."

"Abandonment my ass," spat Julius, "have you forgotten our many conversations?"

I looked at Julius, shocked by his statement. "Excuse me? You talk with the Devil?"

"And why shouldn't he? He talks to you, does he not?"

"As I was saying! We built the Vatican to be our doorway to God, but, on occasion, we must consult with... him.

Christianity has been plagued with corruption throughout its tumultuous history—you know this, Gaius, better than anyone. Do I really need to bring up the Borgias?"

"I told you."

"Shut up, Melek. Go on, Julius."

"This site upon which we built our shrine, is the site of much atrocity. St Peter himself died on this ground."

"Ah yes... I remember it well!"

"Really, Melek?"

"Just saying, Barbarian."

"So, to understand God, we must also understand the Devil, must we not? For light cannot exist without the dark. So we allowed him to install a door, a direct link to hell if you will. Only I have access, and it is a terrible burden, known only to each Pope, and one that we keep secret until the day we die."

"Oh yes dear heart, God forbid that you should have a civilised conversation with me. Tell me, does God pop in for a chat at all? No? Well, there's a surprise."

I had to admit it, Melek was right. God did not speak to the Pope or any of those who showed him such devotion. God remained but a matter of faith, of belief in something unobtainable.

"Well, quite. So, on occasion, we converse, on matters of history, religion, or particular... cases."

"I'm sorry? Cases? I don't understand."

Julius caressed the golden cross, refracted light splattering across his white robe in a dapple of red. I had never seen the man so troubled. He glanced at Melek, and something passed between them, some kind of mutual understanding that left me feeling like the odd man out, that something important escaped me.

"Yes. Sometimes... very rare you understand... something comes up that we need to... consult on."

"What? And I am one of these cases?"

Julius laughed gently, a kind sound that immediately seemed to sooth my worried soul. No wonder the man became Pope — he had that effect on people.

"No, my friend, no, not you, never you. This involves... someone else, someone from your past. We decided, that is Melek and I decided, because of the nature of the problem, and because of who, what you are, that you should be consulted."

I snapped. I couldn't help it. All that cloak and daggers shit, it gripped my tit. I was more of a stab now and ask questions later kind of guy.

"Will someone please just tell me what the fuck is going on!"

"Ah, there he is, my little Barbarian. Well then, Julius, if you please?"

Julius kissed the ruby at the centre of the cross, and then he walked over to the wall where faint outlines of cherubs awaited Raphael's immaculate touch, and he pressed the cross against the plaster. To my astonishment, a door appeared in the wall, a golden door studded with precious stones that glittered with an internal light, dazzling to behold.

"Ostentatious anyone?" I quipped in a sad attempt to hide my nerves.

"I do try, Barbarian, I do try. Come on then, let's follow the brimstone road!"

I tried to open the door, my hand wrapped around the ornately carved, golden handle, but it would not move. Melek brushed me aside.

"Allow me dear heart, after all, beast before beauty, as they say."

The door swung open at his touch, a theatrical belch of smoke hissing through the opening. Poor Julius paled, and he smiled at me weakly as I walked into the bank of roiling smoke, the door closing behind me to swallow me in darkness.

In my head, I expected a long, steep staircase of roughly hewn rock, flanked by spewing flames and the stench of sulphur. I walked into a garden. Huge trees, unlike any that I had seen, flanked a rough path that wound into a vista of lush green foliage with leaves bigger than a man, reaching into a sky of the most perfect blue. Colour exploded throughout in the form of huge waxen flowers that opened their deep throats to the sky, water droplets sparkling against their immense petals like diamonds. It took me completely by surprise, and it took my breath away.

"Wow. So not what I was expecting."

"Fire? Brimstone? Yeah, I get that a lot. Hell is a state of mind dear heart, not a place. When I released those dark souls from their captivity in Heaven, I built them a place of beauty, a place from my happier days on Earth, when beasts the size of mountains roamed that virgin ground. I am many things, Gaius, but I reserve my cruelty for those who deserve it."

"But demons, there are demons?"

His face twisted into a scowl, a dark thing that masked his immaculate beauty.

"That is Father's doing. He denies us the beauty of the Angels and inflicts upon us the image of the damned. Some punishment, do you not think? Such beauty, crippled by such ugliness. Have no fear Barbarian, it is a state of being that I intend to rectify. One day."

We walked through that forest of a garden, as two friends would walk on a sunny day, and it felt so surreal, to be at the side of such fathomless evil, and yet feel so at peace. The dichotomy of it fucked up my head. "You continue to surprise me."

"Why? Because I am not the monster you would all have me be?"

"Oh, you are, but you have... layers."

"It bothers you, doesn't it, my little conversations with the Pope."

"No... yes, I don't fucking know. I don't know what to think anymore."

"Good start. It is funny, is it not, that God does not show himself to those who love him most, and yet, it is my existence that fuels belief. How can you believe in God if you do not believe in me? That is why I talk to him, to Julius, to all the Popes. It gives them faith."

"But why?"

He turned on me then, and I saw the beast ripple across his features, a flicker of the thing that lurked beneath, and it still terrified me.

"Because it will hurt all the fucking more when that shit comes down to Earth to face me, and I kill him. The Church is mine. They just don't know it yet."

"The more I know you, the more I realise I don't understand you. You are one complex man."

"Thank you, I will take that as the compliment that was not implied. And you, my friend, my immortal Barbarian, are just about to find out how *grey* black and white can be."

Without warning, the forest opened out into a vast grassy plane, a warm breeze fingering the blades of long yellowing grass in great wavering ripples that billowed across the expanse. In the centre of the field sat a large wooden barn, its gabled roof exposed in parts to the elements, a dilapidated mass of old, twisted, decaying wood that looked incapable of supporting its own weight.

"What is this place? Why is it so different here? It feels so, unloved."

"Hell is different for everyone. As I said, we make our own Hell, and for this individual, this represents his lost love. He used to meet his lover in this place, and they could never venture out of that barn together for fear of discovery, and so it became his prison. The only thing holding it together is their undying love for each other. Excuse me while I puke."

"What happened?" I felt the pit of my stomach churn, for it reminded myself of my own experience, my own forbidden love for a soldier.

"Father discovered them."

I felt sick. So many parallels to my own life, to the pain that saw me flee from my home, and something else. Inside that building lay a man that he wanted me to meet, someone from my past, someone who loved another man, a love forbidden, a love discovered. I could barely put one foot in front of another, it scared me so, the thought of what Melek wanted to show me.

"His father discovered him?"

Melek stopped. He turned to look at me, the yellow of his eyes filled with such a profound sadness that my flesh ran cold.

"No. My Father discovered them."

The world fell out of my asshole. If my mouth opened any wider, I could have swallowed that barn in one gulp.

"Fuck me seven ways to Sunday..."

"I already have, dear heart. So, are you ready for this?"

No, I was not ready for it, I would never be ready for it. Every muscle in my body told me to turn around and run, to head back into that forest, to run through that door, back into the Vatican, back to the safety of Michelangelo's arms. Yet, part of me needed to know. Melek had brought me there for a reason, and no matter what the consequence, I had to see it through.

"Ready for what?"

"To make history, dear heart, to make history."

The front of the barn consisted of two huge doors, rotten with time, barely clinging to their rusty hinges. Set within one of the big doors sat a smaller one, and Melek pushed it inwards and beckoned for me to enter.

The inside had been beautiful once. Someone had made an attempt to make it a home, and furniture, once shimmering with a layer of gold, lay faded and worn, decaying. The upper level of the barn had long since collapsed in a tangle of rotting wood, and the whole place felt used up, hollow somehow.

One point of light, a shaft like the finger of God himself, broke through the shattered roof to illuminate a crisp, white bed, and lying on the bed, his arms crossed over his chest, lay a man so beautiful that I gasped. A man that I knew.

I thought the world would collapse around me. I thought that it had to be some joke, some cruel trick to torment me, to remind me of my life, that the Devil had finally beaten me into submission. I clutched at my knees, bile filling my throat, stinging my mouth, and my tears fell fierce down my face as I stared at him, at his beauty, at his sadness.

"What the fuck is this" I gasped, barely able to stand on my own two feet.

"Is he not a sleeping beauty? Here, come closer, look into his face. Tell me who you see."

I dragged my body to the side of the bed and forced my eyes to look down on him. Even though his eyelids remained tightly closed, I knew them to be the brightest blue, for I had looked into those eyes, at the moment when he killed himself.

"Judas. I see Judas."

"Yes, my Barbarian friend. Judas. The man who betrayed Christ. The man who loved Christ. He went to Heaven, you know. They say that suicide is a sin, but that is man's rule, not God's, and he was doing God's work, even if he did not understand it."

I could not tear my gaze away from Judas. His strong cheekbones, his thick, plump lips, his muscular arms, a chest chiselled and deep, his pale skin clinging to the hard musculature of his body. So beautiful in life, and even more so in death.

"You said that he met his lover in here, that this was the only place they could meet..."

"Yes. Even in Heaven, they could not stay away from each other, and they paid the price."

"Why? Why are you showing me this? What has *this* got to do with me?"

I felt my anger rising, my outrage, my own bitter experience tinging my emotions, clouding my judgment, and it was all I could do not tear that place apart with my bare hands. My heart broke inside my chest. I could feel it ripping away from my ribs, the pain of that man lying on that bed filling my empty soul with despair, his despair, the agony of forbidden love. A love that even Heaven itself did not understand.

It pissed me off. God made man. To be homosexual was not a choice, it was not a decision — we were made that way. Therefore, God made the homosexual. So how fucking dare he deny us!

"I have a difficult choice to make, Gaius. Oh don't look at me like that, Gideon, Gaius, fuck that. I have a choice to make. Father threw him out of Heaven, much as he did to me, and I am expected to keep him here, in Hell."

"So what's the problem?"

"What's the problem? What's the fucking problem? You surprise me, *Gideon*, perhaps you are not the man I took you for."

"For fuck's sakes, Melek just piss it out, will you! You drag my ass to hell and then show me a man I once watched hang himself! What am I to do about it?"

"Well dear heart, that is pretty much up to you."

"I'm sorry? What?"

"This man, Judas, is one of the most despised men in history. His name is forever linked with betrayal. Yet, we know that is not the case, don't we? They planned it all, together, to *save* mankind... sshheesh. But he has committed no sin. So he loved another man. Tough shit, move on, buy the manuscript. If that is his only crime, he has no place here, and I cannot, I will not take him."

My head exploded. This was not the Devil that I knew, the cruel, calculating, evil creature that tortured me in Judea. He saw my face, and he laughed.

"Let me re-phrase that. I will take him, if I have to, but really, darling, why waste an opportunity to piss off God?"

There he was. "I don't give a rat's ass about your motives Melek, and I don't know what you expect me to do about it."

"Don't you? How did you feel, that day, as he watched you flog his lover?"

I saw that moment, as I saw that moment every day of my existence, as a vivid memory of blood and torn flesh, with his eyes, Judas's eyes, imploring me to stop. I saw so much pain in his face that day, so much grief, and I knew that I broke him, that my actions broke him, and I could never erase that image from my memory.

"I felt guilty. I felt his pain."

"And how did you feel as you watched him hang himself?"

"Guilty! I felt guilty, all right? I took his love away from him! I was the architect of his pain! He killed himself because of what I did! Is that what you wanted to hear? Are you satisfied now?"

"And what do you feel about him now?"

I looked down at Judas, at his beautiful face, so at peace as he lay there, a Fallen Angel, and I wanted him. No words could describe the emotions that flushed through my veins, that pounded through my heart as I gazed upon his perfect form, and I just knew that I wanted him.

"He is not mine to have, Melek, he belongs to another."

"He belongs to no one now, Gideon. He is alone, his love is gone, and when he awakes, he will remember nothing of who he was, Father has already seen to that. All he will see is a decrepit building, and that is where he will spend the rest of eternity, as a mindless, empty creature, in a mindless, empty place. They say that God works in mysterious ways, but if you ask me, God is a cruel motherfucker."

My mouth felt so dry. My entire body trembled. Every night, every day, every moment of my existence, all of it led back to him, to Judas hanging from the tree, and me, powerless to save him. Now, in Hell, I could save him.

"I am going to leave you now, Gideon—show yourself out, won't you?" Melek turned and started to walk away, his boots clicking on the wooden floor. Then he stopped, his long, slender finger against his lips.

"There is a caveat to all this. Of course, there would be. One day, I don't know how, and I don't know when, but one day his one true love will return to him. The Universe is a wonderful thing, Gideon, a powerful thing, but there is nothing more powerful in Father's creation than love, and love always finds a way. So listen to me, and remember my words. If you chose this, if you decide to accept my... gift... one day he will be taken away from you, then, and only then, will he remember. Of course, I will be there, waiting, because when that day arrives, Father will not be far behind."

"Why? Why should he care? If he made them?"

"What did your father do when he found you in the arms of another man?"

"He killed the other man."

"Exactly. Goodbye, my immortal Barbarian, until the next time."

Melek stepped through the door, and I stood looking down upon the most beautiful man I had ever seen.

From within my pants, I pulled out a small golden flask, a flask that I kept with me at all times, a flask that contained the blood of a Fallen God. I sat on the edge of the bed, my arm brushing his muscular shoulder, sending an electric thrill through my body at his touch, and I knew then that I could not turn away from him.

My trembling finger brushed a strand of jet black hair from his smooth marble forehead, and I leaned over and pressed my lips against his, feeling the warmth of his flesh against my own cold hardness. As I watched, his eyes started to flicker open, and they saw me.

My teeth flashed down, slicing through my gums and my lower lip, and then I felt them slide into the soft flesh of his neck, his blood pumping into my mouth in a blaze of hot excitement. My head filled with him, all of him, his life, his love, his death, his unending pain and need, and I drank him until he lay nearly drained, feeling his heartbeat lessen in my mouth, his life pouring away with every greedy gulp.

It made me hard. My cock pressed against the fabric of my pants, demanding freedom, a throbbing yearning to know him, but my work remained as yet unfinished.

I placed one hand beneath his gorgeous head, and I lifted him slightly as I placed the golden flask to his lips with the second. Judas would be no ordinary Vampire, and he would be no Feral, he would be like me, Menarche, magnificent. The flask poured its contents between his blue lips, and once emptied, I lowered him back onto the bed as the transformation started to take hold.

He would awake anew, and I would be the first thing he saw through his new eyes. I would have to give him a name, an identity, a new life, a life in my arms. I would show him the world, with all its wonders, and we would build a home together, he and I, two Menarche, equal in our state of being, equal in our love of each other, and together, we would see, and do, everything.

He sat up suddenly, his eyes wide, seeing the world for the first time, and I knew how he felt, for it was a wonder that I never tired of.

"Where am I?"

His voice, a voice that I had not heard for almost two thousand years, so lyrical, so sensual, it made my flesh explode with excitement.

"Somewhere we don't belong."

"And where else should we be?"

"Somewhere better."

"Who are you?"

"Someone who wants to love you for all of eternity, if you will let me."

"And who am I?"

I brought my hand up to his beatific face, my thumb running across his sensual lips, and I leaned in, wondering what his response would be. His eyes searched my face, so quizzical, but he did not flinch. My lips collided with his, and for a moment I felt him resist, as though uncertain what to do, but then his lips smashed against mine, and his tongue searched out my lips, my tongue, my throat, and he tasted me for the first time. Eventually, and with reluctance, I pulled myself away, afraid that I could not stop, afraid to let him take me in that place, in that Hell where we did not belong.

"Who am I?"

"You are my lover, and your name is Eli."

* * * *

There it was. For all to see. Judas. My name was Judas. The most despised figure in history, ever. Flashes of him exploded through my head, of his life, of his pain, of his love, of his death. I felt that moment when he tied that noose around his own neck, the despair that pushed him over the edge of sanity as he leapt into oblivion, as his neck snapped and extinguished his life. I felt it all because I was him.

Tears poured down Gideon's face, and in all the very many years that I had known him, that I had loved him, I had never seen that look upon his face, a look of complete and utter loss, a look so full of terrible pain, a look that cried a thousand apologies.

"Well, isn't this cozy? Shall we all clasp hands and sing songs? But I'm not here for Eli, hell no, that ship has long sailed. Hello, Ethan."

"No!" Daniyyel blazed before Melek, the silver of his wings flashing with light. "That was not the agreement!"

Melek's face darkened, his mouth rippling with layers of teeth that outshone Daniyyel's wings.

"Fuck off, *brother*. You broke the law when you freed Malachi, I get to choose my own recompense, not you."

Never had I seen the Angel so powerless. His wings folded back in defeat, fading into his body, and he turned to look at me, and I saw upon him such a look of sorrow and despair that marred his beauty.

For an old man, Isaiah could move bloody fast. He stood before Melek, fearless and defiant.

"You will leave my son alone!"

Melek looked down on him, but Isaiah did not move so much as a muscle, so brave and defiant against the Devil.

"*Your* son? Bit of a stretch there, don't you think? He is Redivivus! The bastard reborn."

I looked at Ethan, so beautiful, from the moment I'd found him, buried in his own filth, and I felt him, inside of me, a recognition of something so distant, of something lost.

Melek looked past Isaiah, his gaze piercing into me with hatred.

"Father threw you out of Heaven for loving a man, for loving *him*."

The ground shook. Isaiah fell backwards as the earth heaved, and I rushed forward to catch the old man in my arms. A sound filled the open space of Alte, a terrific rumble that shook every stone in my little castle, and Melek started to laugh.

"See! There he is! Father is coming!"

The sound intensified to a tremendous squeal, like metal twisting, then, with a bang that sent us all flying across the floor, the wall behind Melek exploded in a shower of stone and dust.

Chapter Fifteen: Death Is Just The Beginning

As Related By Eli

My ears rang like the fucking bells of Notre Dame. I pulled myself out from beneath a large chunk of masonry, dust so heavy in the air that it felt like a solid smog. Someone coughed nearby, a thick retching sound that I could almost taste. Gideon lay half buried beneath one of the huge oak doors, blown off of its ancient hinges by the explosion, huge chunks of masonry pinning his semi-conscious form beneath the debris. Ethan crawled across the ruined floor towards his father.

"Papa?"

"I'm fine, I'm fine."

Of Daniyyel and Melek, there was no sign.

Through the gaping hole in the side of my home, light suddenly pierced the night, light so white, and so bright that it hurt my eyes. I brought my arms up to cover my face and struggled towards Gideon, reaching out towards his crushed body, but he waved me away. He lifted the load from around his waist with arms bulging beneath the strain. Pain etched deeply into his face, and as he pulled his legs from beneath the door, he clutched his chest.

"Are you all right?"

"Yes, Eli, get Ethan out of here, now."

"Ding dong! Anyone home?"

I knew that voice, that sly, vicious, monstrous voice. Morbius.

I turned towards Ethan as he pulled his father off the floor. "Move, upstairs, now." I didn't know what good that would do, but it made me feel better for saying it.

Ethan started to complain, but Isaiah knew that voice too, and he knew what it meant.

"Ethan, we must go, Ethan, now, please."

Morbius' voice echoed through the dust. "I rang the bell, but no one answered. Come out, come out, wherever you are! You know, it's not polite to keep your visitors waiting."

Isaiah dragged Ethan up the staircase. Ethan's eyes, his beautiful emerald green eyes, met mine, and I saw so many unsaid words in that look, so much that we needed to say to each other, but we had no time.

Alte lay exposed to the world, her doors, her wonderful façade, shattered into dust and chunks of crumbling brick. As I edged towards the gaping hole, Gideon grabbed my shoulder, pulling me away from the ragged damage.

"Don't go out there, don't let them see you."

"It's better than them coming in here, they can't get near Ethan."

"I know that. Listen to me, before it's too late. Take Ethan and his father, go to London. Find Mary."

"What..."

"Boys, boys, boys, now really, get your fucking tight asses out here... well not you Gideon, you are not really that tight..."

Before I could stop him, Gideon crawled over the rubble and stood in the light, his massive frame outlined black against the white. I crawled over to the side, my hands digging into stone, and I looked out over the edge of the rubble at a site that chilled me to the bone.

Parked before Alte, its surface mottled green, sat a huge tank, the ground torn up beneath its massive treads. Morbius sat over the gun at the point where it emerged from the turret, his long legs swinging beneath the guns long length. He reminded me of a child sitting on a swing, but there remained nothing childish about his countenance, with his long black locks of jet black hair coiling around his shoulders. Even through the settling dust and the bright light, I could see the fierce green of his eyes blazing through the fallout, searching me out.

Behind him, standing on the turret, stood the Mother and Father, glistening from head to foot in black leather. She had one hand draped around his shoulders, while her other hand massaged his engorged dick, bulging tightly through his leather pants. It never failed to make me shudder, the site of them, so far removed from humanity with their half-formed features and inky, expressionless eyes, and yet, their son, Morbius, remained one of the most beautiful creatures I had ever seen. The dichotomy of evil.

Tied to the end of the tank's long gun lay a body, a naked human sausage wrapped around the metal barrel, his skin blistered and smouldering from the heat of the gun's discharge. His blond hair lay matted against his bloodied scalp, and even through the burns that transformed his once handsome face into a mass of weeping sores, I recognised him. Hans, the soldier Malachi had once possessed to gain access to Wewelsburg Concentration camp. Hans used to reside in my dungeon, and now the poor bastard formed some grotesque compass on the butt end of a fucking tank.

"Gideon! Fuck, you look rough. Bad day, hunky?"

Morbius brought something to his mouth, a pinkish red mass of flesh, and as he ripped chunks of meat from the object and chewed, I recognised it as a hand. I think it belonged to Hans, though I couldn't be sure.

"Do forgive me, I'm fucking starving, and well, Mother dearest was never very good in that department, were you Mother?"

Gideon shuffled down the pile of rubble that once made up my front door. The man looked in pain, I could see it etched on his face, in his every move, in the tightness of his flexing muscles, but he stood there, defiant, magnificent.

"Fuck off before I ram your head up you fucking ass, you and your fucking freak show."

Morbius threw his beautiful head back and laughed, the sound echoing around the clearing like a death knell, the monster laughing at my front door. He had knocked, and he had let himself in.

"Such eloquence, such artistry, such a wordsmith. And I know what else you can do with that great big tongue of yours. You know, you are one of the fortunate, to have lived so long, to be part of such an exclusive club, to have *learned* so much... know what I mean?"

"Say what you have to say and fuck off."

"Mother, tell him." He took another bite from the lump of flesh in his hand, his plump lips sucking the meat off the finger bones.

The Mother disentangled herself from the Father, sliding her long tongue across his cheek. She moved like liquid, so smooth, so oily, her limbs all slithering at once, and the sight of her sickened me. There stood the Mother of Demons, and she could shoot monsters from her cunt like a child shoots peas from a straw.

"Well, my sweets, it's like this you see? We want the boy. Just bring him to us and we will leave you alone. Oh, and the spear, of course we want the spear."

"It's not here, and you will never, ever find it. And as for Eli? He goes nowhere."

Morbius snorted, thick strands of bloodied snot shooting from his nose. He wiped the mess away from his face, then licked the back of his hand.

"Eli?" he laughed, blowing thick, unctuous bubbles as he spoke. "What the fuck do I want with that little prick? No, I want Ethan, bring me Ethan."

A flash of confusion rippled across Gideon's face, and I felt it too at the mention of Ethan. How the fuck could he possibly know about Ethan?

"For fuck sakes, Eli, come out, I know you are squatting there like you are taking a shit. Come out, handsome, I won't bite... yet."

I moved to Gideon's side, never once taking my gaze away from Morbius. To see such evil in the body of something so magnificent stood an affront to creation, and he remained an affront to everything in existence. Something touched my hand, and I glanced down. To my astonishment, I found Gideon's hand wrapped in mine, his fingers firmly wrapped around me, and for a moment I forgot the monsters at my door because Gideon held my hand.

"Ah look, how touching. But he doesn't belong to you, does he Gideon? Do you remember, Eli, what I said to you in the Black Vatican, when I said that you are the greatest monster of them all? How right was I! It is a privilege to stand before you, Judas, the great betrayer."

"You think you know so much, and you know fuck all."

"Oh, really?" He threw the severed hand at me, and it landed at my feet, knuckles and finger bones visible through gristly flesh. "Handy snack, you should try it some time. This soldier, Hans, he was in your house. He saw you. He saw Ethan. It's all in the flesh, you know, every detail. How else do you think we found your little... abode. Oh I'm sorry, did I scratch the paintwork? Life's a bitch isn't it?"

Hans squirmed on the barrel, nothing but a pained whimper squeaking through his blistered lips. I pulled myself from Gideon, and in a blink, I had Han's head in my hands, and I twisted his head sharply until it snapped with a loud crack, putting the miserable human out of his misery.

"Ha! Bravo, Eli, bravo, such compassion. So where was I? Ah yes, it's all about the flesh. I saw it, in Gideon's blood, I saw you, weeping, crying as you watched your one true love thrashed to within an inch of his life, and by the man you would call lover! Irony, got to love it. Do you know what else I saw?"

Morbius jumped down from the tank. He stood so close to me that I could almost feel the bulge of his cock pressing against me through his tight black leather pants. Once, so very long ago, we had been lovers, the three of us.

"I saw him, Eli, there upon the cross. I saw the moment that Gaius Cassius Longinus speared him in the side, I saw the miracle of everlasting life that his blood offered. I saw him, Eli, his face, the face of a God, as Hans saw him, here in your shit hole of a castle, so I have come for him, to make of him my pet."

"Over my dead body."

"With pleasure."

I felt the blow of his hand against my chest, a sudden blow that nearly shattered my ribs. My back slammed against the wall of Alte, but it was my Vampire that slid to the floor, my teeth and talons extended, and my inner monster ready to fight.

Gideon hunkered down on his knee, his own Vampire poised to strike, but Morbius just laughed.

"There he is! The first Vampire! Wow, I'm so unimpressed I nearly shit myself. But really, did you think that I came alone?"

Morbius raised his fingers to his plump lips, and then he whistled, a shrill, piercing sound that tore through the night.

They moved in a line, filing out from the tree, moving around the tank until they formed a cordon of dead flesh. The Feral stood looking at us through red eyes that blazed from within their pallid faces, their thin, emaciated arms crossed over their shallow chests, one hand draped over the other with their long, spindly fingers dripping down, twitching. Each one had a Quellor Demon perched upon their shoulder, a bulbous mass of pulsating evil with a single yellow eye that burned with hatred. The Mother gave birth to those things, placing them on the backs of the Feral to control them, making them virtually impossible to kill.

At least twenty of them stood before us.

Gideon turned to me, and I knew exactly what that look said. We were fucked. Us against twenty Quellor controlled Ferals, against Morbius and his satanic parents. We didn't stand a fucking chance.

"Call them," he whispered, "we must call them."

The thought of it sickened me, because what he suggested was nothing short of a death sentence.

"Call them, Eli, we have no choice."

He was right. The two of us could not take them all, and we needed time, time to get Ethan and his father away to safety.

We called them in our minds, our inner voices reaching out to those who dwelt in the darkness, those lost children less fortunate than ourselves. They would have no choice but to obey our command, the summons of a Menarche, and they would come, and they would die for us, die because of us. Yet more blood to add to my already soaking hands.

The Mother squatted down and patted the bald head of the nearest Feral. "Now play nicely boys, and bring me their heads!"

The Feral moved as one, a lumbering sea of languid grey flesh, of red burning eyes, and yellow eyes of hatred perched upon their backs. The creatures pulsed upon their shoulders, their vile, squirming bodies filling with their mother's words, willing their hosts on, and we stood helpless.

Gideon picked up a plank of wood, and I picked up a length of twisted steel, and together we launched ourselves into that sea of grey, screaming into the night.

I brought the steel down on the nearest head, and it split with a loud crack beneath my fury. Gideon swung the wood across another, severing the head in a gush of black blood and sinew.

"Oh bravo!" clapped Morbius with glee, sitting between his parents with a leg draped across each of them as they watched the unfolding melee. "Good shot sir! A palpable hit! Bravo!"

"Eli!"

Gideon lay on his back, grey limbs and white teeth snapping at his flesh. I felt the itch between my shoulder blades, and as I raised myself into the air, I realised for the first time what that sensation was, the ghost memory of my lost Angel wings.

I plummeted to the ground, the metal in my hands spinning, and I knocked three of the bastards from Gideon's chest with a crunch of bone and a spray of blood. I grabbed the fourth one by the head and lifted him screaming into the air, throwing him at the Mother with all my strength, sending the two of them sprawling across the turret of the tank.

Morbius howled with rage. He picked up the stricken Feral and held him above his head, while the others turned slowly to watch him as he pulled the poor creature in half, blood and rotten innards spilling down his face in a river of putrescent gore. Bits of stomach and intestines slithered down his face as black fluids poured over his eyes and over his mouth. His long, lascivious tongue lapped at the grunge, sliding over his lower and upper lips, tasting the creature that thrashed in his arms.

With a piercing howl, Morbius threw the torso at me, and the abdomen at Gideon. The body hit me so hard that I crashed to the floor next to Gideon, who did his best to struggle out from beneath the twitching limbs. The torso half grabbed at me, the Feral wild and slathering, teeth snapping at my neck. Strands of flesh started to wriggle out of the torn remains of the body, reaching out towards the legs as the thing began to pull itself together.

I grabbed at the Quellor Demon on the Feral's back, squeezing the vile thing between my fingers, my thumb pressing into its one yellow eye, which exploded in a black mess beneath my nail. The Feral howled, and its teeth sank into my neck.

Pain shot through my body as it ripped at my throat, my own blood pumping into his face as I felt my skin tear and rip. Blood exploded across me, cold black blood that sprayed across my body and my face as the wood pierced the Feral's chest. The Vampire fell limp across my body, and standing above me stood Ethan, a wooden stake in his big, strong hands. He pulled the Feral from my body and helped me to my feet, as Isaiah helped Gideon.

"You shouldn't be out here."

"Shut the fuck up and fight!"

Ethan spun around, just as another Feral launched himself into the air, fangs and talons extended towards the gorgeous hunk of flesh. Ethan threw the stake with such force that it pierced the Feral's chest, exploding out of its rotting back in an explosion of blood that sent the creature sprawling to the ground.

"Eli, where are they?" cried Gideon desperately.

"They'll come, just keep those grey bastards back!"

The Feral lunged towards us as Morbius clapped with glee. With a howl of defiance, Gideon ran forward and plucked a Feral off its feet and swung him around into the charging mass, sending grey limbs and grey bodies to the ground in a heap of writhing dead.

Morbius got to his feet up on the turret. "Mother, Father, let's finish this."

As one, the three Menarche leapt from the top of the tank and landed before us. We shrank back, and I pushed my way to the front, shielding the two humans with my body... for all the good it would do them.

"Aww, how adorable, look, Morbius, my son, see how the betrayer defends his pets."

"Yes, Mother, I have eyes, you stupid fucking bitch." The Mother withered beneath his scorn and backed away slightly. "You see Eli, even my own parents are afraid of me, so what makes you any different?"

Behind them gathered the Feral, their bodies swaying hypnotically as the Mother swayed, their red eyes pulsing with hunger.

"I'm not afraid of you, Morbius, I pity you."

He wiped the remains of the blood from his face, flicking off bits of gristle and gore.

"Pity me? Oh, now this is something I just have to hear."

"Because you are nothing but Melek's bitch."

His wide smile faded slowly, and I saw the anger building behind his emerald green eyes.

"I am nobody's bitch!" he spat, phlegm spraying across my face.

"Then stop this madness!" Isaiah pushed his way to the front, a tiny old man against the raging Demon, and I loved him for it. "Just stop it, leave them alone, forget about the spear."

"And do what, old man? Grow sweet peas?"

"Be happy. Go out into this wonderful world and be happy. Live, love, find your own version of Eden again. You don't have to do as Melek says, you don't have to do this."

Morbius looked down upon Isaiah, but I could not read the expression upon his face. It was almost as though, just for that smallest moment in time, he was actually considering Isaiah's words. He snapped out of it in an instant, and before I could move, his hand wrapped around Isaiah's throat.

"Don't you ever mention love to me, *ever.*"

"Papa!" I had to pull Ethan back, and I pushed him into Gideon's arms as I launched myself at Morbius. My talons flew at his neck, and we fell backwards into the Mother and Father. All I could see was his face, laughing at me, taunting me, and then my fingers were in his eyes, scratching at his skin, my teeth just inches from his neck.

All around me exploded in grey and black leather. I saw Gideon fly at the Mother, I saw Ethan reach for a brick and attack the Father, and I saw Isaiah holding up a cross against the horde of Feral. They were going to die. Gideon stood pinned against the tank, the Mother slicing into his chest with a knife. Ethan lay on the floor, the Father pinning him to the ground with a booted foot. And Isaiah, poor Isaiah, he stood surrounded by Feral, grey limbs slashing out towards him, ripping at his coat as he desperately tried to fend them off with nothing more than a little wooden cross.

I never thought it would end like that. Had I endured that much, only to see it all ripped away from me in a frenzy of tooth and claw? I wanted to be human once, to live, and to love as a human. But, in that moment of pure clarity, in that dark second before the extinguishing of the light, I realised that being a Vampire was the best thing that could ever have happened to me. To live such a long life. To have loved for hundreds of years. To have seen so much of the world. All things beyond the human experience. It took me until that one moment to achieve that epiphany, a moment too late.

They came out of the trees, skulking through the shadows, my dark children, the forgotten remnants of our shameful lineage, Feral Vampires summoned by our call. The night erupted with their shrill, inhuman cries as they launched themselves upon their controlled brethren, dragging the unsuspecting creatures away from Isaiah in a frenzy of snapping teeth and snarls.

I leapt away from Morbius as grey fingers wrapped themselves around his neck, dragging him away from me.

As I watched, more grey bodies scurried over him like a mass of hungry rats, ravenous for flesh. Morbius kicked and screamed, but my Feral had him pinned to the ground.

The Mother and Father ripped and tore at every grey appendage within their reach as the world filled with the sound of tearing limbs. Ethan pulled Isaiah to the side as Gideon picked up a huge chunk of fallen masonry and used it to smash one of the Mother's Feral to a black sticky pulp. All around me reigned chaos as Vampire ripped apart Vampire and everything seemed coated in a layer of thick black blood.

I could no longer tell who belonged to them, and who belonged to us, I could only stand back as death painted the clearing. Victory seemed at hand, a moment of respite in that raging battle, and I gestured to the others to make a run for it, towards the trees. Just as Gideon pushed Isaiah and Ethan away from the carnage, Morbius heaved himself off the ground, his hands pulling the Feral from his torn body, and with a bang, his fist shot through a Feral's chest, and I watched powerlessly as the creature disintegrated before my eyes. He pulled another from around his neck, the Feral's teeth ripping away a ribbon of bloodied skin from Morbius' throat, and with a wail of pure rage, Morbius twisted the Feral's head on his shoulders and pulled it away from his body in a tangle of sinew and windpipe. Before the headless corpse hit the ground, it evaporated in a cloud of glittering dust.

"Run!" I shouted at the others, as all around me Feral parts began to wriggle and squelch in their own blood, pulling their bodies back together before my horrified eyes, tentacles reassembling the grotesque jigsaws as the Quellor Demons repaired their hosts. The Mother and Father grabbed one of my Ferals between them and pulled the poor creature apart until he too vanished in a cloud of sparkling dust.

I ran, fear snapping at my heals as I turned away from my home, from the place that kept me safe for so many years, and I ran. As I caught up with the others, I screamed for them to head for the trees, but luck screwed us with one more twist of its cruel knife.

They appeared before us, a trio of evil, Mother, Father and son. I saw their flesh healing, their own blood crawling back into their wounds as their skin knitted back together. I turned around, looking for a way out, but the Feral were already back on their feet, the Quellor Demons pulsating anew upon their humped backs.

We had nowhere left to run. Monsters before us, rotting monsters behind us, trapped between two extremes of total evil.

Gideon and I corralled Ethan and Isaiah between us, giving them seconds of stolen time before the monsters tore their way through us. We could offer nothing more.

Someone took my hand, a warm hand holding me tight, thumb caressing my palm in a gentle circle, and I turned my head slightly to look at Ethan, and I found his lips there, lips that flew against mine in a moment of desperate passion. They moved across my mouth with such urgency, with such emotion, and my heart exploded at his touch, as his tongue sought out mine and became one. It took all my willpower to pull away from him, and I looked into his green eyes, and I saw the love that nestled within them, and I knew that I belonged to him.

"Must you betray me with a kiss?" I whispered.

"I didn't want to die without kissing you."

They moved all around us, a circle of death, of tooth and claw. I thought, in that moment of utter hopelessness, to snap the necks of the humans, to extinguish the life of Isaiah and Ethan Silberman in a flash of mercy, to spare them the agony that surrounded us with such unrelenting hunger.

Daniyyel would come, and he would take them home, he would give them peace. I could give them that much.

They broke through the dark green backdrop of the forest like a sigh upon the wind, translucent bodies shimmering in the air above the unsuspecting cabal of hate. The sky filled with their spectral forms, a floating battalion in spirit form, and I thought that Heaven had finally gone too far, to disgorge its dead at such an inopportune moment, that Heaven should inflict upon us such a final insult.

I heard his dulcet English voice, and it filled my heart with overwhelming joy.

"Hell is empty, and all the Devils are here! Once more into the breach, my friends!"

The trio of Menarche saw them for the first time, and something akin to alarm danced across their triumphant faces as the ghostly horde descended upon them. The Mother screamed, a shrill cry of rage that ripped open the sky in a flash of blinding lightning. Her hands wrapped themselves around my neck, and I could feel her nails digging into my hard flesh as she tried to rip my head from my shoulders, and all the while the world around us erupted in an outpour of cries.

She stopped suddenly, and her face twisted, and I saw the shock that bloomed behind her eyes and the sudden fear that ripped away her smile. Her body shimmered, and then I saw him, smiling out at me from behind her features, my best friend grinning from ear to ear.

"Bitch, if anyone is going to kill him it will be me! So get your bony-ass fingers away from his throat!"

The Mother shot backwards, tumbling to the ground in a jumble of limbs, and with a sickening pop, Malachi extracted himself from her body.

"Hell hath no fury like a spirit scorned!"

"Mal! I could fucking kiss you!"

"Been there, done that... oh... duck!"

I threw myself to the ground just as a Feral launched itself towards me. To my amazement, Malachi shot forward in a blur of speed and entered the monster's body. The Feral froze, its body as stiff as a statue, and I watched transfixed as the light faded from his eyes, the fierce red dimming to a dull grey. The Quellor Demon thrashed upon his back, tentacles squirming around his neck as it fought to regain control. But as I watched, the Feral's body began to splinter, fissures creeping across its dead flesh as chunks of its body fell to the ground, turning to ash that melted into the rain-sodden earth. The Quellor Demon gave out a hiss of agony as its single yellow eye exploded across the devastated corpse. With a hiss of steam, the Feral disintegrated, taking with it the monstrosity on its back.

Malachi brushed himself down and grinned at me.

"Look at me saving your bum. Who knew?"

"Bum?"

"Eli!"

The urgency in Gideon's voice made my flesh turn cold, and to my horror, I saw him pinned to the ground by two Feral, their teeth embedded into his muscular body, blood pumping across their pale grey bodies, ripping Gideon's skin away from his frame in great bloodied shreds.

I could not remember moving, but my hands tightened around the Feral's neck, tearing him away from Gideon, who thrashed in such agony beneath them. My own teeth pierced the eye of the Quellor Demon, sinking into that yellow mass with a sickening pop as warm matter exploded across my face. The Feral loosened its grip, and I pulled the Feral away, landing on my back with a cry of rage as tentacles reached for my face. I heard the howl of agony explode from the other Feral as Malachi dealt with it, and then Malachi hovered above me, gazing down on me with his wonderful cow eyes, his gentle voice a whisper on the wind.

"Hold on handsome, I'm going in."

The Feral melted across my chest, its body nothing but dust as it withered, the Quellor Demon melting away with it. Malachi lay across my chest, his lips so close that I could almost feel them, as I could feel his ethereal body pressed against mine.

"Well, here we are again. On our backs." I felt his lips press against mine, a soft shimmer of sensation that made me shiver. "Never stare a gift horse in the face, Eli, you never know when it may be your last." With that, he lifted into the air, my friend, my saviour, and dived into the body of the nearest Feral.

The dark night shimmered with glittering ash. All around us the Feral fell apart as Malachi and his ghosts tore through the horde without mercy, bodies shattered out of existence as the Feral fell at their touch. Everything seemed swathed in a layer of grey, and the night sighed with the sound of death.

A loud rumble echoed across the clearing, the sound of some immense engine grinding into life, and I realised with horror that the turret of the tank was swivelling around. The world exploded in a ball of flame as the ground beneath me heaved. Everything turned black as the earth broke apart beneath my body, and I flew, the stars reaching out to touch my skin as the blackness moved in to consume me.

Someone called my name, a muffled sound that barely penetrated my skull. Oblivion started to lift from my eyes, to reveal dark shadows that looked like broken limbs against the stars, but they were trees, just broken trees, wood splintered and torn beyond recognition.

I sat up suddenly, awareness jolting me back to life.

"Eli?"

"Mal, fuck me Mal, what happened?"

"They got away, Eli, the Mother and Father got away... but..."

Something in his tone frightened me. I turned to look at him, his pretty face so full of concern.

"What Mal? Tell me!"

Malachi drifted away from me, and sitting on the ground sat Isaiah, his hands hammering at the dirt with every wail that howled between his lips. Terror gripped my chest, tightening around my heart, his agony ripping away at my soul with every single, pained breath he inhaled. I crawled across the ground towards him, my body still pulling itself back together as bones clicked and skin healed, but I could only see Isaiah, I could only hear Isaiah, and I could only feel his pain.

"Isaiah?" His name fell from my mouth in a terrified whimper, almost too afraid to make itself heard, afraid of what it would find.

Isaiah turned towards me, and I stopped in my tracks, for he wore on his face a look of such despair and his eyes looked so wide and lost, his tears streaming unchecked down his reddened face.

"They took him... my Ethan, they took him..."

Time seemed to freeze, the world stopped turning, and the rain hung glittering before my horrified gaze. I heard his words, but they did not sink in. The words formed in my mind, but I could not accept them, I could not believe them. I looked around the field, a desperate search for that which I wanted to see, that I needed to see, but I only saw death. So many bodies, my Feral children were torn apart, layers of ash and lumps of fathomless things, the ground a pot-marked crater of devastation, but no Ethan.

Isaiah's hand gripped my arm, his fingers wrapped around my hard muscle, and I pulled the old man to me, cradling his head in my chest, his tears streaming down to land upon my hands, and my tears were quick to follow.

"They took him... Morbius... I couldn't stop him."

Light broke apart the night, a star that descended to the ground in a flourish of silver feathers, and Daniyyel stood before us in all his Heavenly glory. I wanted to speak, I wanted to call him a bastard for letting us face that horde by ourselves, for letting Morbius take Ethan away from us, but as I looked into his face, the sadness that looked back at me froze my accusations to my trembling lips.

"Eli, I'm so sorry."

"What?"

"Eli, Eli come here quickly!" I heard Malachi's voice calling me, but I could not tear myself away from the grief-stricken Angel, from the look of such heartfelt sorrow that tumbled down his handsome face.

"Eli!"

Malachi sat in a shallow crater, with Gideon, torn and bloodied, lying before him. I ran to his side, my knees sliding through the mud, and I pulled his body onto my lap, holding the man I once loved beyond life itself.

"Gideon... come on Gideon, get up... heal."

His eyes flickered, those beautiful eyes that I had loved for so long, and a single tear fell down his cheek.

"It's over... I'm so sorry Eli... it's over."

"No, don't be stupid... of course it's not over, look, we won, Malachi saved us..."

A smile crept across his pained face, and his hand, his trembling hand, clutched at his chest.

"I'm so sorry Eli... my Eli... but it's come, my end... the splinter..." I felt the pain rip through his body and he convulsed, his entire body curling into me. I pulled him close, and I looked at Malachi, at Daniyyel, pleading for them to help me, to help Gideon.

"No... no, no, no... there must be something we can do... there must be something you can do..."

Daniyyel bowed his head in shame and wept. "I'm so sorry Eli, this is beyond anything that I may do."

Isaiah slumped to the ground and took Gideon's hand in his, bringing it to his old face, clutching it against his cheek.

"My friend, oh my friend, do not leave us now... not now..."

"Isaiah, you have it... do you still have it?"

"Yes my friend, I still have it."

I could feel the relief through his muscles as his body lay limp in my arms, and then he looked at me, his eyes so big, eyes that already dimmed.

"You must promise me to finish this Eli, do what we were made to do, destroy them, the Mother and the Father, Morbius... that's what we are for... that's why are... don't you see? We are the only ones strong enough to do it."

"No... Gideon, we will do it together, the two of us..."

"No... there is another. You must go to London, Eli, find her, find Mary, she can help..."

Another spasm coursed through his body as he went rigid in my arms. His hands ripped at his chest, tearing the cloth away from his torso, and what I saw made me cry out. An intricate network of black veins pulsed outward from his heart, creeping across his body, the skin blackening around its path. It crept down his arms, down towards his groin, towards his neck, and there was nothing I could do to stop it.

"Tell me how to help you?"

He lifted a hand towards my face, a finger wiping away the tears that tumbled from my eyes.

"You already have, you gave me love when I did not deserve it, you gave me a life when I had none to live. I did love you... despite all the lies... see that I loved you..."

"Yes, I know, oh my lovely man, I know."

"Did you love me? I always thought that you... I always hoped..."

"Yes, Gideon... oh God yes, I loved you so very much, I still do."

"Gaius... my name is Gaius... please, let me hear you speak my name, just once... please..."

Fingers of black licked around his lips, snaking towards his eyes, his flesh breaking around the edge of his once perfect mouth. I leaned over, and I kissed those broken lips.

"Gaius... my Gaius... how I loved you."

His body crumbled at my touch, and Gaius, my lovely Gaius, was no more.

I cried into the night, my voice a wail of despair that shattered the stars as his remains crumbled between my fingers. Heaven trembled at the sound of my grief.

The ash stirred, it glittered, a swirling vortex that moved away from me towards the Angel, and then I saw him, the man behind the legend, Gaius Cassius Longinus in all his mortal beauty, kneeling before Daniyyel.

Daniyyel reached out a hand and placed it upon his head, his voice so full of emotion that I nearly died along with him.

"Are you ready my friend? Are you ready to go home?"

Gaius turned and looked at me, and then he smiled, a sight so beautiful, so human, and then he spoke.

"Yes."

Silver wings unfurled from his back, huge glittering things of iridescent beauty, and he stood up to embrace Daniyyel, and together they lifted into the air, their arms wrapped around each other, and Gaius, my Gideon, was gone.

Epilogue

New Reich Chancellery, Berlin, 1945

The power burned me. I could feel it surging through every nerve ending of my body, a living thing squirming inside of me, making me a God amongst men. As I looked down into the faces of the mindless masses, my adoring masses, their love for me, their Fuhrer, filled me with yet more power, and I sucked in their love as I watched them, as I thought about devouring them, as I thought about devouring all of mankind. They mocked me once, and they would never mock me again.

I felt my companion move on my back, a constant reminder of my elevated status. If I closed my eyes, if I thought about it hard enough, I could still taste her on my lips as she smeared her garden all over my mouth, as she gave me that dark, blood-infused kiss. Her child sat on my back, her blood ran through my veins, they made me their Black Messiah, and I would take the world for them, wipe it clean of the human infection, make it paradise for them once more, a new Eden.

What a wonderful job that Architect Speer did to build me such a place, a place from which I may fashion a world, and a throne from which I may rule that world. Four thousand men to build one Palace, but what a Palace, lined with marble and wood as it was, a perfect blend of Deco and Modernism, a shrine to the new age of technology and design. Leather, steel, chrome, glass, and marble. I lived in a world of such luxury, me, the homeless vagrant who once scavenged for handouts in the workhouses of Vienna.

Me, who now sat in my own Palace, overlooking the pathetic remnants of a race that did not know it was already dead.

If they could see me, those nuns. If Eva could see me. Would she love me as she looked at me with her rotting eyes? Would those lips, grey and corrupted, taste as good to me as I always imagined them to taste? The cock teasing bitch lay dead, so it no longer mattered to me. The bitch could feel nothing rotting in her grave.

The Chancellery Office echoed with the sound of a fist hammering against wood, a hollow, empty sound inside such a vast space.

"Enter." My Angel of Death bounded into the room, the three black pips glinting off of the black collar patches of his stiff grey uniform. He seemed deeply agitated as he ushered in two SS guards behind him.

"Have you heard, Mein Fuhrer?" he asked after making the customary salute. How I did love that one-armed salute.

"Spit it out, Josef. And you had better hope that I like what you have to tell me, because I am starving."

That made the sycophantic fool squirm, I could almost smell the shit hit his pants as he hopped nervously from foot to foot. He indicated for one of the soldiers to move forward. Both men looked far more terrified than Mengele, and with good reason. Josef Mengele I needed — the others existed to feed my hunger.

"Mein Fuhrer... Wewelsburg has fallen... the camp is burning."

I had not eaten for over a day, not real food, the stuff that sustained me, so I picked the terrified runt up off the floor by the neck and pulled him towards my face.

Josef and the remaining soldier backed away, and I looked at them, feeling their fear shudder through their delicious bodies, and it made me smile.

"Stand your fucking ground. You will watch your Messiah feed, and know that if the next thing that leaves your mouths displeases me, that you will be next!"

The man in my hand could not breathe, and already his face had turned a shade of sickly blue. I loosened my grip around his throat slightly, to allow air into his windpipe, and I felt most gratified to see the colour return to his bulbous face. I liked my food alive.

I pulled his face to my own, my gaze burrowing into his, at the terror inside him, at the futility of his life balanced within my grip.

"You are nothing! You are an insect, you and your kind infest the face of this planet with your filth, and I am here to cleanse the planet of your obscene existence! You are a man, an aberration to the Mother and Father, and I am their hand, and I will pave their way towards a new Eden!"

His face touched mine, my lips against his, and the stench of his humanity filled me with disgust. I opened my mouth over his, feeling my lips slide across his flesh, creeping across his face, smothering him with my hate. My jaw cracked, a loud snap that echoed around the office, and my upper lip extended to cover his eyes, his huge, terrified eyes, and then he could see no more, devoured by my blinding superiority as my mouth completely enveloped his face.

I could hear him whimpering, the sound a meek trembling inside the depths of my throat. As I began to feed, as I felt his flesh part from his skull, his whimpering turned to an agonized howl as his limbs thrashed so violently below him. I breathed him in, sucking on his flesh, on his soul, feeling his life fill me, his humanity leaving his weak, mammalian body until he remained nothing but an empty sack of skin and bone, for all that he was, all that he could ever be, now sat inside of me.

I dropped the empty husk to the floor, and I had to take a moment to savour the kill, to feel the thrill of his death escape my lips in a scream of triumphant victory. All men would meet such a fate, and I would feed until nothing remained of their defiling presence, until Earth returned to the naked state from which they came.

Not a sound came from the two remaining men. As I turned to them they saluted, their cries joining the echoes of my own.

"Heil Hitler!"

A faint flicker of a smile curled at the edges of my lips, a small token of satisfaction at their devotion.

"Now, the rest, tell me the rest. The boxes?"

Josef Mengele stood there sweating into his pants, and the coward pushed the remaining soldier forward.

"Some were lost, Mein Fuhrer, in the initial attack. But the rest were destroyed during a failed assault upon the Vampire's castle. They say that ghosts, spirits came out of the forest and laid every Feral beast to dust. It was a massacre, Fuhrer."

I stepped forward, my hand extended towards his neck, but the human cowered away from me, and I liked it.

"But we have him, Mein Fuhrer, we have him," he added quickly.

I stood before the soldier, so close that I could feel his panting breath against my face. He would make a delicious meal, a satisfying second course to my meagre entrée, but I needed to hear the rest of his words.

"Explain to me, give me a name, who, who do we have?"

"The son of God, Mein Fuhrer. Ethan, we have Ethan."

A thrill of pleasure trickled across my skin. Redivivus, the child reborn, and I had him. Now, not only would I bring mankind to their knees, but God too, and he would rue the day that he turned his back on his creations. The Mother and Father would be Adam and Eve once more, in a world of my making.

"Come with me, both of you."

I led them to a wood panelled wall where I pressed my palm against one of the panels. Josef knew of the bunker beneath the complex of course, but I enjoyed the look of surprise that flashed across the soldier's face as he saw the wall slide away to reveal a metal lined lift.

The journey into the bowels of the bunker lasted but a few short moments, and when the flat, expressionless metal doors slid open, I stepped out into a corridor of immaculate white. I called it my workshop, my homage to a story I once heard, and it never failed to amuse me.

Our heels clipped satisfactorily against the hard ceramic surface of the white floor, the sound echoing endlessly in all directions as I led our party to a large window overlooking another brightly lit room below us.

"Look inside."

The soldier edged forward nervously, but what met his gaze shocked the living daylights out of him. Josef Mengele stood by me, his gaze looking down longingly into the room below, and a sly smile crept across his human face.

"We have done well, Mein Fuhrer, to have made so many of them. Wewelsburg was but the tail end of an operation already in the last stages of completion, but I have made you this army, my Messiah, hundreds of them."

As I looked down into the room, I felt the moment fill me, my pride, a swell of pleasure at the many hundreds of wooden boxes below, each one sealed with a large wooden crucifix.

"Look at them, my army, my Feral love letter to a dying world. It is time to let loose my love upon this world. We will start with London, raining down upon the infidels a living death from the sky, until that bastard city lies in ruins at my feet! Death is but the beginning, love is the end!"

About The Author

I am a 46-year-old gay guy living in Cardiff, Wales, with my partner of 27 years, Derek. Oh, and our two cats, Rita and Harry, and a load of tropical fish! I have worked in retail most of my life, and for the past eleven years, I have run my own Interior Design business with my fabulous business partner, Jayne. I am a huge sci-fi and horror fan, Doctor Who being my first love in television, and Alien my first love in film. Sigh. How I would love to write for them both, but we can all dream.

Working for yourself, and trying to pay yourself, is not easy. Bit like being an author. In an ideal world, I would love to see our shop managed by someone else while I spent my days writing, but that, sadly, is unlikely. I love the design industry, and I love writing, but if I had to choose out of the two, writing would win every time.

Writing has always been my passion. I never thought, in a million years, that I would one day be published, and here I am with book 3! When I started this series two and a half years ago, I wrote to every Agent in the Artists and Writers Yearbook, and then some, and I have a pile of *nos* that could dwarf Everest! Just when I thought there was no point, I found eXtasy Books, so I thought, one more try, just one more. They said yes!

To say that I screamed a lot would be an understatement, and yes, there may have been a few tears involved. I signed with the wonderful eXtasy Books, and boy are they fabulous. My editors, cover designer, all of them, just wonderful, talented, incredibly supportive people, and I feel mighty privileged to be a part of them. I owe them everything, for making my dream come true, and I hope we will be together for many years to come.

Printed in Great Britain
by Amazon